"With its star-crossed lovers and fickle downtown art scene, *Lines* is a sweet, sharp-eyed New York fairytale bound to appeal to fans of smart romantic comedies. While Sung J. Woo's deft use of his fugue structure will remind readers of *Sliding Doors*, his feel for Josh and Abby as they navigate their many missed connections recalls the pure, exalted yearning of Haruki Murakami."

—Stewart O'Nan, author of *Ocean State* and *Last Night at the Lobster*

"A thoughtful exploration of the choices we make, and how one chance meeting (or lack thereof) can change your life in complicated and unexpected ways. Smart and meticulously crafted, *Lines* is a story that will stay with me long after finishing the last page."

—Brenda Janowitz, author of *The Liz Taylor Ring* and *The Grace Kelly Dress*

"A witty, observant, exhilarating pleasure, with much to teach us about the complexities of loving and the complexities of living a life devoted to art."

—Brian Morton, author of *Starting Out in the Evening* and *Florence Gordon*

Also by Sung J. Woo

Deep Roots
Skin Deep
Love Love
Everything Asian

LINES

a novel

SUNG J. WOO

ARTWORK BY DINA BRODSKY

LINES
Copyright © 2024 Sung J. Woo
All Rights Reserved.
Published by Unsolicited Press.
Printed in the United States of America.
First Edition.

Paintings in the book are the property of Dina Brodsky. Non-exclusive, irrevocable, and royalty-free permissions granted for the sole production in this book.

No part of this book may be used or reproduced in any manner whatsoever without written permission except in the case of brief quotations embodied in critical articles or reviews. People, places, and notions in these stories are from the author's imagination; any resemblance to real persons or events is purely coincidental.

The flash fiction stories that accompany the paintings throughout the novel were previously published in *Juked*, *Columbia Journal*, and *Slice*, in slightly different form.

Attention schools and businesses: for discounted copies on large orders, please contact the publisher directly.

For information contact:
Unsolicited Press
Portland, Oregon
www.unsolicitedpress.com
orders@unsolicitedpress.com
619-354-8005

Cover Design: Jun Cen
Inner Cover Design: Shahbaz Qamar
Editor: S. Stewart
ISBN: 978-1-956692-50-1
Library of Congress Control Number: 2023945448

For

Dawn

and

Dina

I don't want to hurt you
I just want to be your friend
Even though we draw our lines with very different ends
Do you believe me
Have I even earned your trust
To ask you for it now, would it ever be enough
With all the words to say
Surely we can find
A place to leave our past behind

Oh our worlds collide
When they can't survive
On their own precious lies
Oh we make mistakes
Find what it takes
And make an honest try

—Katie Herzig, "Lines"

Prologue

OUR STORY BEGINS five years ago, on a cool and damp Saturday morning in the city of New York. The street is Fifth Avenue, downtown. Parked cars line both sides of the road, their windshields dotted with dew. We're a block away from Washington Square Park, the imposing arch squaring up its shoulders. The first sentence of the inscription engraved into the stone at the top of the monument reads:

Let us raise a standard to which the wise and the honest can repair.

The second sentence is shrouded in fog along with the rest of this famed structure. In fact, the mist is so thick and pervasive that the few natives who are out at this early hour of seven o'clock walk at a tourist's pace. The rising sun is burning off this white cloak that has descended upon the city, which will remain for another three minutes and twenty-six seconds. That's not much time, but enough for what is and isn't about to transpire.

If we keep walking on Fifth, we'll pass right through the arch. But we won't do that. Instead, we're going to watch two people approach one another.

The man who enters our view from the left is Joshua Kozlov. Five-ten, clean-shaven, of Belarusian origin but by name only, i.e., his favorite dessert is apple pie and he wouldn't know a babushka from a balaclava. He turned forty yesterday. He wasn't happy about it then, and he isn't happy about it now. He hates his birthday. He hates all birthdays, but that's a rude thing to say to people who like their birthdays, so he keeps this opinion to himself. Not that he cares about what others think. (Actually, he does, more than he cares to admit.) What's important is that there's no birthday he hates more than his own, and a milestone one like this makes it a hundred times worse. *The big four-oh! Where's your cane? Don't forget your Depends!* Friends and family have been gushing, prodding, joking all week. At least it's over. He wants to start the new decade of his life with purpose and meaning, which is why he's now marching down Washington Square North with grim-grave determination.

The woman who enters from the right is Abby Kim. Five-three, long-haired, a methodical long-distance cycler, of South Korean origin. Twenty-nine, her family immigrated when she was twelve, so she remembers the old country, but far less than one might imagine. Like she's unable to recall a single student in fifth grade, her last class before she departed for America. Not one, and not even the teacher. She must've had friends, right? Maybe not. Maybe she ate lunches by herself, at her desk, staring at the blackboard. Except she can't remember what she ate, the desk where this alleged consumption took place, or the vaguest notion of a blackboard.

Instead, what has been indelibly etched on her brain is a walking bridge she used to cross with a tin container in hand, about the size of a cigar box. On the other side of the river was an old woman who squatted against a crumbling brick wall and sautéed slivers of rice cake in hot pepper sauce. Abby gave her five hundred won (about fifty cents) and the empty container and watched the woman, who was toothless and always humming some unfamiliar song, ladle up steaming scoops of the *tteokbokki*. The woman filled the container to the brim, too much, as when she closed the lid, some of the red goop squeezed out, but that was just fine with Abby. She didn't even wait until she got home to eat, just used her fingers to extricate one red medallion at a time, tangy, spicy, gooey goodness. Abby isn't hungry, but as she nears the midpoint of Washington Square North, her mouth waters and she's delighted by this Pavlovian response. Her mind, telling her body what to do. She walks a little faster.

Fourteen seconds from now, enough of the fog will have lifted that the island of Manhattan will come back into focus. The second sentence of the arch's inscription, shorn of the haze, now proclaims:

The event is in the hand of God.

Is it God? Or are we in the realm of brain-cramping quantum mechanics? Doesn't matter. Let us observe the events as they unfold, two of them, occurring simultaneously.

We know. This is not what we witness in our daily, quotidian lives. But take our word for it, both lines are happening right now. If this were a movie, the screen would split in half.

Joshua and Abby run into each other.

And:

Abby and Josh miss each other.

In the first line, upon impact, they fall to the ground in an instinctually protective hug. The fog dissipates, and they stare into each other's eyes in disbelief, at the physicality of their bodily collision and their subsequent, spontaneous coupling. They laugh. They rise and dust each other off. Joshua invites Abby for coffee and they end up talking until lunch. They date. They fall in love, hard. They marry just two months later.

And:

In the second line, they pass through the fog, oblivious of each other's existence. Until five years later, when Josh, in his suburban home in New Jersey, finds himself in front of his computer to peer at an oval-shaped locket no bigger than his thumbnail, at the impossibly tiny white dress painted within the boundary of its golden border.

apart

The Garden State

THE DRESS IS beautiful, but the dress is sad. Lacy and white and wispy, it's something a young girl might wear…in her coffin. Sometimes white can be blue, like the glacier he saw two years ago when he and Marlene took a cruise around Alaska. Those grand and funereal icy floats felt like the end of the world, and now here is that same feeling inside this locket, a silent sort of death. Against the black background, the tiny painting of this dress has a wealth of miraculous details, like the frayed ends of the frill on the bottom where each thread is thinner than a strand of hair. Even the wire hanger that the dress hangs on is comprised of multiple hues, only noticeable after Josh clicks on the high-resolution version of the picture and blows it way up.

Item 37, titled "Sometimes I Forget." Next to the photo on the gallery's website is a name, Abby Kim. He's about to click on the hyperlink on her name when he hears:

"Honey? How's it going?"

Josh's mouse pointer jumps to the top-right corner of his screen and closes his browser.

"All done!" he shouts from his basement office. "Shutting down now."

His face flushes as he waits for his computer to wind itself down, then he chuckles. It wasn't like he'd been looking at porn, but it felt something like it. As he switches off the power strip, he considers the chain of human links that got him to the locket a few minutes before bedtime. His wife's birthday was two weeks away and he'd been trying to find her a gift, and he'd gotten an email from his sister, which consisted of a Facebook message she'd received from a friend of hers, who knew a gallery owner who knew the publicist through Twitter. God bless the internet.

As he makes his way up the stairs to their bedroom, the miniscule dress follows him like a ghost. Marlene is in her pink nightgown, leaning over the sink as she washes her face. He imagines giving her the locket at the restaurant after dinner. He'd stand behind her, unclasp the gold chain. As she holds up her strawberry-blonde hair to expose her throat, he'd lay the locket against the soft dip of her collarbone, the part he treasures to touch with the tip of his index finger. Even though they've known each other for eleven years and have been married for five, there's still a mystery to her naked body, hidden curves he has yet to discover.

He sneaks behind her for a hug as she pats dry her face with a hand towel. He places his head next to hers, and they stare at each other in the mirror. His hands slide up from her waist to cup her breasts. Underneath the silky fabric, they strike the most feminine balance between soft and firm.

"Hello, beautiful," he says.

Marlene smirks. "Somebody's happy," she says, then presses herself against his erection.

The following morning, sitting in his cube, a bit groggy after the previous late-night extracurricular activities, he sips his coffee and waits for his computer to boot up. He's read somewhere that men think about sex once every fifteen minutes, which seems patently ridiculous, but then again, during his half-hour commute, the walk from the car to the front door of PayRight in Jersey City, and the walk from the lobby up to his cubicle, his brain plays out last night like snippets of video: Marlene's curls splayed out against her pillow, her breasts bobbing with each thrust, her right hand bunching the bedsheet when she comes.

"Hey, get me for our 9:30, all right?"

"Absolutely," Josh says. As he watches his boss Harold walk down to his office, he imagines delivering the following version of his status report during the morning standup meeting: *Client was very satisfied with the speed and force of the live presentation; we achieved full market penetration late last night; repeat business is a certainty.*

He has twenty minutes to kill before the meeting, so he fires up his browser and types in abbykim.art and sees an image of a circular painting that depicts a room inside an abandoned building. The window is broken, the wallpaper is peeling, and shards of glass and pieces of plaster are scattered across the well-worn wooden boards. Everything here should be ugly, but it couldn't be more opposite. Abby finds beauty in decrepitude, in places and things discarded and forgotten. In the bottom corner of the painting, there's a haphazard pile of fabric that has got to be the same white dress from the locket. Josh leans closer to the monitor, his nose almost touching the screen. The same lace, the same delicate fringes, yes! It's like he's discovered a secret, a furtive bond between the locket and this painting, and in a way, between himself and Abby.

Her website is no-nonsense, with a menu up top that features her C.V. and links to her previous projects, from her most recent works to landscapes from her college days. Trees are her latest obsession, a hundred and one of them drawn with a ballpoint pen. Funny thing is, they all look like they're on the brink of death, shorn of leaves, their branches skeletal, and yet there's an undeniable strength in these bare trunks, too. Together, these drawings are like an arboreal army standing together as a testament to time. This is her specialty, her focus: small-scale works about decomposition and ruin that defy their innate negativity and reach a kind of quiet majesty.

"Josh? Let's not keep the team waiting."

It's Harold again, holding up a manila folder.

"Sorry, Harold," he says, and bolts up from his chair. He follows his boss to the conference room, his mind trapped inside that painting on her home page, circumscribed within that poignant circle of decay.

*

Outside Abby's window, snow falls in temperamental whorls, tiny white flakes reflected by the street light below. Sometimes it looks like they're falling up, because here on the third floor, the wind is wilder, taking the ice crystals for an extra ride. A sharp blast of an arctic chill whistles the sill, as the bottom frame has never sat even. There's a brown water stain on the ceiling shaped like Florida, a crack in the plaster wall that runs from one corner to another, and the outlet near the closet has never worked. Still, it's her place, her little Manhattan apartment, one she's been able to make rent every month for seven years through pure scrappiness: teaching classes at the 92nd Y, giving one-on-one lessons with mostly spoiled brats of one-percenter parents, and selling her paintings. She sells them through the SoHo gallery that represents her, but sometimes customers find her website and contact her directly.

Which was the case earlier today, when she received an email from a Josh Kozlov. She's not fond of email because it makes her feel dumb. English has never come easy for her, even though she's now lived in America for more than twenty years. Still, she finds the language confounding, with its many exceptions and nonsensical rules. Like why should there be subject-verb agreement? Why add an "s" at the end of a verb when it's a "he" or a "she"? Korean is way simpler; even the alphabet itself is self-explanatory, the letters shaped to resemble the position of the human tongue. So when she receives an email like the one from Josh Kozlov, she's immediately put on the defensive.

What a pleasure it is to be ensconced within your private world, Ms. Kim. How exquisite your lines, how vibrant your colors. Your work is simply disarming, and I would like nothing more than to possess your locket that was on display at the Peregrine Gallery last month. As you can surmise from my introduction to your work, my path to you has been a zigzag of fortuitous connections that only the convoluted internet can provide.

And that was just one paragraph of six! After reading that email, it took her an hour to compose a reply that she hoped would mask her lack of linguistic grace.

Email, the bane of her existence. Her inbox is a mess, with messages that date back to the beginning of the Obama Administration. When she first got her Gmail account, she promised herself this wouldn't happen, that she'd be better with her correspondence than her Yahoo! Email (there are unanswered messages from her college days in that vast ether), but alas, organization has never been her forte. It's especially difficult right now because she's putting together a gallery show with her fellow Schoolers, her inbox dinging almost continuously.

Speak of the devil — Ding!

Abby, Franny's Big Bird with Roadkill 1 *is still stuck in Customs. Fuck we do now?*

Ding!

Need a rough headcount. Don't wanna run out of white wine like last time. What's with the mass hate for red? Anyway, ASAP, yo!

There's only one way to quell her exhausted brain, and that is to work. Abby zips up her hoodie, sits down in her wooden chair over her desk, and picks up her 2/0 pointed round brush. It's seven thirty. Half an hour to lose herself into her latest painting, a two-inch Plexiglas disc that's beginning to finally look like the scene in her mind, a narrow asphalt bike path snaking through a sun-dappled forest. It was just last summer that she went on her month-long European cycling trip, but it feels like a lifetime ago, someone else's life.

Josh said he'd ring her at eight, but her iPhone rings now. Ted.

"I know you're working, so I'll keep this short. Good luck and call me as soon as you're done? Please, my dear future wife?"

"Of course, my dear future husband."

He keeps his promise of brevity and hangs up without saying goodbye, and she loves him for it. He called because he wanted to express his concern, which is sweet but unnecessary. In all the many times she has met a prospective buyer in her apartment, not once has she ever felt like she was in any kind of danger.

Still, Ted has asked her to keep the front door ajar, so even though she disagrees with him, she'll make good on her part of their agreement. Before Ted, she never would've done something she didn't believe in, but things are different now. Is it because she's months away from becoming a bride? Possibly. At thirty-four, she's at the midpoint of her fourth decade, a time when one is supposed to make mature decisions about the life ahead and not just do things on a whim...such as stuffing a trio of shorts, underwear, and t-shirt plus a giant bag of trail mix into the backpack, her only check-in luggage her disassembled bicycle. With her windbreaker on and her rolled sleeping bag strapped to the bottom of her backpack, she would leave JFK Airport as a civilized human being and return four weeks later from the European countryside as a vagabond gypsy drifter.

LINES

Goodness, was she ever filthy when she came back! How thoroughly thorough was dirt, embedding its granular blackness into the very pores of her skin. Even though she took the occasional camp shower, stepping into the warm bath in her apartment, watching the water slowly turn gray, scrubbing her fingernails with a toothbrush because there was no other way to remove the grime — that feeling of cleanliness she achieved after her multi-country sojourn…it must be what the butterfly feels as it breaks free of its cocoon. And it went well beyond the physical, this refreshing, resetting, renewing. A month of sleeping and waking and riding, sketching into her journal with her Zebra pen of the places and people she'd observed, this was how she restocked her creative stockpile that fed her for the rest of the year.

Every journey was transformative in its own way, but on her last trip, for the first time, she felt like she was riding toward something instead of riding away, headlong into a future instead of dodging the past. It had felt like the beginning, which is why she now feels so bereft because it was actually the ending. Yes, she could still go. That's what she used to do — just up and leave, decide in the middle of the night, take the LIRR to JFK next morning and get on a standby flight to Frankfurt.

Why not now? She could do it. She could.

But she won't.

Stop, Abby thinks. *Stop thinking about the past or the future. Your painting awaits you. If you aren't going to do this, who will?*

Dip the brush into the green paint. Touch the brush to the surface.

Dip the brush into the white paint. Touch the brush to the surface.

This is her mantra. When she loses herself in her work, she feels beautifully numb. She blends into the background of the universe, becomes a vague splotch of color, a nameless blob. This is her peace, more serene than any drug.

She hears her phone's notification chirp but ignores it. She wants to stay here, in the tight space between her brush and the surface. When she meets people for the first time and they find out she's a painter, they all assume it's the creativity of the profession that attracts her. That is not a falsity, but it isn't the truth. More than anything, what she loves is this mechanical repetition, the accrual of a thousand strokes onto a single canvas. If this were fifty years ago and she and art never got together, Abby could easily imagine spending her days at a factory, nailing a bolt onto a metal plate, hour after hour, and loving it.

This time the phone rings, and then she remembers that she's supposed to meet someone tonight.

"Hi," she answers.

"Miss Kim?"

It's weird to be called that, but she's been called worse.

"Josh?"

"I'm outside your apartment building."

"I'll come down and let you in."

He descends downstairs to his computer, thinking about a girl in New York City getting ready for her wedding, which might be happening right now. He did gush in his email about her locket, so he's probably excited about meeting her. She needs to perk up here, play the part of a grateful artist. Not that she has to play it hard, as she is absolutely, totally grateful. The number of people who support art — and let's face it, the only way to support art is to buy it — is so infinitesimally small that she still finds it a minor miracle when she does sell something.

She opens the door to the vestibule and there he stands. She sees him before he sees her. Unlike 99% of the people who wait, he's not staring at his phone. Instead, he leans against the door and takes in her view, which isn't much, just 28th Street downtown, a boring red square of a building across the pavement, the fluorescent glow from the windows of a D'Agostino Supermarket a block away that reflects the falling snow. Standing in profile, Abby sees the smile on his face. It is such an unguarded, genuine smile, and she almost feels embarrassed that she's bearing witness to it.

And now it is her, standing inside, knocking on the window of her outer door, as if to ask him to let her in. Maybe in a way she is asking just that, to be let into his preoccupied, exhilarated mind. He turns. Through the clear glass, she meets his pale blue eyes, the color of an arctic iceberg.

together

The Big Apple

THERE WAS A time when Joshua's cool blue eyes calmed her, but now, all she sees is his disappointment.

No. Stop. She will not be distracted, not again.

The baby portrait Abby should be working on, an eight-foot by six-foot canvas of stretched linen hung on the wall, hovers over her like a reproachful giant, reprimanding her for the last two hours. Cecilia is the baby's name, and her pouty smile is almost there, almost memorable.

You're so close, the smile says. *Why are you wasting your time on that stupid locket?*

From an outsider's point of view, the portrait looks done, but Abby does not feel it. It is a gut thing, unexplainable. She's obsessed 24/7 when she's on a project, but then there comes a time when she can't even bear to look at it again, and that's when she knows a painting is finished. She's not at that point yet with Cecilia. Almost there, but right now, she really, really wants to work on the tiny little dress inside the locket, and she feels terrible about it.

Abby looks up at a snippet of lined yellow paper taped at eye level, one she reads every morning, or sometimes in the middle of the day like now, a quote by the writer Paul Bowles:

Because we don't know when we will die, we get to think of life as an inexhaustible well. Yet everything happens only a certain number of times, and a very small number really. How many more times will you remember a certain afternoon of your childhood, an afternoon that is so deeply a part of your being that you can't even conceive of your life without it? Perhaps four, five times more, perhaps not even that. How many more times will you watch the full moon rise? Perhaps 20. And yet it all seems limitless.

This is why she's painting the locket, because life, as infinite as it may seem, is hardly that.

"...some gold in our Roth?"

"Let's have you sleep well at night, move a portion of your immediate-term bond allocation to a gold ETF. BIV to GLD..."

Abby catches the conversation between Ted and his clients as they pass by her door. They may be speaking English, but it might as well be Swahili, financial jargon of indecipherable acronyms. But she likes eavesdropping nonetheless, because they're words she's not meant to hear. More than any other definition, that's what she believes an artist's job to be: to capture the unseen, or the obvious that escapes everyone's attention. Or at least that's the excuse she gives herself for snooping.

She smiles as she works on the right sleeve of the dress in the locket. A small dab of gray, a tiny line of red, looking good, no, now looking bad — *focus, goddamnit!* — it's because her mind is on her door, or more specifically, a pair of quick knuckle raps emanating from the other side. She's never seen Ted in this position since her door is made of solid wood, but she can imagine him, loosening his tie, putting his left hand in his pocket, while his right hand hovers over the grained surface.

Why is she picturing him on the other side? What is wrong with her?

LINES

There's nothing wrong with her, it's just science. She read about it on the internet: operant conditioning. As it turns out, nothing makes you crave something more than an inconsistent schedule of reinforcement. She and Ted don't always eat lunch together, but it seems like lately they do, and she looks forward to them, a little too much. Which is why she ended up on the Wikipedia article about B.F. Skinner and cognitive behavior therapy yesterday, waiting for the knock that never came.

It doesn't help that her studio is an unused extension of Ted's office, something the original owner had built but never finished. She has her own entrance, but she sees him every day. Proximity breeds familiarity, and familiarity breeds…

Knock, knock.

She sighs, the force of the expelled air surprising her.

"Come in," Abby says.

When the door opens, he is as she envisaged him, the top button of his shirt freed, the knot of his blue tie hanging slightly askew.

"Feel like eating?"

"Sure, why not," she says, her voice forcibly nonchalant.

They walk over to his closet, which houses the breaker box, cleaning supplies, and a small fridge. They both brown bag, Ted with his ham and cheese sandwich, potato chips, and brownie, Abby with her beige Tupperware container of chicken Caesar salad. Their lunch is not much to look at, ever, and even where they eat isn't anything special, the two-seater leather couch and matching armchair in Ted's office, where he breaks the ice with his clients before they move over to the big desk for the real work of financial planning. Ted sits in the armchair while Abby takes the couch, their unspoken designated places.

"You look a little down today, Ms. Kim," Ted says.

"Do I, Mr. Wingfield."

Ted offers her the open bag of potato chips. Abby fishes out two curved discs. They're salty-sweet, laced with barbeque flavoring.

"Is it because you're spending time with your Lilliputian locket while the massive baby awaits?"

Abby, her mouth full of arugula and chicken, stares at him, dumbfounded.

"Surprised at my Sherlock-Holmes-level of detection, I see," Ted says. "Don't choke now — finish your bite so you can praise me appropriately."

"You're hilarious."

"I try."

"I don't know if it's, what do you say, greener grass, but if I could, all I'd do is make small stuff."

"Why don't you?"

"Not enough pay."

"Ah — money. Everybody wants more than they have. The couple that was here last? Their portfolio is pushing fifteen million, yet they pine for more."

Ted takes his brownie and splits it down the middle.

"Let my wife's mad baking skills give you a spiritual boost," he says.

Dark, dark chocolate, so dark it's almost sour, coats her tongue like poured paint. Abby closes her eyes and sinks into the couch cushion.

"This is no dessert, it's a drug."

"Beth knows her chocolate."

"Thank you, Beth."

"She loves to hear her treats are doing good in the world, so she'll be thrilled. But back to your cash flow problem — why can't you just crank out more of your smaller paintings?"

LINES

"The rich want big things. In business, no scale? Doesn't scale." *And Joshua didn't get his promotion,* she doesn't say, even though she wants to. She wants to tell Ted about his bitter moods, his moping around the house when his writing isn't going well, the way he shuts down. But no, she's already dumping on Ted as it is, and this is one subject she really doesn't want to get into, because she knows once she starts, she'll never stop.

She feels a buzz in her pocket. Her phone. A text.

"Shit," Abby says.

"What's the matter?"

"This gallery show I'm curating — one fucking problem after another. *Big Bird with Roadkill 1* is still stuck in customs."

"That sounds like a very interesting painting," Ted says.

"Franny is one very interesting painter. You will come? Bring along Beth? Maybe the kids, too, though some art might give them nightmares. Anyway, I must deal with this. Thank you for my venting."

"Happy to perform my designated duty," Ted says.

She rises. "Not your duty to hear me bitch. Next time, your turn, okay?"

"Sounds fantastic. I'm meeting with the Robertsons tomorrow morning, so I'll be armed with venom."

"So we'll do it again tomorrow?" Abby asks.

"Same time, same channel."

Tomorrow, noon. As she walks away from him, down the hallway and back into her studio, she already looks forward to it.

*

Hold the door, hold the door — that's why his name is Hodor.

Goddamn.

Joshua has just finished reading the recap of the latest episode of *Game of Thrones* from the AV Club website, and now he's filled with awe…and pity. Awe for the show, pity for himself, that is. Before he gets too wrapped up in the drama, he remembers to close his browser window and pop up the Word document in its place, some dumb-ass internal memo that he was supposed to have finished editing yesterday.

He pushes off from his cubicle desk and makes his way to the water cooler. Up ahead on his right is the conference room, where raucous laughter erupts just as Joshua passes by. He catches Harold, his fat prick of a manager, with his head tipped backward, mouth wide open, his teeth on full display. Fucking Harold.

If there was someone he hated even more than Harold, it was Walt, who of course is right there, draining the water tank into his enormous pink bottle.

"You catch the ep last night?" Walt asks.

"Hold the door," Joshua says.

"I swear, the cinematography of *Thrones* rivals anything at the movies."

"Right on."

"Uh-oh," Walt says. "I think it's tapped out." He leaves, sucking on the nipple of his bottle like an overgrown baby.

The last thing Joshua needs to do is to replace the tank, because he tweaked his back yesterday, but he needs to drink so he can poop without straining. This is the sad truth as he has firmly entered his forties, that water is no longer just for quenching thirst, according to the gastroenterologist he saw last month after a nasty bout of hemorrhoids, the doctor who charged $437 to speak to him for five whole minutes.

LINES

"Hey, what about your back?"

The voice of friendship, the voice of reason, Marlene. Before he can even respond, she moves past him to pull out the tank by its neck.

"Wait," Joshua says. "Let's do it together."

They lift the jug and heave it onto the stand and watch and listen to the glug glug glug as the water rushes into the unit. And it might be the sound of water or that he's just sad, but tears well up and overflow and breach his bushy salt-and-pepper beard.

Marlene hands him a Kleenex without a word. How does she have a Kleenex when she doesn't even have her purse with her?

He dabs his eyes and waits as the spout flows cold water into his blue bottle. Printed on the side are tick marks:

Tolstoy 32oz

Bronte 28

Dickens 24

Austen 20

Faulkner 16

Steinbeck 12

Hemingway 8

Morrison 4

It's from Powell's, the gigantic bookstore in Portland, Oregon. It's one of the many places he wishes to visit. So many places he'll never get to because he's poor and stupid and Jesus, what a fucking pity party he's having all by himself at the water cooler.

"You got me this," he says, pointing to his bottle.

"A while ago. The letters are starting to rub off."

Joshua turns off the spigot and takes a long drink from his bottle. A fun fact: the physical act of crying is impossible if you are drinking. Is this the reason why the depressed often become alcoholics?

"I hope I thanked you when you gave it to me," he says, screwing the bottle closed.

"I'm certain you did," she says. "Come with me?"

Joshua follows Marlene to her office, which is located on the pretty side of the PayRight building, showcasing the verdant green of Jersey City's Liberty State Park. She became Senior Vice President of Client Services last year, and deservedly so. Every time Joshua has stayed late, Marlene has as well, which undoubtedly means she stays late all the time. They started at PayRight on the same day, a decade ago, sitting through the idiotic sexual harassment video during orientation ("No, Mr. Whitaker, that is very inappropriate behavior"), making silly comments like the hosts of *Mystery Science Theater 3000*. Ever since then, they've been best work friends.

Marlene closes the door behind her. Instead of sitting behind the desk, she sits in one of the two chairs in front and guides Joshua to sit in the other one.

"What's going on?" she asks.

"Hodor," Joshua says.

"What the fuck is a Hodor?"

"*Game of Thrones.*"

"Please don't tell me you're shedding actual tears over the fate of a fictional character in a TV show."

He tells Marlene that the night before, he stayed up until two in the morning fighting with his computer. At the beginning of the season, a tech-savvy friend of his told him how to download the latest episodes using something called BitTorrent, but then the website where Joshua went to get the file was down last night and he ended up getting some horrible malware or virus or whatever the hell it was from another site.

"Luckily, my shitty laptop is so ancient that the malicious code didn't execute all the way, or at least that's what the tech support people told me. It cost $50 to talk to them for ten minutes. It would've been cheaper for me to just get the online HBO thing."

"I have HBO," Marlene says. "I barely watch it. I read something recently where college kids can use their parents' account or something."

"I read that, too."

"Okay. Let's figure this out so you can cry about something more meaningful in the future."

They move to the other side of the desk, Joshua dragging his chair over, Marlene sitting behind her computer. From this vantage point, Joshua sees the only photo frame on her desk, her miniature brown wiener dog, Bocci, and is not surprised that the password she shares with him is Bocci0417, a combination of the canine's name and her own birthday. The password he uses most frequently is 0902Abby, his birthday and his wife.

"You don't have to do this, you know," Joshua says.

"Don't be silly." She writes her username and password down for him on a Post-It. Over thirty employees report to her but her penmanship is like that of a girl, all exaggerated curves and an empty circle for the dot over the *i*. He's always found this adorable but has never told her and wonders why he hasn't. He could tell her now, but no, it feels wrong, like he's crossing a line.

A loud guffaw draws their attention to the hallway, at the two men sauntering by, Harold and Walt.

"Your BFFs," Marlene says.

"God."

"Still pisses me off when I see them together. I can only imagine what you feel."

Joshua plays with a pen on the desk, a black and gold thing with some expensive heft.

"It's all right. It would've been a nightmare dealing with Harold on a daily basis. Though I could've used the pay bump, obviously."

In his heart of hearts, Joshua knew he wouldn't get the promotion, but it still hurt to have it come to fruition, to have his hope officially dashed last week when Harold made the announcement at the all-hands meeting.

Marlene peels off the note and hands it over. "Guard that with your life."

"I don't know if my life is worth as much as this."

"Hey."

"Kidding. Thank you, Marlene. Starting next week, I won't have to pretend at lunch that I've seen the episode and carry on a fake conversation with my fellow cubemates."

"If you haven't seen the episode, how do you know…?"

"Recaps."

"Recaps?"

Joshua laughs. "You're like the smartest person at PayRight, but sometimes it amazes me how there are some things you have no idea about. Recaps — so there are people on the internet who summarize the plot of TV shows. Recappers."

"And people get paid for doing this?"

"The ones with talent," Joshua says.

"Or the ones who got lucky."

"Sometimes it's one and the same."

"And sometimes not."

Joshua knows what Marlene is doing, and even though he appreciates her morale boost on one level, it also just makes him feel worse, like an even bigger failure as a novelist than he already feels. And now he can see Marlene feels badly, too, recognizing she's had the opposite effect.

"Okay, moving on. That thing you told me about a few weeks ago, the art show that your wife Abby put together?"

This is a funny habit of hers, always referring to Abby as "wife Abby," almost like a title.

"*Barely Imagined Beings.*"

"Right — you'll be there?" she asks.

"Why? You're not going, are you?"

"Now wait a minute. Why would you tell me about it if you didn't want me to go?"

"One, I didn't think you would go. Two, I was asked to ask because Abby's afraid nobody's going to show. But believe me, people always show, the worst kind of people, especially the artists themselves."

Marlene tilts her head and smiles. "Now I want to go more than ever. What's the matter with them? The website looks good…"

She navigates her browser to Abby's website, because the gallery show link is there. And for a moment he sees her home page, an image of a circular painting that depicts a room inside an abandoned building. The window is broken, the wallpaper is peeling, and shards of glass and pieces of plaster are scattered across the well-worn wooden boards. Why she still insists on keeping this particular eyesore as her representative work, Joshua cannot fathom. She is literally painting garbage, wasting her obvious talent on decrepitude and decay.

"You look like you're in pain," Marlene says.

Joshua rakes his fingers through his beard.

"This. This does not bring home the bacon."

"I thought she's taking on commissions now."

"She's got one now, but she hates doing it. She's obsessed with painting these ridiculous things that could sell on Etsy, you know? Trinket-like tiny stuff that no serious collector wants. That's the problem with all these artists, Marlene. They're all obsessed within their own tunneled vision, and I swear, it's a sickness."

He begins his diatribe with Franny DelMonico, the gal who paints roadkill into all of her scenes. Whether it be a couple sitting down for a dinner or a shelf of a child's room full of stuffed animals, there's always a bleeding, often disemboweled carcass of a squirrel or a bird or even an eviscerated deer embedded somewhere on the canvas, akin to a *Where's Waldo* of the grisly grotesque. Then there's Roberto Vasquez, who uses a four-colored ball point pen, the familiar white and blue cylinder with red, black, green, and blue triggers that teachers used to use to grade homework, to inscribe meticulous side portraits of people into a pocket sketchbook. These pictorials are as finely detailed as presidential heads on paper currency, but he has now veered off into only doing farm animals.

"I don't know. It's kind of neat, the way they really go into something," Marlene says.

"See, they got you, too." Joshua opens his eyes and mouth wide and points with a blank look on his face.

"Some other reference I don't know."

"Donald Sutherland in *Invasion of the Body Snatchers*. One of these days, you and I are going to sit in front of the television and binge through all the essential cinema. Hey, it's almost lunchtime. Let's go out. I'll do everything I can to steer you away from attending this horror show of an event."

As they head toward the elevator, Marlene asks, "But aren't you going to be there, at the show?"

LINES

Joshua stops, smiles, his grin as wide as a clown's.

"Not if I already have plans with my best friend from work," he says.

apart

The PATH Train, Hoboken to 9th St.

JOSH STARES AT his smartphone like everybody else riding the jerky PATH train. *Barely Imagined Beings*, the PDF reads. *A group exhibition featuring 17 artists using animal forms and imagery in various media including: video, installation, painting, and sculpture. Guest curated by Abby Kim.* The two pictures on the document are a painting curiously called "Still Life of Toys with Roadkill" and an impressively detailed ballpoint pen sketch of a goat's head.

With a screech and a burnt rubber smell, the train comes to a stop. "Christofuh," the staticky voice yells out. "Christofuh Street, Ninth next."

On this Thursday at 7pm, the train car racing from New Jersey to Manhattan is almost empty. Across from him are two men with a vacant seat between them, their eyes closed and their heads tipped back against the window, both drowning out the outside world with their white earbuds. Josh, on the other hand, is wide awake and excited to be right here, right now. Marlene's attending a Big Pharma conference in Boston, which bummed him out because he really wanted her to meet Abby, the artist who created the locket she now wears every day, but at the same time, there's a part of him that is glad to fly solo. Museums and Marlene don't mix, her patience with the slow walk limited to less than an hour. Even at the Louvre a few years back, Marlene could barely muster two hours. Still, Josh feels apprehensive about going by himself to a place he's never been before, to see people he doesn't know.

Except that's not true — he knows one person, Abby.

As soon as the doors slide open at the 9th Street stop, warm air rushes in.

When he exits the car, he grabs his blue bottle from his messenger bag. The water's still cold and wakes up his throat, his chest. He wants to feel everything, remember everything tonight. He and Marlene have always said they should come into New York once a month, but they're lucky to make it once a season.

Before he puts his bottle away, he glances at the "Nutritional Facts" printed on its side:

Suggested Daily Reading*

Plot 52%

Narrative 28%

Lyricism 12%

Pretense 3%

Hyperbole 5%

* Serving sizes are based on a 1600 page per week diet.

Marlene bought this for him when they visited Powell's Books in Portland, Oregon, together, their first trip as a couple. Has it already been so long that half the printed letters on the bottle have faded away? He could still remember walking along Burnside Street as if it were yesterday, a bookstore so big that it filled an entire city block. It was a curious feeling being amongst all those books. In a way, it made him feel small, that there were all these authors who have already published their works while he still hadn't produced anything. But there was solace there, too, being amongst that vast expanse of printed paper. If all these people had achieved publication nirvana, why not him?

A street away from Powell's was Stumptown, where he and Marlene shared a pint of chocolate cold brew coffee that gave them such a caffeine buzz that they practically ran into the arms of Blue Star with their brioche doughnut. Marlene went for the classic glazed while Josh chose the one coated with green tea powder, and neither spoke a word until they'd each devoured their divine carbohydrate bliss.

Here at the train platform, as he climbs the stairs of the 9th Street PATH station, Josh recalls fondly how life-changing that Portland trip had been. Six months later, he and Marlene were husband and wife, and two years after working steadily on his first novel, he had completed the first draft. Another three years would pass until he finally found an agent dogged enough to sell it to a small independent publisher, but Portland was where it had all begun.

But he wasn't in Portland now, he was in New York City! Across the 9th Street PATH station exit is the Avenue of the Americas, and goodness, does it ever feel like America itself. Within a minute he walks past a Hasidic Jew, a Muslim woman, a Chinese tour group led by a man holding up a red Star Wars lightsaber. He hears a couple speaking French, and on the next block he encounters a silver food truck with a bright yellow sign that screams *Falafel! Kabob! Shawarma!* A pyramid-shaped hunk of slivered meat on a vertical spit lazily spins under a pair of heat lamps that pull double duty as spotlights. Even though Josh ate dinner before getting on the train, he can't pass this up.

"Hello my friend!" the smiling server inside the truck says. "What would you like?"

"One lamb shawarma, please?"

The guy expertly shaves the meat with a mini machete.

Is there anything better than walking and eating on the streets of New York? At night, this city becomes its true self, its cosmopolitan denizens roaming its fascinating streets. Every bite of the pita, with its spiced meat, yogurt, and hummus, is wonderfully foreign and complicated. Josh laughs as he remembers a silly Simpsons quote, Homer's friend Lenny who exclaims in an episode, "It's like there's a party in my mouth and everybody's invited!"

For a late February night, it's surprisingly warm; he unzips his jacket to cool off. By the time he finishes his shawarma, he's made it to 3rd Street, with a row of tattoo parlors to his right and an asphalt basketball court to his left. Up ahead, Josh sees the lit-up marquee of the IFC movie theater highlighting the artsy films he's never heard of — *The Bad Batch, The Ornithologist, Band Aid.* These are movies that he'd never be able to see at home in Basking Ridge, New Jersey. Over on the court, it's a fierce three-on-three game, the men passing the basketball like a hot potato until a player drives to the basket and finger rolls the ball in. And beyond the chain-link fence, a handball court abuts a pale green wall. Handball! New York really has it all.

Josh checks his smartphone to make sure he's not veering off his intended destination. Despite the bevy of distractions, he's still on target, Bleecker Street ahead. A few blocks later, he finds the gallery located between a $1 pizza joint and an Indian restaurant. It isn't much to look at from the outside, the gold and black sign *Torp Gallery* above the glass doors affixed over the unfaded oblong space that used to house the old sign. But none of that matters because through those glass doors, the art awaits. Standing klieg lights, like the ones used on film sets, shine on their assigned subjects, two of them on a painting he recognizes from the website, "Still Life of Toys with Roadkill." From here, standing outside and looking in through the door, Josh sees Abby cross his vision. She's wearing a knee-length white dress with a repeating rose pattern, black stockings, black boots. It's almost a shock to see her so dressed up, because the last time he saw her, the first time he met her at her apartment a month before to pick up the locket, she was in a ratty gray sweatshirt, black yoga pants, and blue flip flops.

He can still remember her knocking on the window of the apartment's outer door, even though he'd been the one outside. She was a short little thing, a girl, looking more like a high school student than a woman in her thirties. Her hair was cut shorter than what he'd seen in a few photos of her on Google Images, not quite shoulder-length, which for some odd reason disappointed him.

He smiled and she smiled back. She opened the door.

"Mr. Kozlov?"

"Please, call me Josh."

He crossed the threshold and towered over Abby. He wasn't that tall, two inches short of six feet, but next to her he felt like a gawky giant. Were you supposed to shake hands with painters? Hug them? Bow? He didn't know what to do.

"I'm on the third floor. No elevator, so we shall climb?"

Shall? Who said *shall* anymore?

"You lead, I'll follow."

The stairs were narrow and creaky and dark, but Josh couldn't have been more excited. He was about to see a painter's actual studio! Abby stopped on the third floor, in front of apartment 3G that bore the following brass nameplate:

JAMESON REHNQUIST
DOCTOR OF PSYCHIATRY

"That looks like it's been there for a hundred years," Josh said.

"It pre-dates myself for sure," Abby said. "Please, come in."

Josh couldn't say what he'd envisioned — perhaps a white room populated with easels displaying paintings in various stages of completion — but it wasn't this. To his right was a tiny kitchen, barely big enough for one person. The hallway opened up to a room about the size of his own kitchen, with a wooden desk in one corner and a futon in the other. The futon was crouched upright with a glittery blue cover thrown over it to turn it into an ersatz couch.

"Could you have some tea?" she asked.

He never drank tea, but it seemed rude to refuse.

"That'd be great."

"Mint or chamomile?"

"Dealer's choice." He noticed her hesitation as she moved toward her cupboard. "Either one is fine. How about mint."

"Of course. And if I may ask, what is this dealer and what is the choice?"

Even though she spoke English well enough, it was obvious common phrases escaped her knowledge. When Josh explained the idiom to her, she picked up a pen and notepad to jot it down.

"My brain is not as dependable as it once was," she said.

"That makes two of us. Google Calendar reminders run my life. So you paint your paintings there?"

It was as ordinary as a desk could be, built out of an anonymous dark brown hardwood. A scuffed brass knob protruded from a single center drawer. On its surface were two Solo plastic cups of paint brushes, a roll of paper towels, and a colorful slab of an angled particle board with two of her paintings stuck to it, the left one a forest fire, the right a path in a sunny forest. The board served dual purposes, her workspace and her palette.

"I require but a limited area to work," she said.

LINES

As Josh now pulls open the door to Torp Gallery, he remembers the sorrow he felt as he stood over her desk. Why sorrow? It was unmistakable, his sadness, and also the wish to help her in some way. Not that she needed his help — she was making her living as an artist in New York City, no small feat. No, she was doing just fine…but standing there next to this tiny girl in her tiny apartment with her tiny paintings, Josh had felt such a profound sense of longing.

"Josh!"

The gallery is packed with onlookers, but she's found him. She walks over to him with open arms.

*

The artist Abby introduces to Josh first is Franny DelMonico, not because she's her best friend but because Franny is as interesting as an artist can get. She can depict anything on any scale, one of the most versatile painters in Abby's MFA graduating class at the School, but what separates Franny from everyone else is her artistic purpose.

They are standing in front of a 20x30 painting that features SpongeBob SquarePants, Donald Duck, and a pair of princess dolls in ballroom gowns, one blonde, one brunette. The level of detail is nothing short of astonishing: the red bow on Donald Duck's lapel is painted with such verisimilitude that it looks as if an actual tie is attached to the canvas. These toys are set upon a white tablecloth atop a dresser, in various scattershot positions — the blonde princess is lying on her side, Donald Duck is almost upside down, leaning against the brunette. Sitting upright and center-left is a plush SpongeBob, its fabric folds almost touchable in its realistic illusion, no doubt the focus of the painting because of the disemboweled, bleeding squirrel draped over his spindly arms, as if he's cradling a dead lover.

"I feel like laughing…and cringing…at the same time," Josh says.

"That's the right response, Josh," Franny says. "You pass the test, my good man."

"I'm sure you've answered this question a thousand times, but why the carcass?"

"Back in the 17th century, many painters, the best were Flemish, painted hunting still lifes. Hunted animals hanging on hooks amid bowls of fruits. This is my way of satirizing that."

"The juxtaposition of the infantile and the gruesome — it's just absurd, isn't it? Funny but also sad."

Abby catches Franny's eyes, the way she's looking at Josh. Her friend is not easily impressed.

"Where did you find this fine fella, Abby?" she says.

Before she can answer, Josh and Franny are bathed in alternating lights of red and blue. She must be, too, because when she turns toward the entrance, she shields her eyes as a pair of police officers come through the doors in silhouette. Abby hurries over to the older uniformed officer who stands with his arms akimbo, hands on his belt.

"You in charge here?" he asks.

"I'm the curator," she says. "The gallery owner was here but he left after the show started."

"We need everybody out," he says. "We received a bomb threat."

"I don't understand," Abby says.

Behind them, another officer enters with a German shepherd dog.

Josh, now standing next to her, asks, "What's going on?"

"Seventeen minutes past nine, an anonymous caller rang up our department and reported a bomb in the building. Probably a crank, but procedures, you know. Excuse me."

LINES

The officer draws in a breath then bellows for everyone to exit in an orderly fashion. There's about fifty people roaming the gallery who indeed file out calmly.

"What the fuck," Franny says. "This is nuts."

"I believe it's good it happened now instead of earlier. In thirty minutes we were going to close anyway," Abby says.

"Art show receives bomb threat — could be a headline, you never know," Josh says.

The German shepherd, clad in a harness of black nylon straps and chrome rings, begins his sniffing at the full-scale cow sculpture made out of papier-mâché. The cow is on its knees with his two front hooves together, a position of prayer; "Holy Cow" is its tongue-in-cheek title. The dog spends a few seconds on its exposed pink udders.

"Either there's a bomb there or that dog wants some milk," Franny says.

"You guys, too," the officer says. "Out."

They grab their coats at the entrance and make their way out to Bleecker Street. Abby buttons her black pea coat all the way up to her neck; she's always envious of just about everyone when it comes to body temperature. Neither Franny nor Josh have their jackets zipped up, comfortably chatting with each other in the winter night.

Abby feels an arm wrapping around her waist.

"Hey sugar!" he says.

"Roberto! I'm so glad you came!"

"Except it looks like I missed the festivities."

Roberto, in his stylish blue porkpie hat with a yellow feather in his brim, gives Abby a squeeze. She knows of no one with a higher degree of mastery than Roberto when it comes to ballpoint drawings, especially portraits. Using a limited palette of four pen colors, he renders expressions rivaling Norman Rockwell's. The first time Abby saw his skill, at the School's mid-level drawing class, she was filled with admiration and envy. After almost a decade of practice, she's become a good pen sketcher of buildings and animals, but Roberto was a genuine prodigy. For his final project, he created a one-dollar bill that could pass for real with Barack Obama as the portrait president. No matter how much she draws, Abby believes she'll never be as good as him, but how fortunate they were great friends and she got to see his works before the public. The unfairness of the universe may be writ small inside the Moleskin sketchpad that Roberto carries with him in his back pocket, but having a peek at that book always makes her day. She dearly hopes he brought it with him tonight.

"Roberto! Hey, now that the gang's complete, let's all go Peculiar!" Franny says.

"Peculiar?" Josh asks.

"Peculiar Pub, three blocks up," Abby says. It is their de facto hangout around these parts, a chummy bar with a white tin ceiling and church pew booths.

"You're coming with us, Josh, no excuses," Franny says.

"It's an honor," he says.

"I need to wait to close up the gallery after the cops are done," Abby says. "It shall not be long. You all proceed, I will follow."

"Let me make your wait worthwhile," Roberto says. He pulls his sketchpad from his back pocket and hands it to Abby.

"I may stay in this spot for the next couple of hours," she says.

Roberto tips his cap to her and joins up with Franny and Josh. Before they disappear completely into the gaggle of Saturday night pedestrians, Josh looks back and Abby smiles and waves. It's nice to see him getting along with Franny; her works are larger in scale and way more expensive than Abby's small paintings, but who knows, he may be interested in buying something from Franny as well. Abby isn't a fan of the business side of art, but it has to be done — like this show, which has driven her to the edge of her sanity. But she wants to support her friends, and the best way to support them is to publicize their talent.

She blows into her hands to keep them warm. Through the glass doors of the gallery, Abby watches the bomb dog and his handler walking to the back of the space. They're about to enter a mess in the storage area, mostly because Brenden the gallery owner hadn't put away a single one of the fifty folding chairs that had been set in the middle of the space. That Brenden, what a piece of shit, just like every gallery owner she's ever dealt with. No matter the kind of gallery, whether they be an entry-level space like Torp or catering to hedge fund millionaires like some Gallery Row establishments in SoHo, they are all helmed basically by con men. For his exorbitant 40% cut of any sales, Brenden had promised promotions on radio, print, and art websites, had even specified the frequency and timing with which these advertisements would run, but he'd crafted the contractual language in such a way to get away with the barest of minimums. He hadn't even bothered to put away the chairs, which Abby had to fold and drag over by herself an hour before the show opened.

But enough, enough with the negativity. In her hand now is the reward for her valiant efforts, opening the sketchpad and letting Roberto's art take her away. She leans against a lamppost and lets its luminescence shine onto these hallowed pages.

"Hey."

She looks up and finds Josh. Framed against the yellow glow of the light above him, he looks angelic, blessed.

"I didn't want you to wait here by yourself. And if I may be perfectly frank, I want a peek at Roberto's sketches as much as you do. Last time we met, you told me so much about him."

"There's room for one more on this lamppost," she says.

"Goodie!" he says, unbridled with joy. It's been a long day, but Abby draws strength from Josh's ardor, the faint flowery scent of his cologne, his jacket brushing against hers.

"It's like we're having our own little gallery show, isn't it?" he says.

Abby nods. She opens the sketchpad with a flip.

A small boy standing on a dining room chair, one bare foot on the cushion, the other foot and his little hands on the wooden back of the seat, his head turned right to the viewer: It's like gazing upon a hidden treasure that gazes back at you.

Abby feels Josh's breath on her neck.

"Oh wow," he says.

"His face," she says.

"That smile!" they say at the same time.

They turn to each other. *Right here,* Abby thinks. *There's no place I'd rather be than right here.*

together

NYC Subway, Bleecker Street to 28th Street via 6 Train

A DISASTER, FROM beginning to end. As Abby rides the 6 train back to 28th Street, her mind lands on the final humiliation of the night: a pair of NYPD officers shutting down the gallery show. The one in charge, the older one, he was clearly enjoying his power trip, bellowing to everybody to get the hell out. There were only a handful of patrons left, and when they were gone, the two cops walked around the gallery like they owned it.

"Get a load of this cow," she overheard him say to his partner, the younger guy, who was an even bigger asshole.

"Our tax dollars at work, sarge."

What Abby wanted to say was *We paid for this space with our own money*, but of course she stayed silent as a third cop joined in the needless bomb detection effort, holding onto a hundred-pound German shepherd dog that looked like a wolf.

The threatening crank call the cops had received was no doubt Brenden's fault. The reason why Torp Gallery was a cheaper rental than every other venue Abby had checked out was because her show was a last-minute replacement for the space. After what happened tonight, Abby dearly wished she had asked more questions, but now it seemed clear that Brenden had cancelled the previous reservation, not the other way around like she had been led to believe. So Brenden screwed the guy over, probably because Abby was willing to pay a little more. To get back at Brendan, the guy called in a fake bomb and ruined her show.

But who was she fooling? Having the opening night end early was the best thing that could've happened, a mercy killing with a chance for media coverage, which is what artists need almost as much as money. Jackson Pollock may have been a genius, but his genius wouldn't have gotten anywhere without the criticism of Clement Greenberg who bestowed upon him the attention that he deserved. Who knew, if an art critic or a popular art blog somehow heard about what happened tonight because of the police activity, they might write about the show and then delve a little deeper to her friends' works, Roberto's unreal sketches or Franny's striking paintings. Unlikely, but possible. She has to believe in the possible, to keep hoping for better days than this one.

Abby gets off at the 28th Street stop and climbs the stairs to street level. It's four blocks back to the apartment, but after she buttons up her coat, she can't make herself walk that way. Even though she's fairly certain that Joshua hasn't returned from whatever it was he was doing — helping his co-worker Marlene with something or another, she can't remember — he might already be home. In her mind's eye, she sees him sunken on their Salvation Army couch with the lights out, the glow of the smartphone illuminating the sour expression on his face that combines a grimace and a sneer. In her mind's ear, she hears it, *pppfffffftttttt*, the disgusting raspberry of his fart. In her mind's nose, she smells it, the acrid scent of a rotten egg rising like an angry apparition. She should be more sympathetic to her husband's gastrointestinal ailment, which is a genuine medical condition, but oh god, no, she can't go home, not now.

Never have the bright lights of a McDonald's seemed friendlier. She pushes open the door, the odor of grease and fat enticingly off-putting. Abby orders a small cup of black coffee and sits down at a booth by the window that looks out onto the street. She is the only diner at the moment, which makes her feel even worse. It'd be nice to be in the company of other human beings, even complete strangers, because she hasn't felt this lonely in years.

The only saving grace from the evening is on her ghetto LG smartphone, whose cracked screen has gotten even more spiderwebbed since she dropped it on the subway this evening. But thankfully it still turns on and is able to display a snapshot of Roberto's latest sketch, the little boy standing on the chair, his tiny toes pressed against the cushion, his smile a wonder. Staring at this image loosens the knot in her stomach. It clears her head and reminds her that all that matters in this world is the work, her work, what she creates, what she captures. Because that's what Roberto has done here, captured a moment in time and space. That's what great art does, it pauses the movement of the universe and marks it. Everything else is a distraction, including Joshua, especially Joshua.

Just when was it that her husband had become her enemy? It may make logical sense that the one you love the most has the greatest potential to hurt you, but it makes no emotional sense. Five years ago, they'd fallen in love, so hard and so fast that they got married just two months later. Perhaps if she'd been an accountant and had accountant colleagues, she would have received conservative advice against such a rushed union, but her fellow artists considered passion as the ultimate verifier of affection and offered her nothing but praise. Franny was one such memorable offender, romanticizing the comingling of the writer and the artist into a glorious fantasy…

Wait a minute. Is she really blaming her friends for the trainwreck that is now her marriage? What lowly depths has she sunk to. Besides, things were fine for a good long while. Even if their matrimony had been fueled by their initial fire, the first couple of years were solid.

But it's been unbearable for the past twelve months. Something broke inside Joshua, and possibly between them, too. It all started about a year and a half ago, around Independence Day, when Joshua had finally gotten a sliver of good news from his literary agent. His first novel, one that took him nine years to complete, had accrued twenty-six rejections by various publishers, but the twenty seventh wanted it.

This was good news, but Joshua did not consider it as such. In fact, it turned into a source of great resentment. "Three grand," she heard him mutter to himself in the bathroom on more than one occasion as she walked by him in the hallway, staring at his mirrored reflection. That's how much they were willing to pay, Hot Metal Press, an independent publisher located in Brooklyn. Apparently their outer borough location was a knock against them, because all publishers of note were on the island of Manhattan.

But even if Hot Metal was small time, wasn't it better to have sold a book to someone than not at all? Abby knew better than to say that to his face, so she kept her opinion to herself. Which is what she'd done for all of last year and now this year, too, staying out of the path of Hurricane Joshua, who hates his soul-sucking job, hates his irritable bowels, hates the cover of his book, and hates his wife, too. If he is her enemy, surely the feeling is mutual.

It's his darkness that she finds most oppressive. Not that she needs her life to be filled with rainbows and sunshine 24/7, but as someone who tries to paint the fragility of beauty in the world, Joshua's relentless dourness is a chisel that chips away at her optimism.

And then there were his farts, his nasty, stinky, extremely loud farts. They started right about the time Hot Metal bought the book. Maybe they are some sort of a psychosomatic reaction to the stress, but really, something has to be done about them. As long as she's known him, Joshua has had a sensitive stomach, but now, after he eats his dinner, it's like he transforms into the most foul-smelling machine gun. The worst is that at night while he sleeps, his farts change from the *rat-at-tat* to singular, concentrated *booms* that have woken her up.

"Excuse me, but do I know you?"

LINES

Just when she thought her evening couldn't get any shittier, here it was, being hit on at McDonald's. She hasn't even looked up from her cup, but she can hear that *thing* in a man's tone, a certain kind of pleading confidence. But she's wrong — this man is old, possibly pushing his eighties, yet his voice is so young and so is his demeanor. Wearing a stylish black pinstriped suit, he leans on his cane and smiles at her.

"Apologies, but I don't know you, sir."

He snaps his fingers. "Abby Kim, aren't you? The artist?"

Now it's her turn to smile. This is something that happens to her perhaps once a year, being recognized outside of a gallery show. "Yes, thank you, I am she."

"May I sit here, young lady?"

"Surely."

He places one hand on the edge of the table and the other on the cane and slowly begins to lower himself, though about halfway down his descent, he loses control and plops down. Abby involuntarily rises from her seat, but the man waves her off.

"Used to be more graceful than this," he says. "I'm Melvin, Melvin Donovan. That shouldn't ring a bell because I'm just a guy who likes art, one of your many anonymous admirers, I imagine. The last thing I expected tonight was to walk into a McDonald's and find you here. I came from your *Barely Imagined Beings* show. I really enjoyed your last group show at that High Line gallery, too — those tiny little circles of your cycling trip. I even bought the one of your bike."

"Marvin," she says.

"Melvin, my name is Melvin."

She laughs. "No, the name of my bike. Marvin, a character in a science fiction novel."

"The Paranoid Android, of course?" Melvin asks. "Douglas Adams' *The Hitchhiker's Guide to the Galaxy*."

For the next half hour, she and Melvin chat like old friends, about her cycling trip through the Austrian countryside, his love of off-track horserace betting, their shared complaints for the latest delays on the A-C-E subway line.

"I don't mean to pry into your professional life, Abby, but I haven't seen any new posts from you on Instagram in a while. Have you been busy with other things?"

"A commission is taking longer than expected," she says. She turns on her smartphone and brings up a shot of her baby painting in progress.

"It's big," Melvin says.

"A hundred times larger than the actual child, I think," she says.

"I didn't know you created larger works. Nothing like that on your website outside of your early stuff."

"Melvin, you really know my history!"

He places his right hand over his heart. "I'm not just some fair-weather fan, Abby. So it sounds like you're doing this for the money."

"All commissions are for money."

"Point taken."

Abby flips past the baby pics and stops at a close-up of her tiny white dress painting sitting next to the locket.

"May I?" Melvin says, pointing to her phone.

"Of course."

He stares at it for a good thirty seconds.

"To go into the locket, I presume."

"Correct."

"For a show?"

LINES

"Supposed to be, but I missed the deadline. But I liked the idea and wanted to do it anyway."

"How much?"

Abby tells him four hundred. Melvin takes out his billfold and writes her a check.

"My address is on the check. When you are done with it, you can mail it right there. I wrote it out for $420, which should be enough for shipping insurance and all that."

Melvin rips the check from the pad and hands it to Abby. She stares at it, the faux parchment background, Melvin's flourished signature at the bottom. As a child, she hardly cried. *Jang-goon*, her mother used to call her, the word for a general in Korean. But right now, she cries, silently. Why the tears all of a sudden? She's grateful but not *that* grateful. It's not like this check is necessary to pay the rent or buy food — there's still money in the bank for the month.

No, it's like there's someone else inside her body, making her do things she doesn't understand. She dabs her eyes with a napkin. Melvin looks away, gives her the space to compose herself.

"Thank you," she says.

"You're welcome. You've made my evening."

"I say the same."

With both hands on his cane's handle, Melvin lifts himself off the chair. "I turn eighty-six this year, so when I tell you that time goes by fast, I know of what I speak. Do what gives you joy, Abby. You won't regret it. Good night."

Abby bids him the same. What remains of her coffee is cold, but she drinks it down to the last sugary drop. Home is a ten-minute walk, so she could get back without having to pee, but she kind of does feel like peeing now that she's thinking about it.

She pushes open the door to the women's bathroom and to her right sees an angry-looking sign over the tampon dispenser.

!!! OUT OF ORDER !!!

Written in red, a trio of exclamation marks bookending the all-caps pronouncement. The notice is huge, poster-board sized, way bigger than it needs to be. Kind of like her baby painting.

As she pees into the bowl, her mind on tampons and babies, a thought occurs to her:

When was my last period?

*

To fart or not to fart — that is the question.

The answer is yes. And once the intent is established, what comes next is as natural and inevitable as a cool breeze after a rain.

A good, loud, solid fart is not only a physical release but a metaphorical one. Out out, damned gas! With every thunderous dispersion of the foulness within, body and soul start anew, tabula rasa, a clean and well-lighted rebirth.

But sometimes the moment requires a different kind of a fart, an insidious fart, a sneaky fart. And that moment is now, because since the stop at 14th Street on the PATH back from New Jersey, the lady standing above where Joshua is seated has poked him in the head with the umbrella sticking out of her purse three times. Inadvertently, but that doesn't matter. An unaware sin is still a sin, and this encroachment is overdue for a reckoning.

LINES

The steak sandwich he had for dinner a couple of hours ago gave him the usual IBS discomfort, but it has finally fully digested, a meal that also featured caramelized onions with slices of roasted garlic. He feels it, the gaseous payload working its way through his colon like a self-satisfied snake, locked and loaded, his weapon of mass olfactory destruction.

Ready when you are, sir.

Joshua presses down one buttock to assure a silent release.

Fire!

The challenge is to keep a straight face, because Joshua never tires of its noxious effect. The man sitting to his right jumps, literally jumps, his feet leaving the floor of the subway car for a moment as he leans away. The woman to his left lets out an involuntary moan, but then she throws a hand against her mouth to close it, because the last thing she wants is to taste this awful inescapable fart.

Come on, my little invisible monster. Show this old bag what you're made of.

It takes a few more seconds, but the umbrella woman wisely scoots over to the exit doors. She turns back at Joshua's direction, but his face betrays nothing.

How do you like them rotten apples?

"33rd, final stop," the conductor barks. Everybody gets out, but nobody gets out faster than the two people flanking Joshua. Another job well done by his devilish digestion.

As he walks up the stairs to street level, he considers letting out another one. That'd be cruel, wouldn't it? On the staircase with your ass in someone's face and just letting them have it. But no, there's no call for inflicting such trauma, not tonight. After all, he did have a nice time with Marlene, watching *Wonder Woman* with her. It was quaint going to the suburban movie theater to see a blockbuster, a nice change of pace. His fellow writers from his graduate school days wouldn't be caught dead seeing something so popular, opting for the likes of Angelika and IFC to watch some foreign documentary about a genocide no one's heard of. So much cheaper, too, though that didn't even matter because Marlene generously picked up the tab.

He'd told Abby that he had to help out a work friend in need, which wasn't exactly a lie, was it? No, it was not. And it got him out of having to go to her ghastly gallery show opening. If there were people Joshua hated more than his fellow workshoppers, they were Abby's painter freaks.

Joshua walks along 32nd Street, through the hustle and bustle of Koreatown. A biting gust of wind brings the intoxicating scent of *bulgogi*, the marinated beef dish that is always a failsafe option for non-Koreans. One of the more recent incarnations of this carne is as taco filling, but really, there's no bad way of eating *bulgogi*. After being with a Korean woman for half a decade, he should have become a more adventurous eater of his wife's national cuisine, but that hasn't happened, much to the chagrin of her parents, who still try to push the hot stuff on Joshua, like *kimchi-jigae* during last Thanksgiving, a peppery stew so hot that he couldn't taste anything for the rest of the meal.

His phone buzzes, an email. A Google Alert on the name "Deborah Kieslowski."

A thought comes to his head: *Jesus Christ, what now?*

Though what he really should be asking himself is, *Why are you doing this to yourself?*

He wishes he wore something more substantial than a hoodie, because now that it's nine at night, it's fucking frigid. Joshua ducks into Koryo Books, the Korean bookstore he visited with Abby last Christmas, when she was looking for a gift for her father.

Joshua always feels weird whenever he comes to a Korean establishment by himself, because he feels like he belongs here more than a regular white guy. But in order for this to be recognized, he'd have to voice it, which would be super weird. But not saying it feels weird, too. He knows a few Korean words, yet stumbling through his butchered pronunciation of *ahn-nyung-ha-sae-yo*, the Korean equivalent of *how are you*, may be, in the current ultra-PC environment of our modern times, quite likely racist.

"Hey," Joshua says to the reedy-thin guy at the counter who looks up from his smartphone with sleepy eyes.

"Hello," he says.

Did he just wink at him? Does he remember him? Or is it some kind of a tic? Or is the guy *hitting* on him?

Whatever. As usual, Joshua is overthinking it, overthinking everything. He needs to underthink, ignore, be as obtuse as an unacute angle. That's a good line, he should write it down before he forgets. Though he's sure unacute is not a word.

So many books here, wall to wall books, but not a single one is competition because they're all Korean. Though it's probably just a matter of time until Deborah Kieslowski's powerhouse of a debut novel is translated to twenty languages, including Korean, and finds its home here. Now that his fingers are no longer freezing from the cold, Joshua leans against the monumental display of K-Pop-branded pens and pencils, a little makeshift area of scattered scrap paper where customers can test out their writing instrument of choice before buying such tasteless junk.

Up until last year, Deborah was a member of his writing group. But since Deborah's first novel *Days of Wren* was sold to Knopf for what *Publishers Lunch*, a trade magazine equivalent of film's *Variety* for the publishing industry, anointed "a good deal," Deborah has abandoned them. According to the legend on the website, a good deal meant a sale between a hundred grand and a quarter of a million dollars.

Joshua closes his eyes for a moment and imagines an old-school scale, two golden shallow dishes suspended on the opposite ends of a beam — Deborah's egregious pile of cash on one end, Joshua's pitiful sheaf of bills on the other, an epic unbalancing. Two books, yet two wildly different monetary compensations. Was Deborah's book 83 times better written than his? Worth 83 times as much? Nobody in their group thought so. And stranger still was that neither Deborah's nor his was the group's favorite: that was another writer's zany novel about a science teacher moving back and forth through time with a talking monkey, which still hasn't found an agent after two years of searching.

The business of publishing makes no sense. It is less a business and more a casino, but even knowing that doesn't mitigate the frustration of what could've been. Why not him? Why couldn't Joshua be the one who hit the jackpot? God knows he can use the coin, while Deborah lives on the Upper West Side with her cardiologist husband, a Mercedes-Benz, and a doorman.

But back to the Google Alert that raised all this bile. Since Deborah's success, Joshua has been keeping tabs by putting a news alert on her name. It's a kind of self-torture, really. Why be reminded of her good fortune over and over again? What Abby says of him may be true, that there's a part of him that welcomes misery, relishes being a victim, being pinned down against the weight of the world. There is a nobleness in victimhood, isn't there? To be Job, to be a martyr?

Lucky him, there are two Google Alerts, one for an upcoming reading at Strand Books in the city, and a review from *The New York Fucking Times*. In the *Books of the Times* section, which is as high an honor as an author can get in the newspaper because it means it's reviewed by the chief critic and that it appears in the paper itself, not the *Book Review* supplement on Sunday. Not only did Deborah hit the monetary lottery, she hit the literary one, too.

But did she?

LINES

After a couple of paragraphs, Joshua realizes that this is a takedown of the worst kind. "This first-time author has made the gravest of sins, confusing sentiment with sentimentality, equating drama with melodrama." *Contrived, schematic, rootless, obvious*...the negative adjectives pile on and on and Joshua doesn't even realize that he's laughing until he hears himself echoing in the empty store. He looks over to the cashier, who watches him with a curious concern.

"Sorry," Joshua says, holding up his phone. "Just saw something funny."

"We close in fifteen minutes."

Yeah, well, then I'll leave in fifteen minutes, fuckwad.

Just as he's feeling mighty refreshed from this great gift of schadenfreude, his phone emits another short vibration for an email notification and he imagines it must be good news. It is — until it isn't.

Hello Joshua, yes, the honorarium for your short story was sent to you via PayPal. We transmitted the $100 to your email yesterday — it is this email, correct?

Here he stands, laughing at his former colleague who was most likely, to quote Liberace, crying all the way to the bank, while he had sent two emails to *Whirlwind* this week, a literary magazine that no one reads, desperate for the hundred bucks they owe him because he can really, really use it right now to pay the minimum balance on his Visa card.

And as if that strain of thought isn't humiliation enough, the fart he's been holding captive since his subway ride, a bodily function he thought he held dominion over, whistles its escape through his clenched sphincter. It isn't that loud, but in this mausoleum-quiet store, Joshua sees the cashier slowly turning toward him.

If there is a grimace or a look of disgust on his face, Joshua remains oblivious to it, because he keeps his head down and exits as quickly as he can.

Now almost ten o'clock, the unseasonable warmth that had soothed the wintry city earlier is nowhere to be found, replaced by a brittle iciness. Utterly asinine of him to leave his jacket at home — what the hell was he thinking? It's still February. He cinches his hood's strings as tight as he can around his head, but his teeth still chatter as he walks double-time down the street in a futile attempt to bring up his body temperature. The last thing he needs right now is to get sick, because he can't afford to go to the doctor, not with the shitty PayRight insurance he has for him and Abby with its astronomical five grand deductible. Last month, between him and his gastro doctor and Abby's sinus infection that required specialized antibiotics which cost more than two hundred dollars, they're tapped out. What the fuck was health insurance good for? The whole industry is just one giant scam.

As he crosses Madison Avenue, a silver BMW, sleek as a shark, pulls ahead and parks in front of The Cutting Room, a concert hall Joshua has only seen from the outside. The driver is a David Beckham double, five o'clock shadow on chiseled cheeks and a European-cut suit; he walks around to open the door for the woman, who's almost as tall as he is and has a skintight black dress and murderous high heels. Like something out of a TV commercial, Fake Beckham tosses his keys to the valet, who hands him a ticket on his way to move the classy vehicle away from public view.

This is New York City, a fine place if you have money. If you don't? If you don't, then it's a fine place of agony. Those great rock stars who come here? All the great chefs who turn cooking into an art form? The best actors, the best comedians, the best of the best of the best?

They're not for you.

apart

Chase Sapphire Reserve Visa: Pay Full Balance

JOSH HAS LOST count on the number of times he's re-written this email to Deborah Kieslowski. Even though they'd both attended New York University's graduate school during the early 2000's, they've never met. This was not an impossibility because NYU's Masters in Fine Arts in Creative Writing was large, about sixty students. Still, it seems odd that they never ran into each other even once. Josh wishes they had, because then this email wouldn't be taking an hour to write.

This morning when he saw that *The New York Times* had reviewed her first novel, of course the first emotion he felt was jealousy — what writer wouldn't? Published by the revered Knopf, reviewed by the biggest paper in the world, it's every writer's dream and Deborah was living it. But then as Josh kept reading, his jealousy turned into horror, then anger, then finally fell into sorrow. Without a doubt Deborah had made a whole lot more money than he did with his novel, but that's just money, who gives a shit. A review this bad could ruin her career. "This first-time author has made the gravest of sins, confusing sentiment with sentimentality, equating drama with melodrama." What the fuck? It was uncalled for, the mean spiritedness of the review. *Contrived, schematic, rootless, obvious*...the negative adjectives piled on and on, each one a freshly thrown dagger to his poor colleague's heart.

No matter how many times he reads through his email, it just feels wrong. Either too trite…or not trite enough? He trashes the email again.

"You look like you're about to throw up," Marlene yells from the kitchen. She's doing up the dishes, the water running at full blast.

"You can't see me from there, sweetheart," he says.

She turns off the faucet and walks into the living room, drying her hands on a towel. Josh is on the couch with his feet on the coffee table.

"Am I wrong?" she asks.

"One of these days, you must share your secrets, my lovely witch."

"Still working on that email."

"I don't know what to say because I don't know her."

"Isn't that the problem, that you need to get to know her? What could be way more personal than an email, let's see…how about that thing that people used to do with phones?"

"Call her, out of the blue? But that's so…" *Invasive*, but no, Marlene is right. And he does have her number because there's a voluntary repository of all the writing program alumni information, and hers is right there, right above his in alphabetical order.

"I'll leave you to it," Marlene says. As she leans over to give him a kiss, her tiny-dress locket dangles from her neck. When the morning sunlight catches the glass and a spark tattoos his vision, Josh experiences one of these rare magical moments where a project comes to him fully formed. Not the locket, but Abby's circular paintings. God, how could he have missed it? They're literal storyboards, and he knows just how to approach it, the voice, the feel, everything. Right after this phone call, he's jumping on his laptop and cranking out some prose.

It's Saturday morning, ten after ten. Not too early for a phone call. He dials the number, a 917 area code, which he believes is New York City, though with cell phones, those numbers no longer serve as geographical markers.

LINES

On the second ring, the phone picks up, an uncertain female voice. "Hello?"

"Hi," Josh says. "Deborah. This is Josh Kozlov, you don't know me…"

"Josh? Sure I know you! Well, not *know you* know you. You're on the NYU listserv. Fellow survivor of the creative writing program."

She reminds him that they have exchanged emails in the past. A few years ago, Deborah had asked the listserv for any novels that primarily take place over a single evening, which Josh now vaguely recalls.

"*The Night Country*, by Stewart O'Nan," Josh says. "Well, I'm glad the ol' noggin was working that day, at least."

"I got it from the library that day and read it in a single sitting. That entire book is like one long song, so lyrical. Just what I was looking for, for the fiction workshop I was teaching back then. I hope I remembered to thank you for the recommendation. So…how are you doing?"

She's asking how *he's* doing. Is it possible he's dialed the wrong number? He didn't expect to talk her off the ledge or anything, but this woman sounds like she hasn't a care in the world.

"I'm okay. I just…well, I've been trying to write you an email for the last hour at least, you know, about the review."

"What review?" Deborah asks.

Silence.

Jesus Christ, Josh thinks. *What do I say now?*

"Gotcha, didn't I?" she says. "That's incredibly sweet of you to reach out to me like this, over the phone. My esteemed agent didn't even do that."

They chat like old friends, about their time at NYU, how they attended half a dozen of the same author readings and yet never met.

"Not as if we'd attended huge venues, either," Josh says. "As I recall, some of those events only had like a dozen people."

"So we must've seen each other, but now that we're Facebook friends and I'm looking at some of your pics here, I must say, I honestly do not recall you at all."

"I should be offended, but then again, I don't remember you, either."

She laughs, then says, "Oh shit!"

"You okay?"

"I gotta go pick up my daughter from her ballet class. Josh Kozlov, you're a peach. You took my mind off of this awful review for an hour, and for that, I'm grateful."

"You're welcome Deborah, but I have to tell you, the whole time we've been chatting, I haven't gotten a single distressy-vibe from you."

"Thank you, thick skin. I was born with it, never gave a shit about what anybody ever said. That's not to say this doesn't sting, of course it does, but really, you write for yourself, right? I know you've heard that a thousand times, but it is true. In the end, it's what you leave on the page that matters. That you wrote what you wanted to write."

They exchange goodbyes and hang up, and as soon as the phone call is over, he lets out an enormous fart he'd been holding in, an expulsion of gas so powerful that the couch cushion vibrates.

You didn't hear that, did you, sweetheart? Josh texts her.

7.5 on the sphincter scale, Marlene replies from their bedroom upstairs.

Josh climbs up the stairs and finds Marlene sitting up with a fortress of pillows against the headboard of their bed, her hair pulled into a ponytail, in a gray hoodie and black yoga pants. In her hands is one of his old Stephen King novels, *The Tommyknockers,* and their Siamese cats Mac and Lily are snoozing in her lap.

LINES

"What's with the big smile, big guy?" she asks.

"It goes with the big fart," he says, then joins her on their bed. It is soft, generous, and toasty warm thanks to Marlene's body heat. *This*, he thinks. *This is happiness. Try not to forget it.* "With God as my witness, I swear I have not deviated from Dr. Choudry's plan."

"I know your heart broke a little when he said you can't eat kettle corn anymore."

"Don't remind me. Still, I'm fully on the wagon."

"Then I'd say it's time you go back to your nutritionist to tweak something. Are you starting to feel bloated again?"

Josh slaps his tummy like a drum. "No. I think it might have been stress-induced. That conversation was pleasant but still wasn't easy."

"Sounded like you were having fun. Heard you laugh at least twice."

"She's super nice. And super successful — even if the *Times* panned it, they wouldn't have reviewed it if it wasn't an important book."

"No such thing as bad publicity," Marlene says.

Josh scratches Mac's head and revels in the feline's purring.

"Didn't it cost like four hundred dollars to see Dr. Choudry last time?" he asks. "I know you explained this before, but I thought the deductible..."

"You're thinking of last year. We wised up and opted for the traditional plan this year, which is more expensive up front but ends up costing less in the long run. We already met our $250 deductible last month when I went for my bone density scan, so an appointment with Dr. Choudry will be like fifteen bucks."

"Good thing you're the brains of our outfit."

"It's really all because we're on my insurance instead of PayRight's — which is still crappy as it always was."

His phone dings and he clicks it open, a new email.

SUNG J. WOO

Subject: You've got money
Hello, Josh Kozlov
Whirlwind sent you $100.00 USD
Note from Whirlwind:
Issue 19, short story payment

He shows the email from PayPal to Marlene. "I'm treating us to dinner out tonight, babe!"

"Oh my goodness, Josh, that's great! We'll totally celebrate!"

They may not be living in New York, but there are plenty of lovely restaurants in their sleepy suburban town of Basking Ridge, even one where the staff knows them by name: Russo's Ristorante. Josh reserves a table for two via the restaurant's website for 7pm.

For lunch, Josh and Marlene chow down on last night's leftovers, an excellent spinach ravioli dish that they made together that's gotten better after sitting in the fridge overnight. Now there's four hours to kill before dinner. On the living room couch, Marlene has her company laptop open, eager to dive into her PowerPoint presentation for next week. She's one of those lucky people who loves their job so much that it's not work at all. He sits next to her.

"Oh, I like the background you chose there," Josh says, pointing at the photo of a little boy eating a crepe in front of an old church. "Wait, that looks like Paris?"

"I think you took that picture."

"Shouldn't I get royalties?"

She gives him a kiss.

"There you go," she says.

"Worth every penny."

LINES

"In a couple of hours, would you mind reading over my deck?"

"My pleasure," Josh says. He rises and heads for downstairs, but before he climbs down, he turns and pauses to appreciate everything he has: his wonderful wife, their two cats who get along like best friends, their quaint house in this quiet, leafy neighborhood. Five years ago, Josh was living in Hoboken with two unkempt apartmentmates. He'd turned forty that year — the day after his milestone birthday was when his life changed. He was in New York, and there had been that fog, and as the fog lifted, so did his fate. The next day at his job, he and Marlene began working on the Zabriskie Pharmaceuticals account. It was the trip to Zabriskie's home office in Chicago that turned a work friendship into something more.

Their cat Mac follows him down to his office, his writing space. It isn't much, just an antique secretary in the corner of the finished basement, no windows, just the way he likes it. Windows are a distraction. The secretary is about the size of a human being in both height and width; a door at the top, two drawers on the bottom, and a door in the middle that flips down to become a desk.

"This is gonna be epic," he tells the cat.

"Wooo-aaa," Mac yowls.

After the laptop boots up, Josh beelines to Abby's website, right to her collection of mini paintings called "Cycling Guide to Lilliput." They're all smartphone snapshots, like a selfie for paintings. Often they are accompanied by the paintbrushes and sometimes include the tips of her fingers, as if to add a level of authenticity to the work itself. Josh clicks on the first one, which he recognizes — there were two paintings when he visited her studio, and it's the one on the right, a path in a forest, except it's sharper, more detailed, like a lens having come into focus. What he finds most enticing are those splotches of sun on the ground; they're just white blobs of paint against a gray background, but damn if they don't look like morning light. He stares into the painting, willing himself into her mind.

For the next two hours, he writes, deletes, rewrites, deletes. Writes some more. Deletes some more. Edits.

The Path (I)

When people find out about her long-distance cycling trips, they ask her questions.

Why do you go on these trips by yourself?

What are you thinking about when you're on that bike of yours for hours on end?

Don't you, like, get lonely?

She supplies them with satisfactory answers, sensible words.

So I can immerse myself in nature.

I think about the colors I see, the shadows, the light.

My art keeps me company.

None of these statements are false, but they aren't exactly true, either.

LINES

    The truth is, she rides because she can. She rides because it is what she wants to do. She rides because she is *not* not riding.

    When she is on her bike, *she is on her bike.* When she sees the sunlight filtered through the leaves, *she sees the sunlight filtered through the leaves.* She is there, right there, slipstreaming through the wind. She feels that wind, its heat, its velocity. Blowing by her cheeks, raking through her hair, tickling her eyelashes. No past, no future, just the present, the omnipresent, the now. She follows the path. The path follows her. Off she goes.

    Mac jumps on his lap, seeking warmth.

    "Not bad, right?" Josh asks him.

    The white cat goes in for a closer look, smack in the middle of the round little disc, his nose leaving a wet mark on the laptop screen.

    "You have excellent taste," Josh says.

    Mac jumps off and races back upstairs, off to his next adventure. Josh reads over the story for what seems like the hundredth time. It feels right, feels like he's in her frame of mind. Of course it's not *her* frame of mind, it's his fictional version of what he believes is a faithful representation of Abby's state, though it's not really Abby, either, at this point, it's a character, his character.

    Now that he's written this piece, he realizes he needs to run this by Abby, because it's her painting. Not only does he need her blessing, he needs her actual permission because if this ends up somewhere, both of their names are going to be on it. Underneath his story, he types:

words by Josh Kozlov
art by Abby Kim

Why are his cheeks warm? Why is he blushing?

"I think it's almost time to go?" Marlene calls from upstairs.

Once again, Josh feels embarrassed at what's on his screen, like he's doing something illicit.

But I'm not. This is art, this is work. There is nothing funny going on here.

"Coming," he says. He snaps his laptop screen shut, swings his secretary closed.

You're just excited, that's all, he tells himself, and it might be true. The outset of a project is when he's thrilled by it, and this most definitely feels like love.

But there's a part of him that wonders, that brings forth doubt:

Exactly what, or whom, is this love for?

*

"What do you think?" Ted asks, holding up two ties, an iridescent blue one with flecks of yellow and a solid wine-red silky strip.

Abby stares at them, hoping it is sufficiently long enough to feign interest. "Both are spectacular."

He sighs. "As someone who uses color and light in ways I can't even fathom, I'd appreciate your professional opinion."

He gets like this, her future husband, before an important event. He thinks he's being generous, giving her the choice of what he should wear, but to her it's a burden, much like the event itself. It's his annual class party at the Cornell Club in Midtown, for the alumni of the esteemed university. Mostly Abby feels guilty about the whole thing because it's not like Ted drags her to these affairs that often; in fact, this one and the Christmas party at the Union League are the only times they doll up and spend the evening with polite rich people. There's little reason why she should resent this at all, because this is a part of Ted's job, to drum up investment clients, and she should play the part of the good fiancée. And the food is great, with tiny delicious hors d'oeuvres brought out on silver trays by uniformed caterers in the woody and leathery Andrew Dickson White library, the impeccable meal served in the summery Cayuga Room, drinks and ice cream and cake and live music, too, a jazz trio or a small orchestra…

No. No matter how much she tries to convince herself, this is definitely not something she's ever going to enjoy.

She tells Ted to go with the blue, and he happily complies. While he ties his tie in the bathroom, Abby sits in front of her makeup mirror to apply her mascara. She's one of the lucky Asians when it comes to her eyes, large and round without needing the double-eyelid surgery her mother got, to give her the sought-after folds. She could still remember it like yesterday, her mother's eyes like a beaten-up boxer's the day after going under the knife. Abby had been nine then, a few years before her family emigrated to the United States from South Korea. Her mother had wanted to look her best before the move, hoping to make a good impression on the people of this new land. She'd been a senior saleswoman of the Lotte Department store in Seoul, the top seller in young women's clothing department. She took a conversation English course for a full year prior to their departure, but despite her efforts, she ended up cleaning houses for four years before landing her job at JC Penney.

Her mother, who had lived through the Korean War as a baby, had learned to drive a car for the first time in her forties, a new life in a new country…and she did it all without complaint. And here was Abby, whose most difficult part of the day would be spent in a posh New York City landmark, sipping champagne and nibbling on filet mignon. *Oh, the guilt! Just lay it on, slather it, let me drown in it.*

Her phone chirps. She sees the sender and the subject of the email:

Josh Kozlov — A Modest Proposal

"How's it going over there?" Ted says from the bathroom.

Abby swipes at her phone, removing the notification.

"I'm ready," she says.

They pick up the 5 train from Union Square, and it's just one stop to Grand Central. They are the best dressed in the car, Ted in his black three-piece suit and gray overcoat, Abby in a brand-new knee-length black velvet dress with rhinestones tracing her neck and hem.

"Thank you for this," she says.

"It's the least I can do," he says. "I know this isn't your jam. Really appreciate the support, my dear."

He squeezes her hand, and she squeezes back, but the guilt she felt while putting on her makeup returns. There are two things she's keeping from him now, though the first thing, the bigger thing, the biggest thing they'll ever experience as a couple, is technically conjecture. She doesn't know for a fact she's pregnant, although now her period is a full five days late, and she's never late. In fact, for as long as she's been menstruating, she's been synced with the waxing and waning of the moon, which is why they always use a condom for a week after the full moon because that's when she's ovulating. She and Ted have been having sex for two years now without any repercussions, and now this, though she feels even worse for labeling her possible pregnancy a repercussion. But it is, because she was still hoping against hope that she could make one last solo cycling trip, before she became a wife and had a family.

They walk up Vanderbilt Avenue holding hands and hang a left onto 44th Street at the MetLife building, its wide base and impossibly high skyscraper stacked on top structurally embodying the message of all insurance carriers: we're your bedrock. They walk by Coach, Allen Edmonds, then a Brooks Brothers shop that threatens to take over the entire block. This is most definitely not Abby's jam. These high-end retailers lead right to the red awning of the Cornell Club and its gilded door.

"Three hours tops," Ted says as they approach the entrance. "About the length of *Titanic*."

"Or a third of *The Lord of the Rings* trilogy."

"Now that's an excellent way of seeing it. Way better than sitting through orcs and hobbits, right?"

A doorman in a smart black suit and yellow buttons greets them, and they are ushered into the warm glow of the club.

What's worse, the milling-around cocktail hour or the sit-on-your-ass dinner? In the cocktail hour, you can duck out of a boring conversation, but Abby's wearing her heels and now that she's firmly into her thirties, standing in these beautiful torture devices for more than an hour make her toes go numb.

Arthur, the old man with a serious mustache who built his fortune in textiles, is one of these talkers who never pauses long enough for her to interrupt him. But now she must, because her poor bladder feels like it's about to burst.

"I'm sorry, but I shall go for a moment," she says.

"Oh, but we are having such a lively conversation, Abby!" he says.

"To powder my nose?" she says, a ridiculous phrase she only utters on occasions like these.

"Ah, of course. Well, I'll be right here and I'd love to hear more about your tree drawings."

Except she hasn't been able to get a word in edgewise. If she were a more enterprising artist, she would leverage this opportunity much like Ted does, since everyone in this room is wealthy. But she's never been good at the commerce side of art. It's not that she feels it's beneath her or anything like that; she's just not an effective conveyer of her skills. Every time she tries to sell herself, it sounds hollow and disingenuous, like she's talking about someone she doesn't know, and wouldn't like if she did.

"You okay?" Ted asks her, but his concern isn't really for her wellbeing but rather her effectiveness as an aesthetic enticement to his client-accruing mission. Her mission is to be an attractive curiosity to these serious business people, his quirky artsy wife. How quaint that she does this painting thing for a living, and how great that Ted snatched her up.

"I'm good, I'll be right back," she says, but he doesn't hear her since his attention is back on the tall Nordic woman with her severe bun.

The bathroom, like every other part of this opulent building, is a throwback to an older, disappearing world. There's seating outside the actual bathroom, with couches and armchairs that look like furniture for royalty. Abby pulls on the heavy wooden door and is invited into the bank of softly lit marble-topped sinks and gold-trimmed mirrors, but right now she needs a toilet.

Blissful relief, at last! Almost on cue, she feels her phone vibrating in her purse. It's just junk email from HGTV, a reminder for her to enter the sweepstakes to win their Dream House, but then underneath that message is the one Josh had sent, the one she's been saving.

Saving because she knows it's going to be something lovely.

"Dear Abby," he writes, "This is about you, but it's not you. Now I'll let my fiction do rest of the talking, okay? Take your time. But not too much time, because, well, I'd love to know what you think…"

What she sees first is her own work, the posts she makes on Instagram of her paintings. This was the first in the series, the first one she ever created — how the heck did he know that? Underneath the image is a story, titled The Path (I), and it is indeed about her…but it isn't about her, because this is an idealized version of her.

Is this the way he sees me?

LINES

When she leaves the stall and sees herself in the mirror as she washes her hands, her cheeks are bright red.

No, this is all in your head. This is a work of fiction. You're a character. Like he wrote, it's about me but not me.

Before she leaves, she sits in the fancy sitting area to compose a reply, but then she sees she hadn't scrolled down far enough, because there's a second story.

The Path (II)

The first day is easy breezy. The second day? Not so much.

On the second day, the giddiness of newness has worn off. On the second day, her legs are sore. On the second day, she thinks to herself, *So why am I doing this again?*

But then she finds her rhythm, or perhaps the rhythm finds her. It starts with the pedals, their simple circular motion, repeated like a mantra. She begins to anticipate the gentle curves of the road ahead, almost as if she's been here before. As she rides over the uneven terrain, each bump is like a gentle nudge from an old friend.

And then, the sunlight. Just a moment ago, it wasn't there, but now, it's as if those rays have always existed.

She downshifts to pick up speed. She wants that light. She needs that light. Her calves burn, she can hardly breathe, but she's so close now. One more push...and she slides into it, the brightness of the beams, the warmth of the air. On her bare arms. On her upturned face.

Oh yes. Now I remember.

This is crazy because this *is* her. This *was* her, last summer, on the second day of her cycling trip through the forests of Germany along the Rhine River, when she rode between Hagenbach and Lauterbourg. As she gazes into her painting and hears Josh's words echoing in her head, she's transported in time. She leans back on the couch, closes her eyes...feels the tacky handlebar in her hands, smells the earthy pine needles, the breeze, and the sun and the...fear? God, absolutely, this is fear, this hollowness in her gut, like her stomach just fell out from under her.

What are you afraid of?

Are you afraid of him?

Or are you afraid of yourself?

She jumps off the couch almost in a panic. She clicks off her phone's display, marches right back into the cocktail party and straight to Ted, who's now chatting up an elegant silver-haired man who looks like all the other elegant silver-haired men in this room.

"Honey," he says, "Let me introduce you to Victor here."

"I think I'm pregnant," she says.

Neither Ted nor Victor speak for a good five seconds. Then Victor laughs.

"You make one hell of an entrance, Ms. Abby Kim," he says.

LINES

The news of her pregnancy is a truth wrapped inside a lie. That's what she thinks as they enter the Duane Reade drugstore on 34th Street. She'd used her impending motherhood as an emotional shield, and it has now been sullied. Her unborn, innocent child has already been sullied.

For as long as she's known him, Abby has never seen Ted so nakedly happy. There's a tightness in her chest, as if fingers are digging into the heart muscle itself, trying to find a grasp.

"It was meant to be, don't you see?" Ted says. "We were going to wait until we were married, but our child found his or her way all by his or herself. A fighter from the very beginning."

They blaze by rows of toothpaste, so many toothpastes, then a phalanx of blue and green bottles of mouthwash, radiating under the harsh fluorescent lights of retail.

"I see," Abby says, not really, but it feels right to agree with him.

"Got it!" Ted says, holding up the pregnancy kit like a trophy.

Does he not notice her distress because he's excited, or is it because she's hiding it so well?

The woman behind the counter, with her reading glasses hanging on the edge of her nose and a condescending frown, asks Ted, "All smiles, are we?"

"Yes ma'am."

Her name is Doreen, according to her name tag. She meets Abby's eyes for a second and gives her a knowing glance, an inclusive glance, a motherly glance.

"It's her carrying the baby for nine months," she says, putting the box in a bag and handing it over. "You have the easy part."

"You're absolutely right," he says. "I'll take care of her. Of them both. The best I can."

Outside, it's sleeting, a thin layer of ice coating the windshields of parked cars. Ted puts his arm around her as they walk back home, already making good on his promise.

together

Citi DoubleCash Mastercard: Pay Minimum Balance

ABBY RESTS HER brush on her palette. Baby Cecilia, one hand covered in soap bubbles and the other clutching a yellow rubber ducky, is done. At last. No more baby.

Except now she's got a real one brewing in her own belly, an idea which is equal parts exhilarating and terrifying. She's going to be a mother.

It's half past noon, but no knock on her door from Ted. She quietly, stealthily walks up to her own door — which makes no sense, so she stomps her feet for the last three steps. Which makes her feel even stupider. She swings it open and sees and hears nothing but the deserted hallway.

She walks over to the bathroom, though she doesn't have to go. But she can wash the paint off her hands with her squeeze bottle of turpentine, streaks and crusts of deep brown and mango down the drain, the last colors she'd worked with on the canvas. As the paint temporarily coats the sides of the sink, Abby feels a sadness. She might have resented painting Cecilia for the last month or so, but now that she's finished, the work is no longer hers, and there's an emptiness in that. Of course she'll be paid for handing it over, two thousand dollars and 100% hers because no gallery was involved with this commission, but still, she feels a loss. She always does after a project comes to an end, even one she didn't love.

That's what this child inside her is going to be, too, isn't it? Her greatest project, one she'll love and cherish, and when she or he leaves, the void will be unfillable.

Goodness, what drama. Her kid is as big as a sesame seed and she's already thinking about an empty nest.

"More fangs, my excellent Ted."

Fangs? That is definitely what she heard. When she exits the bathroom, she sees the young man in the hoodie and jeans and Ted exchange a weird kind of a double-handed handshake.

"Oh, you didn't see that now, did you, girl?" the guy says to Abby. "'Cause if you did, we'd have to kill you."

"Thank you, Linus," Ted says, and Linus makes his fingers into guns and points at him before he disappears through the stairway door. "Sorry about that," Ted says to Abby. "Hey, have you had lunch yet?"

As they walk over to the couch, Ted tells her about Linus, a twenty-four-year-old who went to Cornell and joined the same fraternity as Ted, though two decades later.

"He sold his internet startup for a hundred million last year, so he's swimming in it. What you saw was our fraternity's secret handshake, which I would not have ever remembered. I'm glad I had the foresight to look over my ritual materials last night."

"He wanted more fangs?" she asks. "Animals?"

Ted laughs. "Acronyms make my profession sound more interesting than it is. FAANG stands for Facebook, Apple, Amazon, Netflix, Google. High tech, high risk, something Linus has no need for with his capital, but that's what he wants, so that's what I'll buy."

Her phone buzzes in her pocket, and it's an email from HGTV, the online Dream Home sweepstakes.

LINES

"Do you need to get that?"

"Oh no, it's just junk mail."

But it isn't junk at all. In fact, as she listens to Ted prattle on about his excavation of college memorabilia buried in his basement, her mind drifts to this house on Puget Sound, a 4-bedroom, 3½-bathroom mansion right on the water. Every day for the last two months, Abby has dutifully typed in her email address on the website for a chance to win this house. There's also a cash payout of a quarter of a million dollars and a new car, but the house is what she desperately desires, which is strange because she has never been a fan of big homes. In South Korea, she grew up in a small two-bedroom, sharing her modest room with her younger sister, yet the house never felt cramped. Everything they ever wanted they had, which was why this venal thirst for this gargantuan home with its Great Room and Downstairs Den and Cocktail Lounge and two guest bedrooms made little sense.

Even less sense? That when she imagines herself in this house, it's not with Joshua. No, the man who's waiting for her in their kitchen with its waterscape view and six-burner professional cooktop, wearing an apron that proclaims World's Greatest Cook, is none other than the guy sitting across from her, Ted. Who is happily married to Beth, the world's greatest baker from the brownies Abby has tasted, and not to mention their two cute kids, Tyler and Giselle. But reality does not matter in Abby's fantasy, nor should it. If she can't even have what she wants in her world of make-believe, what good is it?

"You're enjoying my ancient tale of misery and woe?" Ted asks.

"Yes, absolutely," Abby says. He was talking about his senior year in college, where he had to gather mud for an annual mudslide for his fraternity's alumni when they came to visit in the spring. "I enjoy hearing about your criminal activities."

He points a celery stick at her. "You seem distracted today."

She hasn't told him of her pregnancy. In the coming months, it's going to become rather obvious, so she might as well share the news sooner than later. But she doesn't want to, because it would change this thing that they have, this casual kinship, though she doesn't see why it would; if anyone would understand the impact of children, it would be Ted, with two of his own. What's strange is that the core of her reticence is embarrassment, not at the expectant child itself, but how the child came to be: that she and Joshua had sex! She knows how utterly asinine this is, yet the shame is real.

"I shall see a doctor today," she blurts out.

Ted was about to take a final bite of his ham and cheese sandwich but stops.

"Oh. Okay, well, are you all right, Abby?"

His concern for her is so unguarded that it disarms her into a kind of stupor. As she stares at him, she notices how his face is rounder than Joshua's, and unlike her husband's cold and clinical blue eyes, Ted's are the color of coffee with a touch of cream, same shade as what she'd just washed from her hands after finishing Cecilia.

"Abby?" he asks again, now even more concerned.

"Yes, sorry, yes, I am okay, fine," she says. "It's nothing, just a checkup."

The TV mounted on the wall of the obstetrician's lobby is blaring a cooking show. The host is a woman wearing a tight red dress and enough makeup for an opera singer. The chef is a very blond man, even his eyebrows which are too thin to be not shaped by a stylist. As he cuts up a cherry pie, they yuck it up and so does the audience.

Abby's appointment is for 1:50pm. What kind of an appointment time is that? Was there one for 1:40pm? Does this doctor operate on ten-minute slivers of time? No matter. She's grateful it's 1:50pm, because it's now 1:48pm and Joshua still isn't here.

LINES

"Oh, oh!" the host screams in delight after taking a bite. "This is *so* good, so good!"

It does look good, now that the camera zooms on the filling. It's not likely that Abby is already eating for two, as she only found out about her pregnancy a month ago. According to the internet, at five weeks, the fetus is sesame-seed sized, 3 millimeters and resembling a tadpole more than a human, so unless she has a super-tadpole with an outsized appetite, this is just the effect of her throwing away half of her lunch. But she just couldn't eat all of the salad, as the nausea she'd experienced in the morning had returned midway through the meal with Ted. Now her breasts are tender and she's got a headache, symptoms of her hormones gunning into overdrive. She's glad that everything checks out, that she's going through the physical changes that every woman goes through, but there's also a part of her that resents her body's slavish normality, that she's just like everybody else.

The door to the lobby dings, and there he is, her husband. And immediately Abby knows something is wrong.

Joshua sits down next to her, still in his puffy winter coat. Even though it's below freezing outside, there's sweat beaded on his forehead. "Jesus Christ," he says. "Jesus Christ."

"What, what happened?"

"I almost died. Almost fucking died."

"Abby Kim," the nurse announces from the open door next to the front counter.

And now her phone rings.

Joshua's proclamation of his near demise, the nurse with the clipboard calling out her name, the smartphone barking its ear-piercing ringtone — it's all too much, all at once, and Abby just loses it, she buries her face in her hands and sobs.

"Oh no, no no no," she hears Joshua say. He puts his hands on her shoulder, but she shakes him off. "Abby, please, you can't do this…"

He's right. She needs to stop. But she can't. Has she ever cried harder in her life? Never, not even when she had to leave her house in Korea, leave her stuffed animals behind. She'd been strong then, or just young and oblivious. How she longs for that blithe ignorance now, to be without a career, a husband, a child — to be free.

*

Even though Abby has returned to her rational self by the time the doctor arrives, no doubt the nurse (and the support staff behind the counter) informed their boss of what happened in the lobby because Joshua feels the chill here in the examination room from the get-go. Dr. Margaret Chang, with her pageboy haircut and John Lennon-style spectacles, barely acknowledges him when she walks through the door.

"And how are you feeling today, Abby?" she asks.

Abby, sitting with her feet dangling off the exam table, says, "All right, I think."

She looks like a fucking child, he thinks to himself.

In the beginning of their relationship, her reckless youth — she's ten years younger than him — had been bewitching. Last-minute trips, mapless forays, breakfast for dinner — all so charming, but now? Now the shtick has worn rather thin. Now he sees the source of all her irreverent behavior: immaturity. What kind of a mother will she be when she can't even handle a doctor's appointment without bawling like a goddamn baby? A shitty one, that's what.

"Everything that's happening to you is perfectly normal," Dr. Chang tells Abby. "You're going to have your moods, and your dear husband here will just have to buck up and take it like a man. Right, Joshua?"

LINES

He laughs to keep this wolf doctor at bay, but this small pink-walled room with its stool and chair and bed feels even smaller now. Initially he thought it would be nice for Abby to have an Asian physician, but now he's unsure. It's like he's being ganged up, outnumbered not only on a gender level but racially, too, akin to the way he feels whenever they have a family get-together on Abby's side, him being the lone white guy bobbing in a sea of Koreans.

While the doctor and his wife chat about two different brands of folic acid vitamins, Joshua sits in his chair and pretends to listen. He stares at the poster on the wall next to the sink and cabinet, the path of pregnancy from inception to delivery, starting where the sperm meets the egg to the mother cradling her newborn, and seeing this logical progression of human birth calms him down. Abby might have been the one who freaked out in the lobby, but it was he who was almost run over by a truck from the back parking lot to the entrance of the medical building.

Joshua touches the tip of his nose, which had grazed the edge of the side mirror of the truck; that's how close he'd come to his own demise. Of course, it was all a blur, the gray side of the truck filling his entire vision for not even a second when he looked up from his smartphone, and then gone. Which in a way made it even worse, that something that could've killed him happened so quickly. Not that he wanted to die in some prolonged, Shakespearean-soliloquy fashion, but how crazy was it that there was virtually no difference between being alive and dead, just a microscopic moment? He's not being melodramatic here: that truck was barreling through the crosswalk, thirty miles an hour at the slowest. Yes, he was on his phone, but come on, walkers have the right of way!

Standing there with the wind still whipping about him, more than anything, he wanted to run into the lobby, take Abby into his arms, and assure her that everything was going to be fine, that this pregnancy, this baby, this delicate life of theirs would all work out because he was alive and nobody was dead.

Except when he did walk through the door and saw his wife, he came to a realization that was even scarier than what he'd just experienced: his death meant Abby raising their baby by herself. The cold shock squeezed him like a boa constrictor, which is why all he could utter was the name of Jesus Christ twice and then blabber on like an idiot, frightening his poor pregnant wife into a panic attack.

"…which means, of course, a caesarian," Dr. Chang says.

"Excuse me? Did you say c-section?" Joshua asks, and both women turn to him like he is butting into a private conversation.

"Yes," Dr. Chang says. "It's my job as the physician who'll deliver the baby to present all possibilities. Nobody wants surprises on the day of labor, which is why I mention this now."

"I see, now is there anything we can do to make this possibility as infinitesimal as possible, because from what I've read, a caesarian could add another two or three grand to the final bill." From his peripheral vision, he sees Abby looking down and away from him, like she's ashamed or disappointed or something. Why is he the bad guy for asking about money? If there's something they can do to preserve their cash, isn't this a demonstration of his mature sense of accountability? The medical estimator on his shitty PayRight insurance site made this pretty fucking clear, and Abby was sitting right next to him when they both stared at it just last week, the blue arrow of Patient Responsibility expanding fatter and bolder as it grew like a malignant cancer. Were they just supposed to worry about their lack of coin and never speak of it?

Dr. Chang, her eyes leveled on him, taps her fingers against her laptop's mousepad not like a bored person but like she's playing piano. Is this a racist thought he's having, the stereotypical Asian proclivity towards the musical arts?

LINES

"Joshua," she says, then clears her throat. "I've been doing this for a while, and I know a lot. But one thing I do not know is the future. Your wife is a healthy young woman, so as long as there are no complications during the birthing process, I don't see any reason why this wouldn't be a run-of-the-mill vaginal delivery. Still, anything can happen, which is why we should be prepared as best we can. Sound reasonable?"

"Yes. Thank you." It all does sound reasonable enough, but man, her tone — does it give her pleasure to make him feel stupid?

Joshua feels a buzz in his pocket, his smartphone alerting him to probably nothing at all. Sure enough, when he surreptitiously takes it out and looks at it askance, it's some dumb-ass superhero movie that's announcing its arrival into theaters this weekend. He really needs to turn off these meaningless notifications, but he never seems to have the time.

Of course, if he thinks he doesn't have time now, wait until the newborn arrives. He is super late to the game here, some of his friends are already sending their kids to college. By the time his own child graduates from high school, Joshua would be near retirement age. Retirement! Ha! Who the fuck is he kidding.

Just thinking about it makes him feel old, and it doesn't take much for his imagination to nudge the future into ruin. His saggy paunch of now would have ballooned into a formidable belly, rivaling the one that Abby will have in a few months. That occasional jabby pain in his right knee would upgrade itself to a full-blown ache. Perhaps he'll have a replacement by then. His dad got one two years ago, the last time Joshua saw him in person, a thought painful enough that he pushes it out far into the ocean of his mind as soon as it drifts in.

But right now, while his wife and her doctor discuss the results of these screens, so many screens — Rubella, Varicella, Cystic Fibrosis, Tay-Sachs, Sickle Cell — Joshua finds his father floating back towards him, maybe because he'll be a dad himself soon.

The fact is, it doesn't take much to abandon someone, even your own father. But Joshua just couldn't take his bitterness anymore, not when he's drowning in it himself. His father has always been a depressive sort, but things took a turn for the worse when his body started to fail him. First it was a slipped disc that put him on workman's comp for two months, and then the knee replacement, or more accurately, replacements, because he's gone through two of them and he still can't walk right.

"Get what you pay for," his dad told him. "Insurance would only cover the cheapest one, so here's my new right knee, a useless piece of shit. Might as well have a fucking peg leg like a pirate. I swear, Joshy what's the point? All we ever do in this world is struggle. Always scrabbling to get a tiny morsel of happiness, and then when we do somehow get it, we just want more. We're all just genetically programmed robots, and we don't know shit."

This was their conversation last month, which was no different than the one before that one, and the one before that. Listening to his father's rants is particularly difficult because like father like son, Joshua is on board the life-sucks train. Honestly, he doesn't see how his own existence is going to end well, either. Now firmly in his mid-forties, after losing half of his 401(k) during the mortgage crisis, he's been putting all new deposits into a government bond fund, which has hardly grown at all, his total balance still lower than what it was before the "too big to fail" era. He knows he fucked up, he should've been putting it all in the stock market when it was in the toilet, but how do you know when it's safe to go back in? It's all a scam, Wall Street fat cats fleecing "dumb money" people like him.

This past year, Abby's commissions have brought in some money, but all that's gone into their higher rent. They have got to get the fuck out of this city, but there's moving costs, plus having to find a new place which he doesn't even want to think about, not that that's ever happening, anyway. Even though it's bleeding their bank account dry, Abby loves the city and would never leave.

"Names, Joshua?" Dr. Chang asks, loud enough to get Joshua's attention.

Fuck.

"I'm sorry, what…"

"Not yet," Abby tells the doctor. "But we shall, soon."

Names. Baby names. Whatever.

They should name him or her Miracle, because that's literally how this happened, and not in some life-is-miraculous bullshit manner. In January, due to a bad snowstorm, Abby's refill prescription of her birth control pills was late by a day. He and she had just had a fight (about money, what else), so it was make-up sex, which everybody knows is the best kind of sex, and yes, it was his idea, yes, it was his penis, yes, it was his semen, yes, it was his fault because Abby said they should wait and that turned him on even more — and thus conceived, Miracle. If it is a boy, then he should become an NFL running back, because this little fucker sure knows how to find an opening.

When Abby exited their bathroom with the news of her pregnancy last month, holding the white plastic tester like a divining rod as the indicator bled to positivity, he should've blurted out what was deep in his gut.

We should really think about this.

We're not in a good place.

We don't have to do this.

But he didn't, because her face — it was the same face that he ran into that morning so many years ago in Washington Square Park. The face he fell in love with, the face of youth, the face of hope. As hard as their marriage may be at times, that face of hers still retains the power to make him want to be a better human.

Abby jumps off the bed and there's Dr. Chang, ready to give her a hug.

"Keep taking those vitamins."

"I will."

No hug for Joshua, which is fine by him.

apart

Something New

DROPPING BY TO see my old man, Josh thinks, and chuckles to himself as he drives down the Garden State Parkway. There are already some buds on the trees, nature doing its thing, earlier than years past possibly due to climate change, though he reminds himself not to mention that to his dad, as he's one of *those* people.

The fact that he and his dad are still talking at all is a marvel. Growing up, they never saw eye to eye on anything, and Josh was certain that once his mom passed away, they'd drift apart. Maria Kozlov, god rest her soul, was the connective tissue between the two men, and because she'd died suddenly (a heart attack while out shopping for groceries), she hadn't had the time to put a plan together so father and son wouldn't lose touch. She was the kind of woman who would've written it all down, bullet-pointed her instructions. Lucky for the Kozlov men, another woman was ready to save them.

"Son!" Vladimir Kozlov says when he opens the door to his apartment. He thrusts out his hand, and they shake like they've just completed a business transaction. This is his equivalent of a hug, which Marlene noticed the first time she and Vladimir met, the type of sage advice that's helped Josh to reframe and soften their strained relationship. Marlene has been the glue, the secret weapon to keep father and son together, more than his dad could ever know.

"Walking good now, aren't you?" Josh says as he enters his dad's place. It's still a surprise that his one-bedroom apartment is so inviting. Who knew his dad had such homemaking artistry, the solid red rug in the foyer picking up the rouge teardrops in the drapes, a framed print of van Gogh's sunflowers in the foyer offering a burst of cheer? He might have missed his true calling as an interior decorator.

"I can even do *this*!" he says, and performs a half-hearted but almost passable Cossack dance, the squat-kick maneuver that's in every Russian-themed movie.

"Okay, okay, please stop!" Josh says, but he can't help but laugh. For the last few years, he's seen his dad's right knee go from uncomfortable to sore to a full-blown limp. His HVAC union used to provide good insurance, but that was years ago when unions still had clout. The only way he could've gotten the better knee replacement unit and the better surgeon was by going out of network, and the only way he could've done that was with money he didn't have.

Except Josh had the money, thanks to Marlene, whose advice he fortunately accepted back when it looked like the global economy was going to collapse. At that point she wasn't a manager, so their cubes were next to one another's, and Josh can still recall that terrifying winter in 2009, his 401k decimated by the mortgage crisis. Not that he had much to lose, but still, seeing his balance cut in half gave him heartburn, which is why when he'd unexpectedly received twenty thousand dollars from his aunt Anna's passing, he wanted to avoid the stock market like the plague. But Marlene, in her infinite financial wisdom, told him to invest the money.

"Ten years from now, your future self will thank you," Marlene had said, but he didn't even have to wait that long. All he did was put it into an S&P500 index fund, and in seven years' time, it had tripled, which is how he was able to gift his dad with free money so he could walk again. Not to mention that his 401k was now higher, too, because

LINES

Marlene had convinced him to keep socking money into his retirement account and ignore the noise.

"How's your better half?" his dad asks, as if reading his mind. He sinks down into his La-Z-Boy and Josh sits catty corner on the couch.

"My better half told me to invite you to dinner."

"Marlena *lapochka*," he says, *sweetie pie* in Russian.

Something shiny on the antique sideboard catches Josh's eye. He gets up and approaches an ornate round dish, an etching of a green forest flecked with gold paint. "This is precious, dad. Where did you get this?"

"Flea market purchase last month," he says. "I have good taste, yes?"

"Yeah, you really do." Josh takes out his smartphone to show him Abby's tiny locket, thinking he'd appreciate the artwork, but before he clicks on the photo app, he notices an Instagram notification. He's been following Abby for a couple of months; she's a steady poster, displaying her paintings in progress every day, except for the last week or so, there hasn't been anything new. But now there is, and he feels almost embarrassed at his thrill as the app pops up.

Except this isn't Abby's notification, it's her friend Franny's, the odd woman who sneaks roadkill into her still life paintings of dolls and stuffed animals. No art, just a grainy photo of her and Abby, taken at night, last night, their cheek-to-cheek faces filling the phone.

My BFF, my gongju, *to be a beautiful bride tomorrow!*, the caption reads. Josh stares, he reads, again and again. These are congratulatory words for a congratulatory occasion; he should be happy for Abby, but what he feels is far away from happiness.

"My son, are you all right?" his dad asks.

How long has he been standing here, peering at his phone? Long enough to give concern to his dad, obviously.

"Yeah, of course, I'm fine."

"You look..." his dad says, scratching at his stubble. "You look sad, my son."

Back in his car, back on the highway, Josh can't shake the faces of the two girls from his mind. Not entirely true, he can excise Franny but Abby is a tougher matter. Now that the surprising wave of her impending matrimony has ebbed away, what's left embedded in the sand is the bitter remnants of deception. Which is ridiculous, because Abby hasn't lied to him, not even by omission, because in the limited interactions they've had — face to face just once and a grand total of half a dozen emails — the subject of her personal life has not come up. Nor should it, since he is the patron and she is the artist, theirs a purely transactional relationship. Except that's not really true now, not after the tiny stories he's written about her tiny paintings. That's more in the vein of collaboration, of muse and writer, and that's what feels most like a trick, that in Josh's vision of Abby, she's a monk-like painter who has married her art, an artistic nun who has devoted herself to the purity of the canvas. Josh recognizes this is completely unfair, even chauvinistic, putting Abby on a preposterous pedestal. And yet this sensation of being wronged feels so real, like he's lost something dear to him.

It's all in his head, of course, but what isn't? Times like this, Josh feels as if he's never actually present in his life. Most of his spare hours are spent in front of a computer, writing about people who have never lived and events that have never transpired. Even his actual experiences serve as fodder for his fiction; in a way, this life he leads is not his own.

He's seeing things this way because he's in a melancholy mood. When he's in a brighter state, he finds writing to be a noble act, an artist fulfilling a purpose greater than his own, but right now, in his car that's following the road ahead like an automaton, his existence feels tragic.

LINES

It's Saturday, half past four, by the time he returns to an empty house. According to Marlene's note on the kitchen counter, she's gone to the mall to look for a new garbage can they talked about last night, one that opens without having to touch it.

Josh walks over to their existing garbage can, a brushed stainless steel cylindrical canister with a mechanical foot, soon to be replaced by the brutal force of technology. For years this container of refuse performed its perfunctory duty, its body tattooed with scratches and dings, the scars of its daily toil — but now its time is over.

Are there tears in his eyes? Why yes, he's literally crying over a garbage can, but before this current hopelessness is trumped by eventual absurdity, Josh makes himself feel, really feel, the pain in his heart, because what hurts isn't what's in front of him.

He descends downstairs to his computer, thinking about a girl in New York City, who is getting ready for her wedding, which might be happening right now. She may be walking down the aisle for all he knows.

*

Her phone dings while she's in the backseat of a taxi cab, on her way to City Hall.

SUNG J. WOO

Demolition Spyhole #1

What bothered her most was not that he lied to her, but that he'd lied to himself. Why she took such offense at self-deception she did not know, but oh, this scalding anger inside her! She picked up a sliver of broken molding, its point as sharp as an arrowhead, and flung it against the half-open wooden door, spinning it end over end. She'd meant for it to smash against the surface, but her aim was off and it sailed out into the hall, sliding harmlessly into a pile of discarded drywall.

Why couldn't he say what was so obviously in his heart? They were such simple words, so basic that they almost superseded the need for language. But they had to be said, didn't they? Of course, because that was the only way she could be claimed, and she wanted to be.

It was Friday, morning. Gray clouds in the sky resembled a bunched bedsheet, pushed haphazardly by a waking god. She stared at the building across the street, what must've been a factory of some kind. It was abandoned, too, like this place. People used to work here, hundreds. Maybe one day they would return. But for now, she was alone.

The story is emailed without preamble, not even a subject line, as if to pronounce that everything that needs to be said is contained within the text. She reads it a second time as the driver brakes and accelerates, jerks the car around double-parked vehicles and oblivious pedestrians until they're on Canal Street.

She closes her eyes and sits back, letting the nausea pass. She's never had trouble reading in a car before, but now that she's two months pregnant, many things make her stomach rumble, like the scent of this driver's cologne. She cracks open her window to let in some air, but not too much as her hair is done, her hairdresser weaving tiny white flowers into her French side braid.

"Here?" the driver asks, slowing down in front of a yellow-bricked building.

"Almost," Abby says. "Do you see the woman with pink hair?"

"Hard to miss."

Franny, in a white dress with pink polka dots, has dyed her hair in a radiant, neon pink to match. She yanks the cab door open and rushes in.

"Oh you beautiful thing you!" she says, and plants a massive kiss right on the lips. "Both of our lips are now hopelessly smudged, but it was worth it. What are these, astrantia blooms? Tiny and pretty, just like you, my sweet."

Of course, if anybody could identify flowers by name, it would be Franny. Abby has never seen these flowers before, but Franny is right, they are indeed tiny and pretty, especially the miniscule pincushion-like bulbs that spring forth from the center of the petals.

As the taxi curls left onto Broadway, Abby holds up her phone to her bridesmaid.

"Wait, is this another story from your Russian not-so-secret admirer writer pal?"

"That is not funny," Abby says.

Franny dons her glasses — unsurprisingly pink — and furrows her eyebrows in concentration. Of all of her friend's gifts, this is what Abby adores the most, how she gives herself fully to a given task.

"Gone kinda dark, wouldn't you say?" Franny says. "Compared to that other one you showed me, that is."

"The feeling I receive is anger."

As Franny goes back to the text, they pass by the flagship Duane Reade drugstore, on the corner of Broadway and Duane Street. *Next block is Reade Street,* Ted told her on their first date, four years ago. He then proceeded to explain that it was opened in 1960 by three brothers, and they named it Duane Reade because most of their employees didn't speak English well and referred to working at their store as going to "Duane and Reade." Ever the chatterbox, Ted had been especially nervous then, which made him more endearing. He had a beard, which she found out later was in reaction to a painful breakup of a long-term relationship. On their second date, cleanly shaven, he looked even taller than his six-foot-two frame.

And now she's going to marry this man, and nothing could feel more right. The pregnancy rushed their nuptials by half a year — they were originally going to wed in the fall — but even this is a blessing in disguise, because Abby does not crave attention and much prefers what they're doing now, an intimate ceremony with immediate family and close friends.

"Screw him, Abby. How do *you* feel about this?"

"About Ted?"

"What? No, this," Franny says, holding up her phone and Josh's story. "I mean it's like he's putting words into your mouth."

"It's fiction, not real."

Franny clicks off her phone's screen and flips it back to her. "And now you're defending him. M'lady, I think this is your cold feet talking."

LINES

Abby leans against the window and lifts her foot from the floor. "Feel the warmth of my foot, my dear Franny. Even my toes are toasty."

Franny squeals and slaps away Abby's ankle.

"Now now, girls, don't make me turn this car around," the driver says. "We're almost here at City Hall. Where should I let you off?"

"In front of the entrance, good sir," Franny says. "It is this beautiful girl's wedding day and she is to be treated like the queen that she is."

Abby stands in front of the altar, facing Ted, as the officiant chants his words of love and devotion. He's a middle-aged mustached man with a strong voice and a stronger Brooklyn accent. She's doing everything she can to be here in spirit, but like a worm burrowing into the earth, Josh's story and her own memories crisscross in her mind.

We are gathered here today, to witness the exchanging of marriage vows, between Abigail Kim and Theodore Wingfield.

It was summer, and she was on her bike, sweating under the hot sun. Nowhere exotic, just ordinary Long Island, but there it was, the dilapidated house with yellow tape around it like a Christmas bow around a present.

Do you Theodore, solemnly declare, to take Abigail, to be your lawfully wedded wife?

I do.

The front door was locked, and the back door, too. But the side window was ajar and she forced it open. Breaking and entering, technically; she'd never done something like this before, but even before she set her foot onto the dust inside, she felt like she was in already.

The house was a gorgeous wreck, with peeling wallpaper and floorboards agape, exposing the ruined innards of what must've been a family home. A door that led to the kitchen hung askew, barely attached by the top pin and hinge. The staircase leading to the second floor was a dangerous game of hopscotch; she'd have to be careful if she planned to climb these rickety steps. Of course she would.

And do you, Abigail, solemnly declare, to take Theodore, to be your lawfully wedded husband?

I do.

Abby sat in the middle of the living room and brought out her pen and sketchpad. She'd take pictures with her phone, too, but sketching was essential. To use her eyes and hands to draw a space was to make it innately hers. This fusion between artist and subject, this was the first act of creation, and the paintings that sprung forth from this union were just fortuitous byproducts.

Do you both promise to love, honor, cherish, and keep, for as long as you both shall live?

I do.

I do.

She climbed not one set of stairs but two, because she could see the light shining in from the attic, whose outer wall had entirely fallen away. The steps here were even more precarious, but she would not be denied, not now, because she knew this house would feed her imagination for months, if not years. For this opportunity, she would risk her livelihood, because to witness and preserve what she saw was her purpose.

Sunlight streamed through in layers, filtered by broken wooden strips of siding like blinds. What Abby didn't realize until she arrived was that there were two levels of decay here. First, the immediate, the cracked wooden post with its white paint chips peeling like tree bark, the water-damaged sheetrock bubbled and stained like a relief map. The second: the abandoned factory below, with its own set of disintegrating bricks and absent people.

As a symbol of your promise, please place the ring on the young lady's finger.

LINES

As a symbol of your promise, please place the ring on the young man's finger.

What is disturbing — and admittedly enthralling — about Josh's writing is how, once again, he has captured her mindset. Standing up in the attic of that broken house, her heart had also been broken, by Jean-Paul, the man-child she'd met and fallen hard for in Paris.

People have often commented that her little circular paintings are like a portal, and it seems as if she's found someone who's stepped through to the other side, to be there with her.

He knows her.

Inasmuch as you both have consented to be united in the bonds of matrimony, and have exchanged your wedding vows in front of us all today, by the power vested in me, by the laws of this great state of New York, I now pronounce you married. You may seal your vows with a kiss.

together

Something Old

FRANNY'S TASTE IN men has been questionable for as long as Abby has known her. All of her relationships have ended in heartbreak, almost always on Franny's side, and truth be told, the current evidence presented here does not assure Abby that this one would end any differently. The problem, though, is that this is no boyfriend who'll ignore her texts, forget her birthday, or cheat on her; this is her groom, her husband to be, her Matthias.

Is it possible Abby is wrong? Absolutely. In fact, she hopes that she's dead wrong about Matthias, but this man in his all-white tuxedo, this walking magazine cover with his manicured five-o'clock shadow and overconfident smile — he looks, speaks, and acts just like the other half a dozen boyfriends who have all left Franny a melancholy mess.

Still, there is reason to be positive, because Matthias, unlike the other metrosexual Eurotrash before him, is not an artist. He is, instead, an architect, so at least he has a steady profession, which Abby dearly hopes will translate to a steady personality, and most of all, steady faithfulness.

If nothing else, the good juju of their wedding's location has got to help, for the ceremony took place in the central gallery of the New York School of Art, the alma mater of more than half of the attending. Not only did this feel like a wedding, it also felt like a reunion, especially now at the reception in the ballroom of the Ace Hotel. Roberto is here with his porkpie hat, of course, with a blonde woman who looks tall and thin enough to be in underwear ads. Her name is Inga, and around this round table for eight, she sits next to Joshua, which, even though he'd never admit it, makes him a little giddy. Her husband has always been a sucker for beautiful women, not in any lecherous or lascivious manner, but more like in the realm of awe, how a boy might act upon meeting his athletic idol. And from the bits of conversation Abby catches, while she herself chats with her rather drunk seatmate, Franny's brother Carl, Joshua's worship may not be misplaced this time, for Inga is indeed a professional model.

"…walking the runway is not difficult, once you've done it a few times…"

And Joshua counters with his artistic status as a writer.

"…my first novel, a family story after a terrible car crash…"

Meanwhile, Carl regales her with his stories of collegiate mayhem.

"…so I jump on my buddy Ray, I mean literally jump on him, and neither of us are wearing any pants at this point…"

Inga cracks up with the laugh of a madman, a laugh that doesn't fit her at all, which means Joshua must've said something really funny. He's laughing, too, the two of them leaning into each other for a moment. Perhaps this is where Abby should feel a pang of jealousy, but she does not. Because for all of Joshua's faults, and there are plenty for her to choose from — his rotten mood, his entrenched bitterness, his unapologetic flatulence — his faithfulness to her is not even a question. It's true he may dislike her at times, but there's something untouchable in him that also provides this unshakable, preordained fortitude of fidelity for her — and his work. It's this toughened core that forces him to write when things aren't going well, which is more often than not. Sometimes she fears this steel of his, but mostly she admires it, and sometimes even loves it, like now.

LINES

"Excuse me, Inga," she says. "If I may borrow my husband for a second?"

"Forgive me, Abby," she says, her practiced frown a thing of beauty. "I'm afraid Joshua here has amused me to the point of discourtesy."

So not only does she look perfect, but she also speaks perfectly, too. Some people have it all.

"No worries," Abby says. "I just want to ask Joshua if he wishes to dance."

"Of course," he says, and gets up right away and even helps Abby get out of her chair like a gentleman.

As nonconformist as Franny is in just about every part of her life, her wedding is a normal affair, with centerpieces, numbered tables, and a DJ playing the expected tunes of the occasion, like "Wonderful Tonight" by Eric Clapton, his wistful croons flowing out of the speaker towers set at the corners of the parquet floor. Joshua takes her hand and wends his way around the throng of slow dancing couples until they find an empty patch of space.

"I've just been chatting like a magpie," Joshua says into her ear.

"That's okay," Abby says. "You are having a good time?"

"Better than I thought I would, to tell you the truth," he says.

"I believe Inga is falling in love with you."

"Very funny," he says, but she can tell that he's pleased by the way he holds her, his right hand between her shoulders, his left on the small of her back, squeezing her a little to bring her in closer. She's forgotten how much she enjoys dancing, all this touching and caressing that seldom happens outside of a quick hug in the morning. There's no reason why they couldn't do this every week; it wasn't as if they lived in the middle of nowhere. The whole point of living in the greatest city in the world was that you could do anything you wanted at any time of the day, and yet…it's fantasy, this vision of swaying to the music with her husband every Saturday night, as fictive as the plot in Joshua's novel, *The Tragic Tolstoys*.

Eric Clapton fades into Seal's "Kiss from the Rose." Oh, the passion of this song!

Baby, I compare you to a kiss from a rose on the gray
Ooh, the more I get of you, the stranger it feels, yeah

"Your book — I'm proud of you, Joshua," Abby says. "I'm not sure if I've told you that before…"

"Of course you have," he whispers into her ear as they dance cheek to cheek, his beard soft like the fur of a cat. He'd groomed it for this evening, because usually it's a scratchy thing. "Of course you have."

He holds her even tighter, and even though she can't see it, she knows there are tears welling up in his eyes. Maybe it's the alcohol or the music or the disco ball painting glitter lights on all the dancers, but Abby is so grateful right now, for everything and everyone.

They head back to their table as Seal fades out, holding hands. He pulls her chair out for her and then gently pushes her in. The DJ announces that the cake cutting ceremony will begin shortly, and a crowd begins to form around the triple-tiered cake that's been rolled into the center of the dance floor on a brilliant silver cart, but Abby doesn't make a move. Instead she watches her husband as he sips on his coffee, basking in a glow of self-satisfaction. She can still make him happy. Despite all their troubles, he can still take pleasure in her company and she in his.

If Joshua's phone, which lays between them on the table, isn't touching his dessert fork, he never would hear its vibration, but that's not the case. It's a cascade of notifications, as the phone chatters the fork which also happens to be touching his water glass.

LINES

Joshua puts down his coffee and picks up his phone, and what happens next makes no sense. It shouldn't be possible for a face to darken against the shine of a screen's white glow, and yet it's as if there's some invisible shade that pulls slowly down until all that remains is blackness.

He puts down his phone. He goes back to his coffee.

Abby knows better than anyone that there is nothing she can say right now that will result in anything but anger, but this is her fate. She is his wife, the one who takes the brunt of his fire and fury.

"Joshua," she says.

"Yes?"

And here, she asks a question for which she already knows the answer.

"Are you okay?"

He drains the rest of his coffee and clangs the empty china against its saucer.

"Why wouldn't I be?"

She should just get up now and go to the cake cutting. Ignore him and his...childishness, foolishness, stubbornness, moodiness — fuck him! And yet when she sees his face, his struggle to keep this façade of placidity, her heart cracks.

"Please," she says. "Please don't shut me away."

"A person doesn't shut someone *away*. A person shuts someone *out*. It's funny you still make usage errors like this, after all the years you've been here."

When they'd first met, he'd found her linguistic quirks and mistakes endearing. Like when she'd first seen Skype, she called it *sky p. e.* Why not? You were connecting with people through the air after all, bits and bytes taking flight through the internet. But instead of berating her, Joshua had kissed her.

"My dear Abby, you look at this world with such freshness and clarity," he'd said.

Where did that sweetness go? Where is that man? Who is this bearded ogre in his place?

"Will you please tell me what happened?"

"It's nothing, I told you," he says. "I'm fine, it's all fine."

It's all Abby can take. She rises from her seat without another word.

"Super mature of you," Joshua says. "Just walk away, why don't you."

She makes her way to the dance floor and doesn't look back. By the time she reaches the cake, Franny and Matthias are arm-in-arm, and it is Franny holding the knife, its chrome blade glinting against the spotlight above.

*

As far as Joshua can see, outside of the cottonheads and baldies in wheelchairs and walkers, everybody else in this entire wedding party has gone over to the cake cutting ceremony.

Good, he thinks. *I'm finally with my people.*

He may be a year shy of hitting his mid-forties, but the truth is, he's always felt like an octogenarian. Like that guy two tables over, his back curled in like a shrimp, doing that puckering and sucking thing that denture wearers do. Joshua has felt like that guy since he's been a teenager. Sometimes he wishes his body would just hurry the hell up and catch up with his ancient soul.

Of course, he feels like this when things turn to shit, and boy, did they ever turn to grade-A, stink-to-high-heaven shit with the arrival of a single email. If he were smart, he would've had his phone in airplane mode, but he's stupid. He's a stupid, untalented hack of a writer, which is really what this email from his so-called publicist of his so-called publisher is about.

Joshua, I hope this email finds you well. We've had a bit of a change in plans. Dominic needs to attend to a family emergency, so he won't be able to participate in the discussion with you this coming Thursday at Nightshade Books — but fear not! As it happens, we have another event happening in Brooklyn that evening with two other Hot Metal Pressers, so why not make it a threesome? A literary Menage a Trois, as it may be (please don't report me to HR!). The time's the same, 7pm, but the location has shifted from the staid island to the hipper borough, and it'll now be held at Mermaid Books. You'll love it! And we love you. See you soon.

Best,

Michaela Schooner
Publicist
Hot Metal Press

    Joshua has known about this other event for as long as he's known about his, because both have been on the "Happenings!" page of the Hot Metal Press website for months. The two authors are graphic novelists, and Mermaid isn't a real bookstore but one that specializes in coffee table/art books. It makes no sense for Joshua to be there, but of course, it makes perfect sense for the publisher since they have to do something for him.

    The only reason why anybody outside of his family and friends would've come to see him at Nightshade was Dominic Gallant, shortlisted for the Pulitzer for his debut short story collection, the flashiest in Hot Metal's stable of writers. Considering he'd never even met the man, Joshua was surprised when he'd heard from Michaela that Gallant would lend him support. What Joshua should've done is email the guy, try to establish some kind of a rapport so Gallant wouldn't just dump him like this, but he never had, because frankly, he'd been afraid of him. Afraid of his fame, afraid of his assessment of *The Tragic Tolstoys*, afraid of being a lesser writer.

It took Joshua eleven years to publish his first book, a decade plus a year. After all that time, he should've written the Great American Novel, but instead what he has is a third-wheel book launch.

Are you okay?

The dumbest possible words anyone could say, and of course, it's his wife who utters them. His artist wife, who wants more than anything to paint her misguided tiny paintings. What a loser couple they were, still struggling to make something of themselves, coming to this wedding with their cheapo gift all wrapped up and tied with a golden bow so nobody could see how cheap it really was. Months ago, on a misspelled auction on eBay, Joshua snagged a brand-new Instant Pot for half price, the popular pressure cooker that was taking the world by storm. At full retail, the thing cost $150; theoretically, that was their maximum contribution to this wedding.

Even at those outstretched valuations, it wasn't even close to enough. Just the fancy silverware alone telegraphs the serious amount of cash that has been spent on this shindig. As far as Joshua knows, Franny isn't rich, so it must be her husband who footed the bill for the flock of waiters who roamed about with hors d'oeuvres during cocktail hour, for the stacked open bar with three bartenders, for the very hip ballroom. Joshua could just imagine him, the tall German, back in his Upper West Side Manhattan apartment and going through the gifts tomorrow, finding theirs and tearing through their wrapping paper and seeing the Instant Pot box.

"How thoughtful of your friends," he'd say to Franny.

LINES

"It is, isn't it, Matthias," she'd say. "You know, they don't have much."

"Which is why we should really appreciate this."

If there is one thing Joshua hates more than being made fun of, it is pity, and this imagined scene in his mind feels so ugly that he drains his full glass of red wine and marches to the bar, walking by the cake ceremony without giving it a glance.

"What will you have, mister?" the girl behind the counter says.

"Mister?"

"My attempt to be retro."

"I like it. Though what I'd really like is a Johnny Walker double, neat."

"You got it."

Joshua throws it back against his throat and it burns all the way down.

"One more for the road," he says.

She pours him one, and to his surprise, pours herself one, too.

"My shift is done, so here's my tip."

They clink shot glasses and by the time he drains this one, Joshua feels the sway of the room. Or, more likely, himself swaying and the room staying put. Either way, it's the twirl he wants. The bartender, now wearing a fur-collared jacket, emerges from the darkness of the serving corner and takes out a pack of cigarettes. When she taps the box against her palm, he can almost taste the tobacco.

"Please tell me you're gonna have a smoke," he says.

She laughs. Under normal lighting, Joshua sees how young she is, at most a year or two out of college. Her blonde hair has red highlights weaved through it.

"If you can make it to the lobby, mister," she says, "you can have a cigarette."

"You lead, I'll follow."

Joshua trudges past the DJ, who stands in front of a wall of old speakers stacked atop each other decoratively, rectangular wooden boxes of all different shapes and sizes arranged seamlessly like a Tetris puzzle. Many of them are without their protective screens, and Joshua notices the woofers look like eyeballs, which is funny because they're actually for hearing.

"They see what they can't hear," he mutters to himself.

"That's deep," the bartender girl says.

If she just heard what he thought he'd whispered to himself, then lord, he's even drunker than he thinks.

It's downright cold on this starry April evening. The bartender leads them a good ten paces beyond the cantilevered roof over the hotel entrance, a beautiful brown slab which is lit up like a Broadway playhouse, a line of yellow Edison bulbs running along the bottom edge. She leans against the papered-up window next door to the hotel, a space being renovated.

"Worked here long?" Joshua asks as she coaxes two cigarettes out of her pack. He pinches and pulls out a tiny white cylinder, a Camel unfiltered. He can't remember the last time he's had a cigarette; at least a couple of years. In college he smoked just three a day, about a pack a week, never getting fully addicted. He's always considered his lack of nicotine attraction as a kind of a superpower. An extremely lame superpower, but in a life of few tangible accomplishments, he's happy to claim it.

"I'm a free agent. Gig to gig, whoever pays the best."

"The brave new economy," Joshua means to say, but he's no longer sure if what his brain transmits to his tongue is being carried out with any level of accuracy. His mouth feels as dry as sawdust, though now that the girl flicks her lighter and pushes the flame to his face, now that he draws in the hot tobacco, everything goes comfortably numb. For a short moment, he can't feel his fingertips, a combinatorial effect of alcohol and cigarette he's long forgotten but now remembers fully. It's delightful to feel so much less, to be cut off from the real world. Another big drag, and his dizziness amplifies to rollercoaster levels. That's all he should smoke because these are unfiltered, as strong as they come…but the naked butt of the cigarette returns to his lips, and now his mouth gains moisture in the worst possible way, that horrendous sensation nobody wants: the gathering of saliva in preparation for vomit.

The gal keeps talking, but Joshua is beyond listening. He looks around, wishing for a toilet to magically appear in front of him, but that's another mistake. Swinging his head around makes the urge to throw up even stronger.

The planters by the hotel.

The cluster of big black pots with their dwarf trees and tasteful bushes.

"Hey, you look…" she says, but that's all he hears as he stumbles forward.

Lips desperately clenched, Joshua lumbers toward the greenery. *Please, please let me make it.* Three steps away, two steps, one — it's almost graceful, his descent to the ground, his hands thrust out like a lover to brace against the rim of the frigid round pot that resembles a squat, oversized wine glass. He kneels in front of the base, the needles of the bush prickling his forehead, as he expectorates the contents of this evening's consumption into the damp dirt. His stomach is a time machine in reverse, the whiskey first, then the main course of pepper-encrusted salmon. A sick waft of half-digested seaweed graces his nostrils, his first bite of the evening. The *nori* had been wrapped around some mystery meat. Chicken? Lamb? Not that it matters. Now it's all part of the pure pungent puke.

apart

Nightshade and Longing

JOSH ARRIVES HALF an hour earlier than he'd thought, the mass transit connection from the PATH to the 6 Train synchronized as if by magic. It was eerie, stepping onto the platforms of both trains just before they left, and now that he's standing outside a pair of brightly lit front windows of Nightshade Books, the May evening continues to feel unreal. He stares at the pyramidal stack of his first novel through the left pane, *The Tragic Tolstoys*, the peak of the pile displaying the black cover with the title in large typewriter font, and his name below it in a slightly smaller font, *Josh Kozlov*.

Seeing his books in public like this, it finally feels real, and a little daunting. The first and only time he's ever given a reading was when he'd received his MFA degree from NYU, five minutes of his thesis, the beginning of this very novel that had been cut from the final version. He'd read with nineteen other graduating fiction writers, and he can hardly remember it, it was so long ago.

He's about to pull the door to enter when he sees his own face staring back at him. In a clear sleeve attached with suction cups to the glass is a color printout of tonight's event:

A literary salon with Josh Kozlov (*The Tragic Tolstoys*), in conversation with Deborah Kieslowski (*Days of Wren*)

Accompanying the advertisement are their author photos, his a simple head shot that Marlene took in front of their dogwood tree, hers a black and white professional job with extremely shallow depth of focus that makes her eyes glow as if powered by electricity. Josh was hoping to enter the bookstore under the radar, to get the lay of the land surreptitiously, but now it looks like that won't be the case.

Except it absolutely is, as no one even gives him a glance, not the patrons, not the workers behind the counter, and not the burly security guard who stands by the door. Josh chuckles to himself. One wallet-sized photo on the door and who does he think he is, Lady Gaga?

Both his and Deborah's books are featured prominently on the front table. Josh takes out his smartphone and snaps a picture. Deborah's is a hardcover while his is a softcover, lower in the hierarchy of publishing since the hardcover means she'll also get a softcover release later down the line. He should be jealous, but in actuality, the overriding emotion Josh feels is gratitude, not just for Deborah doing this gig for him, but for the simple existence of his own book. Of course he'd dreamed it would get published one day, but thinking back to his colleagues at NYU, his workshop class of ten students, he'd never thought for a moment that he would be the first to get a book out. Three other writers from his class were way more talented than him in every way, people who just have that certain flair with words that he's never possessed, and yet he's the one with the book. Even though his novels are right there in front of him, he's still unable to shake the feeling that he's an imposter, that he's tricked his way into his authorship.

It's the first time he's visited this store, and like most indie bookshops, a tall wooden bookshelf stands behind the front table for the employee picks of the month. In addition to their names, each bookseller has a caricature drawing of them. They must be created with a Sharpie, because the lines are thick and black and bold, and really, they're quite good, the two people manning the registers behind the

LINES

counter, Bianca and Rory, their likeness unmistakable. If Josh is envious of anyone, it is visual artists, people who can capture the world with their clean curves and subtle shades while he has to fumble letters into words, take ten times as long to accomplish what they can with a few simple lines. And thinking about art makes him think of Abby and the bitter story he'd sent her before her wedding, which he has regretted as soon as he clicked Send. He's still not entirely sure why he'd felt so angry and bereft that day, when he found out via Instagram that she was getting married. In any case, the day after, he PayPaled her $100 as a wedding gift, monetary reparations if such a thing was possible, and though she did send a thank-you email a few days later, he still feels badly about it and hopes that it did not mar her special day in any way.

Josh slips around the cluster of shoppers to the back of the store, where he finds a woman unfolding gray metal chairs, adding to the rows of white ones already in place. They're all neatly arrayed for the stage with two highchairs, where he would do his reading and he and Deborah would do their talking. There were even a pair of classic theater spotlights on tracks on the ceiling, with black flaps around the bulb unit like an open box.

"Josh!" the woman says.

"Hello Vivian," he says, recognizing her caricature, square-shaped glasses and a short perm plus a sparkly stone for a nose piercing.

"My picks drawing precedes me."

"And my author photo precedes me."

Though she's a bit on the chunky side, her feet are as bouncy as a deer's. Josh extends his hand, but she'll have none of it — she playfully slaps it aside and envelopes him in a bear of a hug.

"Everybody who's ever had the wherewithal to write a book deserves a hug," she says. Her hair smells like strawberry-flavored bubblegum.

"You already have a lot chairs out — are you expecting a crowd?"

"Lots of RSVPs, which is somewhat uncommon."

"If people show up, it'll be for Deborah," Josh says.

"Don't sell yourself short. I read the nice reviews you got from Kirkus and Publishers Weekly."

"I doubt the audience reads those trade magazines."

"Of course they do — the Amazon overlords vacuum up those paragraphs and reconstitute them on their web pages. You haven't visited your own?"

"Not in a while, I guess, because the last time there was nothing but the book cover and the book dimensions."

"Very important to have those dimensions on there," Vivian jokes. "Can't imagine the number of lost sales without the size in full detail."

"Excuse me," another voice interrupts them, a voice Josh can't place. When he turns and sees the skull-capped man standing there, he smiles at him and desperately scans his memory banks for his name.

"Oh my goodness, how great to see you," he says, and though he's not a big hugger, Josh realizes it'll give him a few more seconds to flail around in his brain, and thank goodness the name comes back to him. Ethan, Ethan Roswell, how could he forget when he sat in the same room with him for two semesters at NYU! But it's been more than fifteen years since the workshops, and Josh is not on Facebook enough to be reminded of all the people he's supposed to keep up with. "So how have you been, Ethan?"

"Not as productive as you. Congrats on this little gem," he says, holding up a copy of *The Tragic Tolstoys*.

Ethan was one of the writers in the workshop with undeniable talent; Josh can still recall one of his submissions to the class all these years later, a short story about a Russian monkey going up to space in a rocket, set in the late 1960s, told entirely from the point of view of the monkey. There were rumors that the story was almost taken by *The New*

Yorker, but Josh never knew Ethan well enough to ask, and he certainly doesn't know him now.

"Thanks, man. How have you been?"

"Good, teaching little gigs when they come around, still trying to do what you've done here."

Ethan, whose sideburns have now gone gray, holds Josh's novel with both hands and stares at the cover, as if it held answers. Josh is no stranger to literary longing, wanting his work to be presented in this final paper form like every other writer, but the truth is, the longing never ends. Once he finally landed an agent, he longed for the more powerful agents that passed. And once his agent managed to find a publisher wanting to put this book out into the world, he longed for all the editors of bigger houses who didn't want anything to do with it. And the longing will continue with bookstore readings like this one, press coverage, awards, recognition — it'll never end. What was that saying, to want nothing is to have everything? Only the Zen Buddhists find true peace in this ever-craving world.

Josh considers telling all this to Ethan but doesn't, because it'd sound patronizing coming from him. Even though he got a tiny advance for his novel, just $5000 from the very indie Hot Metal Press, what would Ethan give to be in his place, to be at this bookstore as a featured author? It's not about the money. It's about sharing something worthwhile, something that came from you, with the public.

"It's luck, you know," Josh says. "I found an agent who found an editor. That's what you need to make this happen, two to champion your work, but it's a needle in a haystack situation. Two needles, really. All you can do is keep working and put yourself out there, which is never easy. But if you aren't going to do it, who will?"

While they've been talking, Josh hasn't realized that the room has gradually filled up. When he sees Deborah threading through the thicket of human traffic, he tells Ethan he's got to go.

"Of course. Thank you, Josh. I mean it. You don't know how much it's helped to chat with you. Now I'll take my seat and let you do your thing. Good luck, my friend."

They shake hands, and looking into Ethan's eyes, Josh knows he did something good. He's supported Ethan like Deborah has supported him, writers there for each other, a virtuous circle of positivity. He knows it's silly, but his eyes get misty as they tend to do nowadays whenever something moves him, the gifts of being older and hopefully wiser.

Suddenly it's all a bit of a whirlwind: Deborah greets him and tells him about what they will talk about; his wife Marlene arrives late with the sweet reason for her tardiness, his dad. She brought Josh's dad with her, a total surprise, a lovely one. The manager on duty hurries over with crackly, crystal-clear bottles of water.

Within minutes, Josh finds himself on one of the two tall chairs on stage, the spotlights on the ceiling momentarily blinding him. Someone adjusts the height of the microphone on the stand, then brings it closer to his mouth.

While Deborah introduces him with overwhelming kindness and undeserved flourish, his shaky hands open his novel to the Post-It note bookmark, readying to read. *Breathe*, he tells himself. *You're among family and friends.* His eyes scan the room. All the chairs are taken, there's even a row of people standing one row beyond. There's Marlene, there's his dad, but his search isn't done. He continues to look for a face he knows he won't find, but he looks anyway.

Abby.

She's been here the whole time, hasn't she? Without being here. Inside his mind, inside his heart. Why he wants her here, he doesn't know. But he wants her here. That much he knows.

LINES

*

A pair of human butterflies tower over Abby as they walk on stilts. They're women, gorgeous and lithe like ballerinas, wearing an all-silver spandex catsuit with outsized yellow wings made of some glitzy, gaudy material that glints gold with the tiniest of movements.

"This is balls-out nuts," Ted says, clutching her hand a little tighter.

They've just come through the doors of the New York School of Art, where it only looks like this once a year in May, when the entire building transforms into the Soho Ball. For the school, it's arguably its most important day, as it serves as the primary fundraiser to sustain the institution. During the years that Abby had been a student, this event did not exist, and the school barely stayed solvent. All this happened because a guy who was running PR at Goldman Sachs eight years ago took a drawing class, right here on the second floor of this building. That man, two years later, became the president of the school and was the sort of person who felt equally comfortable in the boardroom as well as the neighborhood dog run, where he would approach an Oscar-winning actress to come to his benefit. The actress invites some friends, the friends invite more friends, and just like that, the Soho Ball was born.

Which is why the lobby now looks like the red carpet of a Hollywood premiere, with a white canvas background stamped repeatedly with the school's insignia and the dressed-to-the-nines guests pausing to pose in front of the spotlights for the official photographer to capture their poshness for posterity.

It's not all vanity, though, as the six floors above, all artist studios, open their doors tonight for the ball participants to see, turning the upstairs into a hive of galleries. The theme this year is animals, so some of the students, also dressed up for the occasion, sit near the bar station by the elevator on the third and fifth floors to sketch live birds brought in from a city animal sanctuary.

Abby no longer knows any current students, as they've all graduated, but tonight she's guaranteed to know at least one other colleague, as her friend Franny has been invited back like her for an alumni highlight. Franny's an obvious choice as she primarily paints animals, some roadkill, of course, but Abby got lucky with the trio of her tiny Lilliputs featuring a goat, a ram, and a peacock, all creatures she encountered in her cycling travels. Thanks to the generosity of the planning committee, they were comped a couple's seat at the dinner table, no small shakes at $2000 a head.

It didn't take much to convince Ted to come, as it is another opportunity for him to talk to the wealthy. This week he lost a client to a "Robo-Advisor," computers who do the stock picking for a much lower cost than people like her husband. Are we all destined to be replaced by technology? It may just be a matter of time until a computer figures out how to draw and paint, though Abby can't see it. How can a machine inject the necessary soul of the artist into the work? Unless, of course, the machine develops a soul, but this line of thinking gives her a headache, and between the DJ blaring out techno-tunes from her neon pink booth and the throng of men in suits and women in dresses chatting and milling about, Abby's got a headache already.

It's likely her profession is safe from the oncoming onslaught of artificial intelligence, but what of her child's? Instinctively, her hand slides to her belly, her tiger-print dress stretched tight against her bump. According to the Baby and Fruit Size chart that now hangs on their kitchen wall, her baby is as big as a turnip, and Abby may sweat excessively, feel constipated, and experience increased vaginal secretions. Her pregnancy has been stubbornly textbook, so indeed right now, her armpits are damp, she hasn't pooped since yesterday morning, and even though she's not on her period, she's wearing a pad because, yes, she's wet down there, too.

LINES

A slim silver-haired gentleman in a white tux and a tiny platinum-blonde woman in a flowy canary yellow dress walk by, and Ted whispers, "Timothy and Imogene Beecher." The woman's scarf of Tweety Bird around her neck hangs all the way down her back.

"You know them?" Abby asks.

"Slightly. I should know them a little more. You think we can chat them up a bit?"

"I'll stand happy and quiet next to you, if that is what you mean."

On the third floor, not far from where her old studio used to be, Ted makes his move. Abby has always been in awe of Ted's ability to schmooze. It's effortless for him, or at least he makes it seem that way, which is why people are instantly at ease when they talk to him. After a quick introduction, it doesn't take much at all until the conversation shifts from art to investments, which makes sense since to some people, they are one and the same. When Imogene excuses herself for another drink, Abby's phone chirps, an email from Josh. Timothy and Ted are so deep in their talks that they don't even notice Abby making herself scarce.

The crowds are beginning to thin, because dinner is to be served soon and they're making their way down to the first floor. It's strange being back here with such a mass of people, because her memory of this space is one of emptiness and silence. Her fellow Schoolers were very aware of each other, so if one listened to music while working, it was always with headphones or earbuds. As she makes her way down the beige corridor, she realizes how much she's missed the smell of turpentine, a blend of pine trees and licorice; oil paint is off limits while carrying her child. And just like that, her throat chokes up and her eyes fill with tears and she laughs them away. These baby hormones, they're like a drug.

Three doors down, Abby finds herself at the threshold of her old studio, 210. It's now occupied by someone named Isaiah Mundy, a sculptor who's carved what looks like a dining set made of human limbs, with sinewy arms as chair backs and foot-shaped feet, plus a table that looks like a giant palm of a hand. It's beautiful and somewhat disturbing, her favorite combination for art. A sign on the table reads:

TAKE A SEAT AND REEEEEELAX

So Abby does exactly that. She takes out her iPhone, opens up her email. There's nothing in the body of the message except for a hyperlink to a website she recognizes, *TNT Journal*. The subject reads: "We're Published!" She taps on the link and sees:

LINES

Insomnia (I)

She should've stopped an hour ago because darkness has fallen, but she doesn't want to. There's a part of her that wants to ride until the sun rises. She could do it. She's done it before. The moon is almost full, enough to illuminate her way. She'll take it easy. She'll take in the shadows, take in the stillness of this forest.

As soon as she makes up her mind to go all night, she sees the sheep. Three of them, in the middle of the path, slowly turning to look up at her as if they've been interrupted from deep conversation.

She glides to a stop and dismounts from her bicycle. She leans it against a boulder, half of its craggy face bearded with moss. The wind rustles the leaves. A squirrel scampers through the thicket of the underbrush.

The tallest sheep, the one out in front, opens its mouth. It yawns.

The two other sheep follow its lead and yawn, too.

And now she feels it, her own mouth opening wide. She breathes in. She holds the air. She holds the world in her lungs, for a moment.

Sitting here in this odd dining room of a studio, Abby feels as displaced as Alice must have in Wonderland. Is this really happening? Is her name and her painting really in *TNT*? *TNT* is perhaps the most sought-after publication for the visual arts, a place in which Abby had never thought she'd appear. Artists who have won the MacArthur "genius" grant regularly grace the glossy magazine and the website. As she clicks through, she sees a literature section she's never known, and because of Josh and his words, now her painting is in here. In *TNT*. She still can't believe this has happened.

She reads the story again. Did he think of her when he wrote this? Is she, as silly as it sounds, his muse? What does that even mean? She feels hot, she feels sweaty, there are too many emotions running through her right now, uncomfortable feelings. She bolts up from her seat to walk it off. She leaves her old studio and enters the next one, which used to be Franny's — and comes face to face with an enormous painting of a baby named Cecilia.

It's an eight-foot by six-foot canvas of stretched linen, the infant's eyes as green as summer grass, and there's no question who painted this: Lynne Priestley. It has to be hers, and sure enough, on the bottom right corner are her initials. Lynne was six years her senior and became known for painting faces under water, and this baby is no exception, though with a slight twist. Instead of just water, now it looks as if Lynne has added swirly, bubbly oil to the surface, lending a fantasy quality to the portrait, though the size is just…too much, at least for Abby. Since leaving this institution, the largest canvas she's worked on was a round eight-inch piece of copper, and even that felt too vast. She can't even imagine working at an overwhelming scale such as this. It just seems wrong, especially the baby's pouty smile, it'd be more effective at a closer distance. It's one of the reasons why the tiny has always been attractive to her, the intimacy, how the smallness draws in the viewer.

"…which is why we want you. Oh, excuse us."

"That's okay," Abby says. It's Imogene Beecher, Tweety Bird scarf and all, and next to her, Lynne herself. She and Abby were in a group show at a small downtown gallery many years ago, but Lynne has since moved on to bigger and better things and does not recognize her. Her long, thick black hair, coming down straight to the small of her back, has always been a staple of her look. In a body-hugging sequined black dress and a diamond choker around her elegant neck, Lynne reminds Abby of the phrase — you can never be too rich or too thin. Abby takes a couple of steps back to give Lynne and Imogene privacy.

"Well," Lynne says. "I have two commissions I'm working on right now, but after that, I have time for you and Timothy."

"And Rascal," Imogene says.

"Rascal?"

"Our Irish Setter."

LINES

"Ah. Whatever you wish."

"I'd want it bigger than this," Imogene says, gesturing to the gigantic babe on the wall.

"Whatever you wish," Lynne repeats.

If there is a hint of sarcasm that Abby detects, it may be in her imagination, because Imogene doesn't hear it. She takes Lynne's arm and they leave together, leaving Abby alone, though not entirely alone. There are two babies with her, Cecilia on the wall and her own in her belly. Next week her fetus will be as large as a bell pepper, and supposedly there could be kicks. There really is a little being living inside her, complete with tiny feet. Most women on the planet go through this natural process, but to Abby, it still feels like a singular miracle.

together

Regret and Mermaid

ABBY IGNORES IT at first, thinking it was indigestion. But then it happens again, a little tap against the inner wall of her belly. A kick. Well, maybe not a kick, more like a tap.

Just saying hello, mommy.

"Excuse me," Abby says to the man who was speaking to her, whose name she's already forgotten. She's never possessed a great memory to begin with, but now with the pregnancy, she's lucky to remember her own name. "I would need to like to sit down?" That's bad English, she knows, but this second language of hers has also deserted her at recent times.

"Of course, of course," he says, and even lends his arm for support and takes her around the crowd to the next studio, which is empty. "Oh look, you can sit on that hand chair!"

Initially she thinks he's joking, but there's a sign on a table that reads:

A HELPING HAND — PLEASE SIT

The table is shaped like a flat face, and the chair is indeed shaped like a hand, straight fingers serving as a back while the curled palm is the seat. It looks creepy and uncomfortable, but once she sits, it's not bad at all, certainly better than standing. The fingers will make weird creases in her little black velvet dress, but so be it.

At this point of her pregnancy, the baby is barely half a pound, and yet she feels like a bathtub, a fully drawn bathtub. Her feet ache, her back has shooting pains she's never experienced before, and at times walking the aisles of D'Agostino's for groceries seems more exhausting than bicycling up a hill.

Now that the tiny kick from her tiny baby has become a memory and the various pains in her body are subsiding, she's able to focus on the matter at hand. She was supposed to meet a couple tonight who wanted to talk to her about one of her paintings, but they never showed. She brings out her phone and looks at her calendar and is reminded of something else that has escaped her addled brain — Joshua's reading, which is no longer at the bookstore in Manhattan but in Brooklyn. She ran the numbers earlier in the day, the 40-minute trip to the borough according to Google Maps' transit logistics, but now those metrics have changed for the worse due to a repair of one of the subway lines. She needs to leave now to make it on time.

Sitting here, the noise of the crowd outside this studio like the buzzing of busy bees, she imagines her underground and aboveground journey, hopping on the E train, then switching to the G. From the Greenpoint station, it is a quarter-mile walk. None of it is particularly difficult, except for the last part of this trip, opening the door to Mermaid Books and coming face to face to her husband's grimace.

Of course, this is all in her head. There's no guarantee that Joshua would be in a rotten mood...oh, who the hell is she kidding. All week she's been immersed in his anger, marinated in his lament, soaked in his regret. Half the time he didn't even look at her as he complained to her, his eyes glued to his phone. She's done her best to be sympathetic, to see his disappointment as her own — if she had worked on a painting for a decade, and then to see that painting regarded with such disregard

LINES

— yes, she'd be pissed, too. But in the end, her empathy can only be extended so long, because the pain is ultimately his. The sooner he takes ownership of his own feelings instead of lashing out at the world, the better off he would be.

But if she were to mention anything of the sort, she knows what would happen, because it's what's happened countless times: she becomes the focus of his ire. Best to just let him stew in his own bitter sauce and let the poison run its course.

Is it any wonder she's still sitting in this hand-shaped chair when she should be getting up and getting the hell out of here?

"There you are!"

"There she is!"

Before she can rise, a well-dressed older couple swarm over her.

"We were hoping you hadn't already left," the silver-haired man says. He's in a dark blue suit with a hint of white pinstripes.

"The blame should go entirely to me," the woman says, wearing an all-black gown with a long yellow scarf worn like a shawl. The work she's had done on her face plus the ultra-dark eye shadow make her look like the wicked stepmother of a fairy tale.

"Hello," Abby says. Stuck in the chair with these two crowding her, she feels like she's about to be interrogated.

"I was just enamored with your giant painting of Cecilia," the woman says. "Why aren't you by your painting?"

"Imogene, you can't expect her to stand next to it all night. This isn't some farmer's market."

"Not all night, but we were there for a good fifteen minutes."

"Fifteen minutes is not a long time!"

"Really? Who made you Father Time?"

Abby, attempting to focus their attention, clears her throat.

"Oh dear," Imogene says. "We're really just carrying on like a couple who've been together for way too long, aren't we. I reached out to you last week, Ms. Abby Kim — I'm Imogene and this is Timothy, my dear husband."

They talk business, wanting her to come and paint their portrait. Abby smiles and nods. They will be in their Upper East Side apartment for another month; when June rolls around, they spend the summer in their Alaskan cabin. So their time is limited.

"You can also take a photo of yourselves, and I can paint from that?" Abby suggests, but they'll have none of it. Because even though they don't say it, what they want is to tell their friends that they are sitting for a painting. Abby's smartphone vibrates, her snoozed alarm for Joshua's reading warning her again that she needs to depart immediately.

"Did Imogene mention Rascal?" Timothy asks.

"Rascal?"

"Our Irish Setter," Imogene says. "I'm sure I did. Didn't I?"

"So your dog will be in the painting, too," Abby says.

"Except he's incapable of sitting down for any more than five minutes."

"This is okay," Abby says. "He can sit, I can sketch quick, and then if you give me some photos, I can put him into the painting."

"But…" Imogene says, "isn't that like…cheating?"

"It is reality," Abby says. "I'm sorry, but I must leave now for my husband."

"Sorry to keep you," Timothy says. "Here, let me help you up. Just one more thing, though, I believe you and Imogene have already discussed the cost?"

"I told you already twice, Timothy," Imogene says.

LINES

"Nothing wrong with triple checking," Timothy says. "Measure twice, cut once, dad always said."

After dealing with rich people for years now, it shouldn't surprise Abby that they, way more than non-rich people, are obsessed with money. After all, it is why they are rich.

"Yes, not a problem, and now I really must go."

Abby bids them a quick goodbye and promises to call to set up a time for their portrait. The ball is in full swing now, many of the lookers happily soused with their flutes of champagne. Like the way casinos provide free booze to loosen the gamblers' purse strings, a similar strategy is being deployed here. If money makes the world go round, then alcohol is its well-greased wheels.

At the coat check counter, she picks up her backpack, plus the gift bag she received for partaking in the ball. It isn't exactly heavy, lots of useful artistic accoutrements like sample pastels, charcoal, Moleskin notebooks, but some bigger stuff like the rolled-up canvas in a poster tube makes it hard to navigate through the crowd.

Outside, the night has cooled considerably; she zips up her jacket as she makes her way up 6th Avenue and finds the E train. Her luck holds on that line, but once she switches to the G, the car's lights flicker at the Flushing Avenue stop. The metallic voice of the conductor announces that there's a power fluctuation and they need to stay here for a few minutes. The few minutes becomes ten minutes, then fifteen. By the time they are moving again, the best-case scenario is a half an hour delay, if she foregoes the walk and finds a taxi.

If she were smart, she would've scheduled an Uber to meet her, but it is what it is. Mercifully, there is a taxi outside the station, but a man is already there and about to get in.

"Excuse me, but I'm pregnant and I must go see my husband," she says.

The guy, in a backwards baseball cap and leather jacket, looks her over. "You don't look pregnant."

She doesn't want to cry, but no, there they go, her hormone-fueled tears. "I'm almost four months."

"Oh shit," the man says. "I didn't mean to...just take it, okay?" And he literally runs away from the cab.

By the time she arrives at Mermaid Books, she's almost forty minutes behind. She flings opens the door, her arms carrying not only her backpack and goodie bag and poster tube but what feels like the anvil of her life. The reading is happening in the back because that's where she sees the cluster of folding chairs, about twenty of them. Joshua is at the lectern.

"Thank you," he says, to a smattering of applause, as he takes his seat.

*

When he sees his wife, gratitude and resentment mix like epoxy. He can feel his heart hardening, his forearm growing taut with tension as he squeezes his book between his fingers.

Sitting behind the spotlighted lectern after his reading, Joshua is grateful for this corner of darkness. Under this inky cover, he breathes through his nostrils to calm himself down. He's never been in a physical fight in his life, yet his hands are fists and they feel enormous and heavy and evil. Right now, he could pummel another human being, swing his arms as hard as he could and have his knuckles break skin, soak in the warmth of a stranger's blood.

LINES

My goodness, what is happening to him? Is this madness? Is that what he is, mad, crazy, insane? Or he's having a heart attack, because his chest still thumps like he's sprinted a mile.

Fist, opened. Shoulders, drooped. Neck, lolled. Finally, his heartbeat feels like his own again.

His eyes hurt because he'd had them clenched for god only knows how long, clenched like someone in searing pain. Which may not be inaccurate. He may not be suffering from a broken hip or a migraine headache, but now that his episode of violence is ebbing, he's left with a numbness that feels very much like the aftereffects of intense physical exhaustion.

When the crowd erupts in laughter, Joshua is forced to reorient to his surroundings: still at Mermaid Books, his opening act concluded minutes ago, exactly synchronized with Abby's belated arrival. Why did she bother to show up at all? She had her own thing tonight anyway, that dumbass Soho Ball with the millionaire and celebrity attendees, which hopefully went well because they could surely use the infusion of cash. It was as if she was waiting outside the door, making certain that he was done to maximize his humiliation.

He wanted her here, his wife, whom he has relentlessly, emotionally tortured. He knows this better than anyone, and this book launch was supposed to be his apology to her. He'd planned to start off by singling out Abby to thank her, but she wasn't even around and now it's ruined.

"So here's what we'll do: I'll read, and Violet will act out my words," the reader says.

The reader is Damien Arturo, and Violet is his sister. They are the graphic novelists, Damien the writer and Violet the artist. The brother is wearing more eye makeup than the sister, liner so thick and dark that it's as if he's wearing a mask like Zorro. In his ratty Iron Maiden t-shirt and black leather pants and streaks of gray in his long brown hair, he looks like a rock star beyond his prime. Violet, in a black hoodie lined with chrome studs and ripped black jeans, gives off a biker chick vibe.

For Joshua's reading, all the chairs had been occupied, but now for the main event, another dozen people crowd around the back.

"I never thought I'd be back here," Damien reads, and Violet, with her hands deep in hoodie pockets, paces back and forth on the stage. She must've studied movement or took classes in dance, because when she turns the make-believe doorknob and walks through and closes the invisible door, it's as if a new room has materialized out of nowhere. She makes a gun out of her right hand, holds it out against the audience, then slowly guides it to her temple.

"This is how it begins," Damien says, and Violet pulls the trigger and slumps to the floor.

For the next half hour, Joshua and the rest of the audience is treated to this strange and engrossing tandem show of narration and mime. It's obvious they've done this before, because their timing is impeccable and the drama drawn from this simple concept is, quite frankly, entertaining as hell. After the character commits suicide, she encounters one weird character after another in the underworld, a modern retelling of Dante's *Inferno* crossed with the playful morality tale of Antoine St. Exupery's *The Little Prince*. Violet plays multiple characters, jumping from one side of the stage to the other, and when Damien speaks the dialogue, her mouth matches her brother's words. When the performance ends, everyone rises from their chairs to give them a standing ovation, including Joshua.

A brief Q&A follows the readings, where the usual questions are asked — where do you get your ideas, when do you do your writing, how do you get an agent. Afterwards, they're shepherded to a table to sign their books. Most of the customers line up on the side of the sibling graphic novelists, but to his surprise, three people queue for him. The first is a bubbly woman perhaps in her sixties, delighted to have him sign the book for her husband, for his upcoming birthday.

LINES

"It's not until August, so I'll read it before I give it to him," she says, then giggles. "I really liked what you read."

"Thank you."

His first ever signed book, to a complete stranger. They'll be reading what he wrote, and he'll never see her again. He'll never meet her husband, the one who'll ultimately hold his book in his hands. Is that sad or is that amazing? Why not both.

The second person is a short fat man who says hello, asks him to just sign his name, and leaves. No muss, no fuss.

"Hello, Joshua," the final person in the line says.

"Hi."

Her eyes turned into pinpricks under Coke-bottle glasses, this grandmotherly woman watches him with a smirk.

"Not familiar?"

"Do I owe you money?"

She laughs and holds out her arm, then lowers her hand to a level slightly higher than the table.

"That's how tall you were when you were in my second-grade class."

"So you were taller."

That makes her laugh again, and then miraculously, he does remember her, that cackle of hers.

"Mrs. Mulvaney!"

"Correct on two counts, my name and the fact that I am indeed physically shorter than I used to be. Of course, you knew me as a child when I must've stood over you like a giant."

"I can't believe you remember me."

"You used to make up darling little stories in your math answers. Instead of answering ten plus twenty, you'd write how ten was mad that twenty was twice as big."

Now it was his turn to laugh. "And I thought I used to be a good student."

She was visiting her granddaughter this weekend and just happened to walk by the bookstore and saw his name and photo on the door. If that isn't the definition of kismet, what was? While he signs his book for Claire, which is her first name, he also writes in between a set of parentheses, *Mrs. Mulvaney*, because there's no way he'd ever address her as Claire. As she prattles on about her visit to the big city from her retirement community in Florida, Joshua's mind wanders to himself in second grade. That would've been Oakhurst Elementary, a squat beige building in his hometown where he spent the first five years of his academic career. Most of that time he's forgotten, but he can still remember those ice cream sandwiches he used to devour, the vanilla in between rectangular slabs of soft Oreo-like cookies. Every day, two kids were tasked to carry school lunches to their classroom, each holding one side of the cardboard box. That's what he now recalls, that lovely feeling of bringing food back for his classmates. It was a primal human response, the satisfaction of providing sustenance, and he wants to share this with Mrs. Mulvaney, but she's in her own little world, talking about her two cats back in Boynton Beach, and it brings her great joy to chat about them, it's obvious, so he lets her. When the conversation peters out, he thanks her for coming, and now she's gone, too, and the last person he has to deal with is his wife, who's still frumpily sitting in the farthest row, holding onto two copies of his book in her lap for some reason.

"Hoo boy. You should see your face."

With her brother in deep conversation with a fan, Violet takes a hit of her vape.

"Only one I got," Joshua says.

LINES

Through the dissipating vapor, she leans in and whispers, "Since my brother's been talking to this doofus for what feels like forever, I've been staring at your face. You have a good, drawable face, in case you didn't know. Anyway, so the whole time you were talking to the old lady, you had this childish glow about you, especially your cheeks. But after she left…it's like you turned into a monster. No disrespect."

"None taken. And I hope I'm not disrespecting you by saying you look like you ride a Harley."

"Those highway death machines? No thank you. The scariest thing I ride is the subway."

"I was looking at my wife. Over there," Joshua gestures to Abby, who picks up on his gesture and smiles and rises from her chair. "Fuck, now she's coming."

"That's a bad thing?" Violet asks.

"Hey," Abby says.

There's really no kind way to say it: his wife is the very definition of haggard, run down, exhausted. Even though she's dolled up in her knee-length black velvet dress with tiny glittering rhinestones around her neck and hem, the bags under her eyes and the slouch in her shoulders make her seem positively geriatric.

"You could've just gone home," he says.

Definitely the wrong thing to say, as he watches Abby clear her throat to fight back tears. "I came fast, took a cab. As quick as I could."

"Okay," he says. "All right. Let's move on. What's with my books?"

She places them on the table.

"Please sign them."

"But that means you have to buy them. I have like ten copies at home."

"Please," Abby says. "Please, Joshua, just sign them for me, okay?"

He does as he is told, because he can plainly see that if he doesn't, his pregnant wife with pregnant hormones would start her pregnant crying right here.

"Thank you," she says, and turns away. The unease in his stomach is pity for Abby, but there's no denying there's disgust, too. Disgust at the fucked-up-ness of everything. And this was supposed to be a happy day.

"It's your beard," Violet says. "When you're in your zone of negativity, do you know your beard raises its hackles like a wild animal? It really pops your whole face."

Joshua turns to her, slowly.

"What the fuck is wrong with you?"

He said that with as much menace as he's able to muster, and yet Violet just keeps on smiling.

"The night isn't long enough for me to get into that," she says, "But I will tell you this. I like your darkness, Joshua Kozlov. Your suffering is beautiful. Your trauma is so fucking pedestrian, but that's what's special about it. We have to find a way to work together."

She holds up her sketchpad. During his and Abby's awkward conversation, Violet had busied herself with her pen. Through the roughly crosshatched shades and the thick bold lines, Joshua sees his contorted visage staring back at him, all his anguish enshrined in black and white. The girl is majorly fucked up, but damn if she isn't good.

apart

Pure Imagination

IN THE MIDDLE of an all-hands meeting at PayRight, Josh's phone vibrates in his pocket. It's definitely a faux pas to look at your smartphone during a meeting, even a bullshit one where their CEO Winston Buck speaks on the projected screen, broadcasting from his Silicon Valley throne in San Francisco about some new initiative that has nothing to do with anyone's job in this conference room. But such is life in Corporate America, and Josh has made his peace with it years ago. Still, it annoys him to be a part of it, which is why he now quietly removes his phone from his pocket and holds it below the table and peeks at the screen askance, as a form of professional civil disobedience, or at least that's how he justifies it to himself. The subject line reads *Letter of Invitation*.

Dear Josh,

We here at the Oregon Institute of the Arts are thrilled to invite you and Abby Kim for our eleventh annual Art and Music Festival in August! I can't express how excited we are to have you both come here for the three-day weekend of festivities. It'll be held at beautiful Breitenbush Hot Springs (near Detroit), and because you'll be one of our featured presenters, we are pleased to provide airfare for you both, in addition to the all-inclusive meals and lodging.

The rest of the email goes into detail about the mission of the Oregon Institute of the Arts, which Josh skims while his brain is preoccupied with Detroit. Why would an organization in Oregon be holding an event in Detroit?

Google to the rescue: turns out there's a town called Detroit in Oregon, about two hours south of Portland.

The meeting is mercifully let out. As Josh makes his way back to his cubicle, his phone vibrates with a text from Marlene.

hows the buckster? ;)

He says he misses you.

ha, such a blowhard...

So lucky you don't work here anymore...

Now sitting back in his cube, Josh starts to type about the email he's just received but deletes it. It's amazing news, but does he even know if he'll end up going? Because this isn't just about him, it's about Abby, too. It's about the two of them, together.

But not like that. Because this is for their art, his words and her painting comingling to form a more beautiful combination than either of them is able to achieve by themselves.

And yet if that's true, if this is a wholly platonic endeavor, why does his heart beat like that of a teenager before his first kiss?

In the eleven years he and Marlene have been together, he has never cheated on her, not even close. Of course he's fantasized about other women, though never anyone he's physically come into contact with in real life but rather actresses who give vulnerable, Oscar-worthy performances on the big screen.

This thing he feels for Abby is most definitely not that.

But then what is it, really?

It's time he stops being a goddamn pansy and faces this head-on.

Is he willing to admit that he has feelings for Abby? Yes, okay. But what does that even matter, because she's married and pregnant and Marlene's his wife and he loves her...so it doesn't matter. Even if the parameters and perimeters of his attraction get established, none of it is actionable, or even desirable.

His mind feels like it's in a loop, returning to the same frustrating signpost no matter how hard or far he sprints away.

Now half past noon, the office floor empties for lunch. He opens up his browser and types "abby kim artist" into Google Images. Most of the photos that come up are of her tiny paintings and tree drawings, but there's one of her that Josh has never seen, Abby looking more a girl and less a woman, in a group shot of nine people, the men in suits and the women in satin dresses. It was for a gallery opening twelve years ago, which meant Abby was in her twenties, barely out of her master's program. He's never seen her hair so long, down to her bare shoulders, and she smiles not at the camera but at something to her left, something outside of the frame. What or who is she looking at?

What if she were looking at him, Josh, her loving husband?

That June morning, they rose from their loft bed in their Greenwich Village apartment. Her studio was a corner of the living room; his office was a converted closet. She used the natural sunlight streaming in through the open window that overlooked the vibrant city; his computer monitor was his only illumination. Two artists in mad pursuit, they worked from daybreak until lunch, at which point they met not in the kitchen but the bedroom, where they wordlessly took off their clothes and made love, quickly and passionately, to release and recharge. Then they'd eat cold leftover pizza from the night before, and once sated, returned to their work. Like regular workers, they knocked off at five, then got ready for the gallery opening, Josh zipping up the back of Abby's golden dress, Abby straightening Josh's tie.

A ridiculous fantasy of domestic artistic bliss, laughable, really…and yet undeniably alluring. Josh ignores his stomach's hungry grumbles, scans the search results, and peers hard at each round painting until one speaks to him.

And does it ever. This one. Because he doesn't even have to think — he knows its story.

The Unseen (I)

She wonders why she's here, at this particular place, in this particular moment. Because she could be anywhere. She could be back home, within the circumference of her everyday life, walking to work,

LINES

greeting her friends and colleagues, sitting on her favorite park bench as she bites into a sandwich.

No, she's here, next to this tree. She lays her hands on the bark and presses, the roughness prickling her palms. She takes in its ancient scent, the coalescing of the aging wood and the decaying understory. The exposed roots of the tree are like fingers clawing into the dirt, and its branches are limbs that aim for the sky.

She removes her sneakers. She removes her socks. She walks barefoot around the tree until she arrives on the other side, the one that faces the river. The earth is softer here, and she feels — she feels...

If someone were to pass by where she'd just been standing, they wouldn't see her at all. All they would know are these trunks, these waters, this solitude.

With her shoes in her arms and her toes in the ground, she thinks: *I am here. And I am not.*

He reads it over twice, amazed at how sometimes the words flow so easily. Josh sits back in his office chair with a satisfied grin, though one that fades as quickly as it came.

Is it possible that this tenderness he feels for her is his mind fooling himself to write these stories? That he's falling in love for the sake of creating fiction?

Josh closes his eyes and cradles his face in his hands. He's thoroughly confused, morally, literarily, emotionally.

"Everything okay?"

Harold, his boss, holds an apple in his hand. He places it on Josh's desk.

"Thanks, yeah."

"Didn't see you at the cafeteria, so I figured you brought your lunch up here, but I see you haven't eaten at all."

Harold leans to his left to get a glance at Josh's screen.

"What is that? Christ, is that thing really that small?"

Josh rolls his chair away so Harold can get a better look. Something Abby does from time to time is to put a reference item with the painting, to reveal its scale. She's used a set of keys, a penny, a pen, and for this one, she personalized it even further by including a set of paint brushes and the tips of two of her fingers at the edge of the photograph.

"And …you wrote this? About the painting?"

"It's just a short little piece," Josh says, but Harold doesn't hear him. He's reading the story, and watching his face moving from curious to enraptured brightens Josh's mood. This is why he struggles and suffers with words, because witnessing his imagined world transferred to another is the highest of highs.

His boss turns to him. "You wrote this?" he asks again.

Josh laughs. "You know that I write fiction in my spare time, Harold. I gave you a copy of my book."

"Which, obviously, I haven't read."

"But now you will?"

"Now I absolutely will," Harold says. He eyes Josh's monitor again. "You just sat here and just banged this out. How do you do it?"

"All hail Nike: I just do it. Don't forget, I've been doing it a long time."

Harold pats him on the shoulder. "Well, don't get too good at it, because I need you here."

"If I had to live on what I make with my writing, I couldn't afford dog food."

After Harold leaves, Josh bites into the red delicious apple. Has he ever tasted a sweeter fruit, or is it just that his ego has been elevated to exultation, thanks to his boss's wondrous compliments? Who cares? The world is a beautiful place, and he'll happily take advantage of its timely generosity.

LINES

Josh clicks Forward on the email from the Oregon Institute of the Arts and addresses it to Abby. He drags the Word doc to the email so it'll attach.

Dear Abby,

I don't think I'll ever tire of addressing a letter to you this way, ever. Anyway — please check out the email below. Like three months ago, you gave me the okay to send our collaboration stories around to literary magazines. As you know, we hit the jackpot with TNT, but it turns out there was an even bigger jackpot in waiting.

I know you feel like these pieces I write are more my thing than yours, but that's simply not true. I could never have written any of these stories if not for your paintings, and your openness — that you were willing to share your art with me this way. Frankly, I'm still astonished that you've let me into your creative space this way. I doubt I would've been as giving.

Anyway, I hope you have the time and the inclination to go. It goes without saying that we either go together or not at all.

- Josh

p.s. I just wrote another one — see what you think. My plan is to write another six before the festival so there'll be ten total to present at the reading. If we go, that is. Which I hope we do. But if we don't, not the end of the world. No pressure! Well, a little. I'll shut up now.

*

She bought her dress last month on sale, a black stretchy tube of a gown that flares out to a frilly skirt, knowing she'll be showing at this point, five months deep into her pregnancy. It still fits her, but barely, and even though it's insane, the dress feels twice as tight around her belly as it had when her solo gallery opening began two hours ago.

Abby has never been more aware of her own body as she is this special evening. For the first time, she feels like someone else — a mother, she supposes. This revelation should usher in happiness, or if not that, at least some form of satisfied maturity, but neither is the case. She wants her body back, one that doesn't need to pee every hour.

"Excuse me for one second," she says to a tall and thin stylish woman she's never met before, whose name she's already forgotten, who was waxing poetic on the current Matisse exhibition at the Met. As Abby makes her way to the bathroom for the fourth time, three of her colleagues stop her for congratulations, her urgency to empty her bladder increasing with each compliment. Finally she's able to make her escape to the restroom, which is thankfully, blissfully empty. And quiet. She wants more than anything to just stay here in this bright, white-tiled sanctuary, but she resists the urge. It is her party, after all.

When she pushes on the door of the bathroom to exit, she almost runs into Eisenhower Wakefield, who's making his own return from the men's lavatory.

"Well," Wakefield says. "The woman of the hour."

In a form-fitting dark blue Italian suit with a red kerchief folded with origami precision in his breast pocket, he's a dashing picture as always. As Abby looks up at his six-foot-four frame, she finds amusement at his positional synchronicity, how the gray letters WAKEFIELD GALLERY on the far wall floats above his head.

"Eisenhower."

From afar, one might interpret from this scene that the owner of this gallery and the representing artist are engaged in pleasant conversation, but nothing could be further from the truth. There are some fortunate artists who float through the business side of art on wings, gathering nary a scratch nor a scar on their flight to their solo shows. Someone like Lynne Priestley, Abby has often thought, who graduated six years earlier than her and has become hugely successful, even getting a series of her paintings featured in a movie last year, though Abby is probably wrong about Lynne, too. No artist she knows has run through the gauntlet of commerce unscathed.

As gallery owners go, she's dealt with far worse than Wakefield, and really, she has no right to complain. What artist would bemoan her gallery selling more than half of her paintings before the show even started? Except Wakefield would not tell her who it was that bought the massive lot, thirty of the fifty by a single person, for the client was a "very private person." Was it Kim Jung-Un, the North Korean dictator? Or some privileged Saudi prince who had people murdered on a whim? Of course, it's not like no bad people owned her art — for all she knew, her paintings already hung on the walls of pedophiles and rapists. But what irked Abby the most was how Wakefield got off on holding this secret from her, an informational power trip.

"Just three to go," Wakefield says. "And the night is young. You might be the first artist I've featured in years to sell out on her opening night."

"A wonderful distinction," she says, her voice level.

It doesn't seem like they're fighting, but oh, they're fighting.

Wakefield gives her a smile that isn't a smile at all. Then he leaves her without another word, and Abby, who is not fond of arguments, expels an exhaustive sigh, but one that elevates to exaltation because there he is, Josh Kozlov. Or are her eyes playing tricks on her?

She hurries down the hallway and, like a spy, pokes just her head out around the corner. It is indeed Josh. In a light-blue shirt and khakis, he looks like he came here from his job, which he probably did, as tonight is Thursday. She's unable to recall exactly where he works; she knows he lives in New Jersey, more than an hour away.

It's been two weeks since he forwarded the email from the Oregon Institute of the Arts, which means it's been two weeks since she's failed to respond. She's started and stopped her reply a dozen times, not because she can't make up her mind, but because…well, she knows now, doesn't she, as she sees him lean in, scrutinize the painting of the story he sent her yesterday. Watching him watch her work, it's so very clear.

Freedom (I)

Fifty-six years from now, she's ninety years old.

It's a Tuesday. The garbage truck on the street below her apartment pierces the calm with its pointed beeps and thoughtless clangs. *I wake to sleep*, she thinks. She pushes down her covers, sits on her bed, places her feet on the wooden floor. Flexes her toes, feels her way into her slippers. She stretches her arms, gently. *And take my waking slow.* She rises. As she makes her way to the kitchen, the light beaming through the small round window above the sink gives her pause.

It may be the morning sun that produces these colors, a burnt orange that fades to a burnished yellow as she leans against the wall and watches, but there's something more at work here, a memory, the rush of her past as she rides into the mist, into her youth, into a dawn when she was a girl so full of nothing and everything, her hair swaying in the breeze, her arms outstretched, in flight.

She hasn't answered him via email because she wants to answer him tonight, right now, in person, to tell him yes, of course yes, and bask in his pleasure, and hers, too. But before she can take her first step away from the safety of this corner and toward the danger of Josh, there's Ted, her husband tapping the shoulder of the writer and extending his hand for a shake.

"Worlds are colliding," a familiar voice says.

"How do you do that?" Abby asks Franny. "You sneak up always when I'm feeling the hardest."

"I'm an emotional ninja," Franny says. "It's my real career. The painting thing is just a front. I was about to apologize for being late, but I see I'm right on time. But before we get to the clusterfuck of your two boys, let's pause and appreciate how fabulous your little round circles look."

Franny is right. In the morning, Abby and two of Wakefield's assistants mounted each two-inch Plexiglas circle on a neutral gray fabric canvas inside a square white frame. Fifty of these gray-white boxes adorn the walls of this two-story Midtown Manhattan gallery; her goal had been to get to a hundred, but she's always been one to overreach. She should be proud of her fifty; none of them were easy, each one requiring hours crouched over her desk, paint slowly encrusting her hands and nails and fingertips as she progressed, art and artist fully alloyed.

Like a movie camera slowly panning a room, Abby takes a deep, long look. These are her works of art; this is her show. She's done good.

"Thank you, Franny," she says, "my fine friend."

"Don't get all weepy on me and run your mascara," Franny says. "Besides, check this out. That last story you forwarded me last night, isn't that where they are right now?"

Indeed, that is where Ted and Josh are, in front of what Josh titled *Freedom (I)*. Her husband says something and makes Josh laugh, and then Josh says something and it's Ted's turn to chuckle, even slapping Josh on the shoulder. It's like they're old friends catching up. She knows it's just politeness masking as instant camaraderie, but it still bothers her.

"Matthias is here somewhere," Franny says, "so before he gets too drunk, I better find him."

"I thought you guys broke up last week," Abby says.

"We did," Franny says, and flashes one of her wicked smiles.

"Hey Abby!" Ted calls her from across the room, having spotted her. He waves her over, then does something out of a TV commercial: take both hands, turn them into guns, and point them at Josh. She almost expects Josh to scream that horribly ubiquitous catchphrase from Budweiser years back, "Whaaaazzzzzup!"

In response to this false chumminess, she pretends to have just seen him and walks up to her two boys, as Franny labeled them. They are just boys, aren't they? All men are boys, while women stay women once they have a child. Even though she's physically younger than both of them, she feels old.

"Josh tells me he just wrote about this one," Ted says.

"He did," Abby says. "Hello, Josh."

"Hi Abby," he says. "This is the first time I've attended a show with the artist present."

LINES

"Definitely not the first time for me," Ted says. "And it won't be the last. But I do have to go, as I'm already late for shindig #2 — I'll see you later, honey." Before Abby can reply, Ted darts in for a quick peck on her lips and is off.

"Where is he going, if I might ask?" Josh asks.

"He didn't tell you? I thought you guys were best friends."

"No," he says, unsure how to interpret the edge in her voice. "We were just talking about what I wrote about this piece of yours."

"Number 24," she says. "I was cycling from Paris to Barcelona. It is based on a sunrise I saw while camping on the bank of the Loire River."

"Okay, well, I didn't know that," he says, his voice small and careful. "I can write a different story, if you didn't like this one. I want you…to be happy, you know?"

And I want you, your full attention, for myself. I don't want to share your devotion with anyone else, not my husband.

Not even your wife.

That last thought startles her and fills her with so much shame that she needs to be rid of it, right now.

"Your wife couldn't make it tonight? Marlene?"

Is it her imagination or did Josh blink at hearing Abby say her name? Is he surprised that she knew it?

"No," he says. "She works another half hour farther away from the city than I do, so…"

"I'm sorry," Abby says.

"That's okay. She's not a huge art fan, I mean she's not against art or anything, it's just she wouldn't…"

Just like that, this is one of the most awkward conversations in history. Abby needs to turn this around, make it right…and then she remembers.

"Yes," she says. "Yes to Oregon. I apologize for not writing back. I am bad with email, better in person."

In a flash, she's in Josh's arms, hard and fast enough that her baby bump squeezes against his body.

"Thank you," he says.

"You're welcome," she says.

They part, and when they look at each other, everything's okay. Better than okay.

"We're all going to dinner in half an hour, when the show is done, my friends and I and family," Abby says. "Shall you please join us?"

together

Reality Bites

THE TEXT FROM Joshua: "just one of those days at the sweatshop, order *bibimbap* ahead for me."

"Everything okay?" Abby's mom asks her in Korean, their secret language to keep everyone else in the dark.

"Yes," she answers, also in Korean. "Stop asking, all right?"

Abby regrets those words as soon as they are out of her mouth. It's amazing how quickly the snotty teenager returns at times of crisis. Not that this is a crisis, even. It's just dinner at a Korean restaurant, an hour before her solo opening. Which may be the real reason of her angst, that she's lashing out because she's nervous about the evening, having to play the part of the artist in a public setting. One on one with people she doesn't mind, but Abby has never warmed up to being the center of attention.

Far across on the other side of this round table, Franny and Matthias chat away with Roberto and his girl. Roberto with his baby face doesn't fit the profile of a ladykiller, but that's exactly who he is, a rotating coterie of pretty female faces orbiting him like moons circling a planet. Abby has seen this twentysomething woman before, which makes it tough to ask her name again. She's the gorgeous redhead, the one with a constellation of freckles. Abby wishes she were sitting between the two couples, but they might as well be sitting at a different table altogether, because she can't hear a thing they're saying.

Abby watches her dad, on his way back from the restroom, stop at a booth and chat with someone he knows. *Kim sun-seng-nim* is how everyone refers to him, that last syllable, *nim*, an elevated term of address because in Korean culture, any kind of a teacher, even one that teaches high school classes in woodshop for druggie burnouts and dumb jocks, is accorded respect. She respects him, too, for who he's always been, an artist. Her dad would wave away such a frivolous designation, and yet if she could point to a single moment in her early childhood when she fell in love with beauty, it was the bathroom cabinet her dad built for Mrs. Lee, their next-door neighbor in the *Ma-po* district of suburban Seoul. A tall tower made to house folded towels and spare bottles of shampoo and conditioner, the cabinet wasn't anything extraordinary from the outside, but inside was the magic, a little wooden box he had made to hide and encase the end of a disused water line. It sat in the back of the second shelf against the wall, and it had no sharp corners because her dad had sanded it down until it felt as smooth as the skin of a newborn. The box was dimensionally a perfect cube, measuring exactly eight centimeters on all sides; Abby knew this because she took her ruler and a flashlight to marvel at her dad's secret artwork.

With every painting she works on, there comes a time when she wishes to abandon it for something else, the whispers of the future lover always more alluring than the complaints of the current relation. But then she thinks about that box, how it sits in the dark without an audience. Knowing this, her dad still made it as perfect as possible. Its beauty exists for the sake of beauty, and there is no nobler act than that. Every piece she works on deserves the same respect her dad gave to the box, a truism that gives Abby the strength to reach the finish line.

"I know you're sick of me repeating this, yet again," she says now when her dad returns to his seat at her table, in their native language. "But thank you for Mrs. Lee's box."

Her dad, as expected, gives her his patented dismissive wave. "That's enough thanks out of you, my daughter. Now it's time to thank *you*." He raises his glass high, and everyone else at the table follows. Her dad speaks in English, "We celebrate tonight: Abby!"

"Hear hear!"

"You're the best!"

"Let's get drunk!"

"My favorite artist!"

For a moment, Abby thinks that voice is Joshua's, because it's so familiar. But then as soon as she has that thought, she corrects her confusion. It's because this man's voice is the one she hears almost as often.

"Ted!"

She jumps out of her chair and rushes up to him.

"Sorry I'm late. This last client just wouldn't leave, but he's almost a billionaire, so you know how that goes."

They hug; she takes him in.

"I'm so glad you made it," she says into his ear.

"Wouldn't miss it for the world."

"Mom, Dad, this is Ted," she says. "We share an office."

"This is the first time I've attended a show with the artist present," Ted says.

Another text from Joshua: "still tied up, ill try to be there before its over."

She's finally figured it out: revenge. That's what this is, petty, stupid revenge for her lateness to his reading last month. Except knowing Joshua, he'll take it a step further and not show up at all. Because escalating a conflict is what he does best.

"Abby," Ted asks, "are you okay?"

"Yes," she says, putting away her phone. "Wait, no." She takes it back out and turns on airplane mode. That's the best way to handle Joshua when he gets like this, to ignore, to disengage completely. "Yes again."

"Good," he says. "Lisa really wanted to be here for your show, but Darla's got her tap dance recital. But enough about my mundane life. What a view, Abby."

They're standing at the entrance of her show at the Wakefield Gallery, the words "Cycling Guide to Lilliput" embossed in a large white Times Roman font against the soothing beige wall. Below the title are two paintings side by side that rightfully launch the series, her bike Marvin which Melvin Donovan graciously lent back to her for the duration of the show, and the first one she painted, of a sunlit bike path through the French countryside.

Below the paintings, each two-inch Plexiglas circle mounted on an off-white fabric canvas inside a circular gray frame, are her introductory words:

The series "Cycling Guide to Lilliput" is a combination of my twin passions, painting and long-distance cycling. Each miniature is an attempt to capture a specific moment throughout my travels that I can return to vividly in my memory. I like to think that the reason my works have gotten so tiny over the years is that painting itself is partially an act of meditation, of being able to hold something still enough in my mind that I can capture an image of it. As it becomes easier to slip into that meditative state, the object I need to concentrate on becomes smaller: economy by way of experience.

Ted pauses to read, so Abby reads, too. Unlike Ted, who takes in the sentences as they are, for Abby the experience is tinged with sadness. Joshua helped her with it, editing and re-editing until every word was

LINES

right, and now her husband is not even going to be here. The full weight of his abandonment hits her like a gut punch, but she'll hold back her tears. This is her night, a rightful celebration of her hard work; she's not going to let him ruin it.

As Abby walks Ted around the gallery, she bumps into a few of her former classmates she hasn't seen in years who shower her with praise. They climb the stairs to the second floor, where ten of her sixty paintings are buckled against a black wall scattered with pinprick LED lights that look like distant stars. These are all her night scenes, each spotlighted right to the edge of the circular canvas, making them glow like tiny precious planets. The standout is the one of the forest fire she saw while camping in northern Germany; it looks aflame, ready to combust.

"My goodness," Ted says. "I keep saying the word beautiful over and over again, but that's what this is, Abby. I can't believe you were able to make all these while still working on that giant baby."

"You helped," Abby says.

"Me?"

"You encouraged me, while…" She doesn't finish her sentence because of an article she read this morning on *BuzzFeed*. The writer of the piece, some marriage counselor who tried to sound like your best girlfriend, claimed that when a husband or wife reveals to a third party something emotionally hurtful about their spouse, that's the very moment when the seed of infidelity is planted. Except hasn't she already complained about Joshua's disdain for her small works to Ted, on more than one occasion? So really, she's already crossed that ugly line.

"I understand," Ted says. "Besides, taking credit where credit isn't due is one of my favorite hobbies, so thank you."

She laughs. He always knows just what to say to lighten her darkness.

They walk the length of the second-floor hallway, Ted spending a good five minutes on the last one, admiring the night scene of a cloudy moon over a lake, almost black and white in its composition, foggy and serene.

"I wish I was there," he says. "You actually were."

"Last August. Though it feels like a lifetime ago."

They're standing closer together, their arms touching, and they sound like the two loneliest people in the world.

"I don't want to leave it," Ted says.

"But we must."

"Pity."

As they approach the staircase on the other side of the hallway, they find Eisenhower Wakefield in a black turtleneck and black slacks, leaning against the wall and amalgamating into the blackness. If he had a cigarette, he could pass for a Frenchman.

"The woman of the hour."

"Ted, this is Eisenhower, the owner of this gallery."

"The last nocturne really spoke to you, didn't it?" Wakefield says.

"Nocturne?" Ted asks.

"Artistic fancy word for *night scene*," Abby says.

"Almost everything on this floor is sold, unfortunately," Wakefield says. "And all but two downstairs. And the evening isn't over yet. You might be the first artist I've featured in years to sell out on her opening night."

"How is that possible?" Abby asks.

"Let's just say we had one devoted collector who purchased two-thirds before we even opened the doors."

"Oh my!" Ted and Abby both say at the same time, making them laugh. "Jinx," they both say, again at the same time, which makes them laugh even harder. Wakefield, however, is not amused. He pretends to be, but he's not much of an actor.

LINES

Once they quiet down, Wakefield says, "The buyer is a very interesting person."

"And I assume a private person?" Abby says.

"Well yes," Wakefield says. "That's right. How did you know?"

"Just a hunch," Abby says. "I just hope my art will bring he or she much joy."

"Uh-huh. Well, good."

And with that, he walks right by them in a huff and disappears into the manmade nightfall of the hallway.

"Is it my imagination or was Eisenhower a little…miffed?" Ted says.

"These gallery owners," Abby says. "Believe it or not, he's one of the decent ones."

*

A quarter before nine, Joshua composes the final text of the evening. It's possible that Abby has switched her phone to airplane mode because she's onto him, but he doesn't care. When she eventually turns her signal back on, she'll see them all, his avalanche of lies under the guise of status updates.

just one thing after another, I'll miss it, sorry

In the prison of his gray cubicle, he hasn't done a thing for the last three hours except surf the internet. He won't miss seeing her stupid tiny paintings that bring in no money, and he's not the least bit sorry.

"Excuse," a squeak of a voice says, startling him from his thoughts. It's a tiny Asian woman, same size as his wife, part of the cleaning crew who comes at night. "So sorry," she says.

"Oh no, it's fine," Joshua says. He pulls out his plastic garbage can and hands it to her.

She nods and dumps the contents into her giant garbage can on rollers then hands it back to him, and now she's off to the next department.

Somewhere in the distance, either up or down a floor, a vacuum cleaner hums its industrial buzz song. Joshua places his hands palm down on his desk to see if he can feel the vibration, but either it's too faint or his sensitivity isn't sharp enough. He closes his eyes and presses down hard against the surface.

"Joshua?"

He yanks back his hands and blushes. "Marlene, hey."

"What are you doing here? And more interestingly, what *were* you just doing?"

Joshua puffs up his chest and speaks in a ridiculous, self-important voice, "What has come to this world that a man can't spread his hands out on his desk like a normal, well-adjusted person?"

Marlene leans her hips against his desk and looks at him askance. "I humbly apologize. You have every right to do whatever weird thing you were doing."

"Thank you. This is America, after all. We should all strive to do our favorite weird things as much as possible."

Marlene laughs her goofy little laugh, a softer version of the Fran Drescher's nanny in that show of hers years ago.

"Do you remember me asking you the first time I heard you laugh?" Joshua says.

"That was like, what, ten years ago?"

"Eleven, but who's counting."

"You thought it was unnatural, studied, like I was consciously making it up," Marlene says.

"You were a little pissed."

"Was I? That's not surprising. I took less shit in my younger days."

Marlene hops on his desk and crosses her legs. She's wearing one of his favorite outfits, one Joshua thinks of as the The Powder Pink. It's a simple two-piece, a tight blazer and an above-the-knee skirt with fine pleats that showcases her long, shapely legs. Now in her mid-forties, she's prettier than when he first met her. She used to have these chubby cheeks that were marshmallow cute, but in the last couple years she's lost them, become more angular and athletic, cut smooth like a gemstone.

Four years ago, when they were assigned to the latest 401(k) project, they traveled the country together to train the satellite office associates on the revamped project management website. They ate dinner every night for three weeks, and by the final Friday, they sat exhausted in the two-seater on the commuter flight back from Boston and fell asleep with their heads leaning on each other. To this day, Joshua still believes that if he hadn't literally run into Abby in New York City next morning on his fortieth birthday, he and Marlene could've...god, no.

Why would he want to subject sweet Marlene to his awful excuse of a life?

"Joshua? Hello?"

"Sorry, a bit lost in my thoughts."

"It's beyond late. Let's get out of here."

As Joshua packs up his laptop and gathers his belongings and on their way to Marlene's office, he tells Marlene everything, from Abby missing his book launch to his final text, almost gleeful in his delivery. This morning he read some garbage thinkpiece arguing that bitching about your husband or wife to a third person equates it to cheating, and it gives him great pleasure to do exactly what that writer warned against.

"Oh jeez," Marlene says. "I'm so sorry."

"This is why I tell you my worst self, Marlene. Because you never judge, you never take sides, you just commiserate. A saint is what you are."

They exit the PayRight building with their laptop bags slung over their shoulders.

"I'm no saint," she says. "But I can drop you off at the Newport PATH station?"

"You can deny it all you want, Saint Marlene."

They walk up to the parking garage across the street and take the elevator up to the fifth deck. Marlene clicks her key fob and her silver BMW blinks its corner lights like a wink.

"Still enjoying your Bimmer?" he asks as they get in.

"I should trade it in before it's too late."

"Still looks practically new."

"Jersey City to Hoboken for seven years, and now Jersey City to Bayonne. It's practically biking distance."

It's a silky smooth ride, even the traffic light stops barely noticeable, good old German engineering. He's visited her old Hoboken apartment once, for a New Year's Eve party, the first year they started at PayRight. He's never seen her house in Bayonne, a place she bought all by herself. Bocci will be waiting for her, he imagines, the little brown dog circling and circling behind the front door well before she arrives, because dogs have the sixth sense, right? He's never had a pet in his life, so what does he know.

"Here we are," Marlene says.

She places the gear in park and presses on the red triangle button, the click-click of temporary distress filling the cabin.

"So very by-the-book," Joshua says, teasing.

"I try," Marlene says.

LINES

And right there, with the gear shifter and the metronomic rhythm of the hazard lights, something unexpected happens: they both reach out, Marlene's right hand and Joshua's left hand, and their fingers lock and intertwine, as if by magic.

"Oh my," they both say, at the same time, another improbable improbability that has just come true.

They stare at each other.

On the ride back from Newport to 33rd Street on the PATH, Joshua can't shake what happened in Marlene's car. What are the chances that they touched like that, and then to utter the same words, at the same time? *Oh my* is not even something he says often, if ever, and as far as he can recall, it isn't Marlene's favorite turn of phrase, either.

Whatever it was, Joshua knew it was something good, and he could tell Marlene felt alike. When he left her car at the PATH station and glanced back, their eyes locked again, and it wasn't awkward. Marlene looked at him with wonder, with longing — with love. It was love, wasn't it? Yes, and he was thrilled to reflect it right back to her. If only he could keep that love, hold that feeling close.

Joshua climbs the stairs to his apartment, and with every step he ascends, the charm of the evening ebbs away, until there's nothing left but dread as he slides his key into the lock and pushes open the door.

It's ten past ten, and the only light in the apartment is the one above the gas range, the bulb Abby leaves on for him when she's gone to bed, and it's like the weight of a planet has been lifted from his chest. He was definitely not looking forward to dealing with his pregnant wife this night, not after bagging on her like the way he had.

His guilt over missing her show is doubled when he sees the container of *bibimbap* in the fridge, in a circular plastic container with a translucent top and a black bottom, resembling a UFO. How strange, his thoughts at night, and the weirdness continues as he lifts open the lid and leaves it gapped for the microwave: what if he's a giant and the rice and the veggies are miniature creatures? Joshua watches the plate spin clockwise, steam fogging up underneath until it rains onto the dish itself, and the scent escaping the microwave is heavenly: chopped fried egg, bits of beef, and butter, the secret ingredient of the best *bibimbap*. He burns his tongue a little as he shovels the mixed rice into his mouth. So good, so fucking good! In the middle of the meal, he belches loudly enough that he's afraid he'll wake Abby.

He should wash his face and brush his teeth, but sunken into the dining chair after the final glorious bite, Joshua can barely make himself sneak into the bedroom. He drops his shirt and pants onto the floor and slides into his side of the bed as quietly as possible.

"Joshua," Abby says, her voice as clear as a bell.

Oh Jesus, here it comes, Joshua thinks, bracing himself for the worst. Can he pretend to be asleep? No, not even someone knocked out with a tranquilizer gun loses consciousness that quickly. He'll have to man up.

"Yes?" he says.

"I want your cock."

Before he can ask *Excuse me*, because for sure he didn't hear what he thought he heard, Abby mounts him, protuberate belly and all. The sheer force of her libido wakes up his penis into instant rigidity, and just like that, they are having sex for the first time in at least a month.

His wife is at 21 weeks, their baby the size of a carrot according to the fetus-veggie chart hanging on their bathroom wall. Her skin is hot, a conduit for her carnal hunger. She plunges down onto him with such force that the headboard groans a metallic wail, nuts and bolts straining to contain each athletic bounce. This female figure atop him is someone he doesn't know, and the recognition of that unfamiliarity rushes his orgasm like a thrown switch.

LINES

When he comes, much quicker than usual, it's Marlene's face he sees, her serenity framed in the side window of her car, reaching out to him with all her tenderness.

apart

Interview with an Artist

WHEN HE COMES, much quicker than usual, it's Abby's face he sees, and as his orgasm fades, Josh's momentary euphoria is replaced with the harsh reality of guilt.

"Holy fuck," Marlene says. In the darkness of their bedroom, she reaches out and squeezes his hand. "Wow!"

"I missed you," Josh says, not entirely a lie, because he did miss her when she was out west last week, visiting her sister in San Diego.

"Awww, my sweet husband," she says. Then, as if reading his shameful mind, she breaks their mutual silence with a question. "So…how's it going with your art project?"

That's how Marlene refers to it, the *art project*, ever since he told her about the trip to Breitenbush. She never mentions Abby by name, surely a sign of her discomfort with the whole thing, but because she's Marlene, she's also been nothing but supportive.

"Trying to get a dozen stories ready for the festival, but because I want this to be reflective of Abby's trips, I thought it'd be good to interview her."

"I know," she says. "You've told me this before."

"I have?"

"Yes," Marlene says, laughing. "I know how important this is to you, Josh. You'll create something meaningful like you always do. I trust you."

Half an hour later, when Marlene's breathing has softened to the familiar shallow beats of her slumber, Josh is wide awake with his wife's final words: *I trust you.*

On his way over to the Lillian Vernon Writers House, Josh keeps having this nagging feeling that he's forgotten something. He reassures himself that the only necessities are the printed photos of Abby's Lilliput series on Instagram, all fifty of them, which he picked up from a CVS on the way up to Hoboken and he absolutely did not leave in the back seat of his car.

He didn't, did he?

Josh stops abruptly enough that the person walking behind him on Sixth Avenue rams into him.

"Dude!" the guy yells.

"Sorry."

He's just a kid, his ears ensconced between enormous red headphones. How did huge, bulky headphones get back in vogue? And aren't they awfully hot to wear on a day like this? The calendar has just flipped to June, but it feels like the middle of summer. Josh badly wishes he'd worn something else than a black shirt and black jeans. He's sweating like he's in a sauna because for once, he wanted to look like he belongs here. Never has he made such an effort to look cool while feeling anything but, buying a new pair of "skinny" Levi's from Zappos last week. He even took half an hour deciding between two dark colors, Ship Yard and Tumbled Rigid. That second one made no sense; how could one derive any semblance of pigment from a descriptor like Tumbled Rigid? They were two nonsensical adjectives, failing to properly modify each other. So he ended up going with plain old boring black, which

LINES

thankfully remained a viable choice. Except now, the fabric sticks to him like glue.

Josh makes a right onto 10th Street, walking by the Joffrey Ballet School on the third and fourth floors of an ornate corner building. On the ground is a flyer from one of their past events, a still photograph of a female dancer in a white tutu in mid-flight, her silver-slippered feet and white-stockinged legs pointing like an arrow. Her placid face makes it seem like she's doing nothing of consequence, maybe contemplating between a bagel or a bialy for breakfast, though someone who looks and moves like this must be on some weird dietary regime Josh can't even fathom.

On the same block as the ballet school stands NYU's Creative Writers House, a nondescript, maroon-bricked building with a stained-glass tri-paneled window as its main distinguishing feature. Every time he pays a visit here, Josh is overcome with envy. This little Writers House isn't anything overtly fancy, with modest faculty offices on the top two floors, a public reading room on the ground floor, and the workshop room in the basement with its oblong table and framed photos of famous authors adorning the walls. And yet this is miles beyond what he had as a student! During his days, the Creative Writing Program never had a proper home, so he and his colleagues were like vagabonds within NYU, squatting in the business school to take fiction craft classes, delving into workshop stories in the recesses of the psychology building.

When he opens the door, a young Black woman sits on the stained-glass windowsill, which is large enough for someone to lean against the wall and stretch out their legs. Like the guy he almost ran into, she, too, is wearing large headphones around her head, lost in her music and the book she's reading. She's probably a current student, one who fails to realize how lucky she is to have a dedicated space for her. He should tell her, impart his wisdom on the youth, but no, that's silly. The fact is, nobody cares about the past because they have enough trouble with the present. His own situation is no exception. It's now half past two, and he's got less than ten minutes to get himself situated and ready for Abby.

Josh climbs down the short set of stairs to open the door to the workshop room, except the knob doesn't turn.

"Can I help you?"

It's the girl he saw at the windowsill, now by his side.

"I'm Josh Kozlov. I'd gotten in touch with Bertrand…?"

"Oh, you're the writer who writes about tiny paintings! Yes, Bertrand is our current program admin. He had to cut out early and left me in charge. I'm Missy, by the way, second year poetry."

Missy takes out an impressively populated ring of keys and finds the right one. "Bertrand shared a link of your *TNT* story with me — if you reformat it, it could totally be a poem, you know. A prose poem, of course, but they're just as valid as anything structured. Anyway, here you go, all yours. Holler if you need anything, I'll be around."

He's been in here once before, and it's exactly as he remembers, a well-lit beige and brown room with a table long enough to comfortably seat fourteen workshoppers, six on each side and two at the heads. On the mantel of the decorative fireplace sit classic black and white photos of Virginia Woolf and Samuel Beckett, and on the far end of the room, atop a set of white built-in windowed cabinets full of books, is one of those enormous dictionaries you only find in libraries and writerly spaces like this. Josh isn't religious, but if he had to pick a church, it would look a lot like this.

As much as he'd like to revel in the grace of his literary gods, it's time to get to work, because Abby's now not even five minutes away. Josh takes out the photo prints of her paintings and lays them down on the table. He has grouped them by theme, "Flow" for river or lake paintings, "Insomnia" for night scenes, "Path" for anything with a road. There are eight themes in all, though organizing her paintings this way has filled Josh with apprehension. Who is he to do this? Abby has been

LINES

incredibly kind to give him free rein to write whatever he wishes, but what does she really think about any of this? That's what he really wants to discover during this meeting, how she feels about this project, this collaboration…and, truth be told, himself.

What do you think of me, Abby?

Do you think of me?

Because when I stare at these paintings, I think of you. When I work on our stories, I think of you. Inside your circular vistas, I become you.

"Josh?"

As if summoned by magic, Abby Kim, in a bright canary-yellow dress, stands before him.

*

It took her an hour to pick the dress, which is ridiculous because she's not that kind of a woman. She's always taken pride in her sartorial low maintenance, and in grooming, too. Makeup is something she's barely conscious of, some eye shadow and blush to liven up her face a bit, but there she was, her bed covered with discarded dresses like dead bodies, her vanity littered with black and green and metallic blue streaked tissue.

After half an hour in front of the mirror, Abby clasped her hands together and took in a long breath through her mouth, then breathed out slowly through her nose. She did this nine more times until clarity reestablished itself.

Josh is writing about me, but it's really more about him.

I am not my paintings.

We are two artists collaborating on a project.

That is all.

Brown eye shadow, brown eye liner, natural and subdued. Light pink lipstick that speaks of the season. A simple tube of a sleeveless yellow dress, hanging loose and comfortable; it's hitting ninety today.

All of it made good sense then. But now, as she stands inside the workshop room of the Lillian Vernon Writers House in front of Josh, his watery blue eyes under the glow of incandescent ceiling lights, she feels wrong on every account. When he rises and gives her a hug, her dress feels paper thin on her skin; she wishes she wore something more substantial, something to provide her protection, against what she does not know. She tastes the fake berry flavor of her lipstick and wants badly to rub it off.

"Excuse me Josh, but where is the bathroom?" she says.

"I think it's right around the corner."

It is indeed, a small bright white room perfect for removal of the unwanted: lipstick, off. She washes off the false rouge on her cheeks, too, and digs through her purse and remembers the blue scarf she has stuffed into one of the zipped pockets. It's gauzy thin but it's big, large enough for her to wrap her bare arms. Symbolic armor, but she'll take it.

"Are you cold? I can have them adjust the thermostat," Josh says when she returns.

"I'm good," Abby says, and realizes that she didn't even notice the table in the center of the room when she first arrived. Covering almost half of its beige surface are her paintings, square photographic prints of her Instagram shots. In almost all of them, her fingers partake in the picture, sometimes encircling her painting like a frame, sometimes posing with the used brushes off to the side.

"Who knew I made so many hand selfies," Abby says.

"I think it's your way of taking ownership of your work, a physical pronouncement of your creations."

"You speak so...rich? Richly."

"Sorry."

"No, do not apologize. I'm getting used to it. And I'm amazed you had all these printed."

"It helps to hold one when I write about it. Gets me closer, having something I can touch."

Even though she saw her own paintings on display at the Wakefield Gallery last month, having them all together in a compact space like this gives an entirely different feel. What if her show had been inside a tiny room, her entire Lilliput series viewable in a single field of vision? There's such an intensity here.

"It's intense, seeing them all in one take," Josh says.

She turns to him, but he doesn't notice because his eyes remain locked onto the table, as if her paintings won't let him go. Abby wants to reach out to him, but she stops herself. Tears well up in her eyes and roll down her cheeks, but she doesn't care. Yesterday the ultrasound tech pointed out that the little black spot on the top of her fetus's head was a sprout of hair. Why that thought just came to her she does not know, but it's been like this for a while now, her unborn baby invading her mind at odd moments. She cried then as she's crying now, and the feeling inside her is the same, a longing to touch the untouchable. How strange that this writer, this Josh Kozlov, this person she barely knows, is the only person beside herself who understands her paintings. How strange, how lonely.

"Oh," Josh says. He scrambles to his messenger bag and fishes out a portable pack of tissues.

"Thank you," Abby says, taking one and dabbing her eyes then blowing her nose. "It is no tragedy. I'm just pregnant."

That makes him laugh, puts him at ease, and her, too. They sit next to each other, and she watches as Josh takes out a notepad, a pen, and his smartphone.

"Are you okay if I voice record our session here? I'll take notes, too, but I don't want to miss anything."

"I doubt I will say anything worth replaying, but if you wish to record, that is fine with me."

"Great," Josh says, then touches the red button on the screen. The timer begins its progression from zero, ticking up every second.

The counter hits fifteen and neither has said a word.

"I should start," Josh says. "Except those numbers make me nervous. Too official. Let me face down the phone."

"Okay," Abby says.

More silence.

"Now I'm wondering how much time has passed," Josh says, and they both laugh.

Once he asks his first question, it gets easier.

Who taught you to ride a bike?

She tells him it was her grandfather, when she was five years old, a stocky taskmaster of a man who pushed her down a path behind his house lined with thorns and nettles. She never fell, but she didn't try riding again for another seven years, at which point her aunt became her instructor. From that point on, there was no method of travel that agreed with her as much as a bicycle.

Have you ever gotten a flat tire? Other mechanical issues?

Josh is delighted that she brought along her tool kit, which consists of a 20-in-1 multi-tool, a tire gauge, a hand pump, and a bag of spare parts of spokes, short chain links, and nuts/bolts. He picks up a rusty set of tweezers and asks if these are what they look like. No better implement than tweezers to remove an offending shard from a tire.

Take me through a typical day on your trip, from waking up to going to sleep.

LINES

She rises at the break of dawn, sunrise waking her up naturally around half past five. While her camping air pad deflates, she packs up her belongings. At home she never eats breakfast, but out here, she needs energy, so she shovels a handful of granola into her mouth, chews, and washes it down with a long swig of water. For the next three hours, she rides, listening to the birds who fly overhead, watching the sun's rays illuminate her path; it is the most peaceful part of her day, her head as empty as possible to take in everything around her. Abby has been on journeys where she sees a fellow rider every five minutes, and on others where she sees no one for days. Doesn't matter to her, either way, because she's in her own world.

It's around ten when she stops, for coffee and four hours of sketching. She's always felt sketching as the most selfish of artistic acts, the purest form of collection. It's not for anyone but herself, and once she sketches something, whether it be a house or a tree or a bridge, it becomes hers. More and more, her sketching is done by memory. Earlier in her career, she relied on photographs from her digital camera, but soon realized that reality can often be a hindrance, preventing her imagination from taking over, and it absolutely needs to take over for her work to be of any worth.

"This is fantastic — please, keep going," Josh says.

"No," Abby says.

He looks up from his notebook and places his pen on the table. "I'm sorry — did I…?"

She smiles and shakes her head. "I don't want to…there's a word, it sounds like cucumber…"

"Encumber?" Josh says.

"Yes, yes, that is it. Like how I don't want to take photographs, I do not wish to encumber you with my facts. I believe you want to bring my reality into this, to make it more true, but that would accomplish the opposite. Just as I had an empty canvas to paint my paintings, I wish you an empty canvas to write your writings."

The only sound in the room comes from the outside, city-slow traffic noise of tires on the road and human feet on the sidewalk. Outside of immediate family, there are only a few people with whom Abby feels comfortable in silence: her husband Ted, her best friend Franny, and now, oddly enough, this writer. With Ted and Franny, it's easy: it's because she loves them. But how to explain Josh? Is it possible she does love him but fails to realize it? There is this ease being with him, but is that because he has written about her, put himself in her shoes, discovered her from the inside out? In a way, he has become her twin, but more like a long-lost twin she's met for the first time: a thorny juxtaposition of otherness and intimacy. She feels like she should know him, and yet she knows nothing about him. There's an imbalance of knowledge here, and it must be rectified.

"Josh," Abby says. "Will you please tell me about you?"

together

Renovation and Remorse

ABBY ABRUPTLY STOPS her walk and narrows her eyes in disbelief. She's almost offended by Ted's question.

"You don't think you know me?"

It's the last week of June. Whether it be the effects of climate change or just bad luck, today's a scorcher, forecasted to reach a hundred and three degrees in the sunbaked city of New York. It's only ten in the morning, but heat already wafts off the asphalt and concrete in furious waves. Shade is of premium importance, walkers crossing streets to gain even the flintiest protection against the broiling rays. Abby's silk blouse sticks to her like a second skin. They've walked two blocks but her lower back is already aching and her ankles throb to the beat of her heart. Now in her third trimester, the effort of carrying a human being inside her, even if it's no bigger than a red cabbage, takes a daily toll and puts her on edge.

"No, I don't think I do," Ted says.

In the four years they've shared an office, this is their first real argument, and how funny it's happening on this day, Friday, which she's been looking forward to for a little too long. Ted is having his office renovated, a fresh coat of paint on the walls and ceiling, new carpet, new desk and chairs. He even sweetly bought a trio of art to put on the walls, small works from her friends Franny and Roberto and one of her newest Lilliputs, a night scene of the forest fire she saw while camping in Northern Germany. It is a time to celebrate, and yet here they are, fighting.

Initially, this day had started out as just lunch between officemates, but then it ballooned into a major day of hooky, a way to celebrate his newly minted digs. So they met up in front of their building this morning and are on their way to the Whitney Museum of Art, walking along the High Line, the still Hudson River to their left, sagging trees to their right. A month ago, when their plan had come together, Abby had imagined the two of them walking side by side on the boardwalk-styled concrete path, chatting like old friends as they took in the best the city has to offer.

The museum is still another six impossible blocks away, but off to the right is a built-in bench with an overhanging tree offering a shadowed respite from this hell on earth.

"Ted," Abby says, but he keeps going. "Ted!"

He turns around, his face flushed, his hair a drippy mess. "What?"

"I need to stop, a little." She points to the shady spot.

Now that he pauses and sees her in full, a six-month pregnant woman struggling to keep up, the kindness she's always known returns to him.

"Of course," he says.

Oh, blessed seat! As soon as she sits on the bench, Abby realizes how exhausted she was. The sandpapery concrete is as warm as a heating pad, but she doesn't mind. As much as she would like to pretend she's still the same person she's always been, the baby has unquestionably transformed her from the inside out, all for the worse. She feels ashamed for this resentment she feels, even if the mommy books and blogs tell her it's all perfectly natural. She'd never consider herself even vaguely athletic, and yet if there is one physical trait she prides herself over, it is her nimbleness. Her hand-eye coordination is laughably inept, but her

LINES

innate quickness has led her to not have a single wipeout on all her cycling trips, and these were not easy rides, tracks with mud and ice, not to mention sheep crossings, gopher holes, even a wild horse that galloped alongside her for a good ten seconds.

But now she's no longer nimble, and she's not sure why. Is it because her center of gravity has shifted? There is indeed a creature inside swimming in her own liquid, though Abby doesn't feel off-balance, just slow, like she's treading water. It's the mother mirroring the child; there is a physical cord connecting the two, after all.

Ted takes out a pair of pint-sized Evian bottles from his backpack and hands her one.

"If heat rises, wouldn't it be even hotter up here on this elevated park?" he says.

"It is logical," Abby says. "This is the best water ever."

"Sticking to the script with this horrendous weather was not a good idea, but we're not the giving up kind, are we?"

"You see? You do know me."

It's strange seeing him out of his suit and tie. This morning he's in a white Polo shirt and sky blue cargo shorts. He could be a tourist, except he possesses the dispassionate air about him that connects all longtime New Yorkers, that this wondrous city is just home and therefore only interesting in fits and spurts.

After the Whitney, they were going to head over to Momofuku Nishi for pork buns and ramen, then to Doughnut Plant for crème brûlée and PB&J doughnuts and cap the day off taking in whatever curious foreign film was screening at the Angelika. A day of fun, as if they were the bridge-and-tunnel crowd maximizing their fun in the city. That had been the plan, but now it feels less like pleasure and more like a job.

"Perhaps we bit down more…" she says but trails off because Ted is no longer next to her. She looks around and finds him through the thicket of trees behind her, leaning against the railing as he stares down at the traffic below.

"Bit off, I think you mean," he says when she stands next to him. "Bite off more than you can chew."

"These phrases always trick me."

"You're doing fine. I can't even imagine what it must've been like to learn a whole new language when you were a kid. How old were you when you came over?"

"Twelve."

Ted returns to staring at the cars and buses below, his hands clamped on the smooth chrome of the railing. His ring finger — where his gold wedding band has always been — is instead a white, untanned strip of skin.

"Do you ever wonder what your life would've been like if you had stayed in Korea?" he asks.

Maybe Ted is having his ring resized. Hers doesn't fit anymore, not with everything having swollen due to her pregnancy, even her fingers.

"I try to stay in the present," Abby says. "I see no benefit in what could be, when there is much to do in the now."

He laughs, not out of humor but exasperation. "No regrets? You're telling me you never dream about what could've been?"

"Ted," she says, feeling another argument coming on. "I am better, more refreshed. We go to the museum now? The air is conditioned there."

When he turns from the railing and she sees his face, she knows what he's about to say. She wants to take her hand and clamp it against his mouth, because once this is said, it's going to change everything.

"Abby," Ted says, "I believe I'm in love with you."

LINES

On the A train to the Upper West Side, Abby has read the same page of the novel on her phone three times now. It is half past one; her mouth still tastes like charred chicken. She's disappointed in herself for eating badly once again, scarfing down two McDonald's crispy chicken sandwiches before rushing to the subway, but she was pressed for time. She's been trying to see the Beechers for the last two weeks to start on their portrait, so she's super lucky it worked out for today. And yet her remorse lingers, for when she eats terrible food, she's also feeding that same garbage to her child. So much for motherhood reining in her selfishness.

Abby leans her head against the window, the vibration of the car jostling her skull. This can't be good for her, either, but she's always found the rattling sensation to be soothing, and after this morning, she can use all the help she can get.

She and Ted didn't go to the museum, and not Momofuku Nishi nor Doughnut Plant nor the Angelika. After his admission, for the next two hours, they sat under the cover of the tree leaves on the High Line and talked and talked. The funny thing, of course, is that she herself has held a torch for Ted for what seems like forever, but never for a moment did she imagine her fantasy ever becoming reality. And now that the unreachable has become reachable, Abby found her feelings oddly distanced. As Ted kept talking about their lunches, their chats, how he's never had an artistic bone in his life but just last week he sat in front of *The Portrait of Adele Bloch-Bauer*, Gustave Klimt's "The Woman in Gold" at the Neue Galerie, for an hour, all Abby could think was how she ever found this guy attractive in the first place.

But now, away from him and inside the quieter confines of her own mind, she knows her reaction was just knee-jerk shock. Of course he's wonderful, he's Ted Wingfield. But all he's accomplished with this declaration of love for her is to complicate matters. Pretty selfish of him, wasn't it? As selfish as her greasy chicken sandwiches.

It's good that she has something difficult to do now, to take her mind off of this mess. Google Maps leads her to a glassy gray building that must be twenty stories high. A doorman in uniform welcomes her in, and the guard sitting in the center of the marbled lobby points her to the second elevator. His key card allows her to press the button for P, Penthouse, and when the mirrored doors split open, she's greeted by a canine ready for the Westminster dog show. When Abby takes a furtive step into the house, she's treated to the dog's long, flowing golden brown fur sashaying like hair in a shampoo commercial as it saunters away. After a few steps, it pauses and looks back, as if to say, *Are we waiting for an invitation?*

As much as Abby finds rich people tiresome, she never tires of seeing where they live. The Beechers have the entire top floor, and the decorator they hired was most definitely a fan of minimalism. The walls and ceiling are bright white, the dental moldings the color of milky coffee, matching the parquet floors. As she follows the dog down the hallway, Abby takes in the hanging paintings and photographs, all of them single flowers: acrylic mounts of sunflowers, lilies, roses, bleeding hearts on one side, still life oil canvases of bouquets on the other. She imagines they change these every so often, most likely from their personal storage. Most collectors she's met have far more artwork than space and rotate their stock either with the seasons or whenever the spirit moves them.

The dog, whose name she cannot remember, turns right at the end of the hallway, and Abby follows.

"Wow," she says to herself.

One wall looks like a single enormous windowpane, but it's a trick of some kind, the seams thin enough to give the illusion of continuity. The clarity of the glass is remarkable; when Abby arrives at the edge of the floor-to-ceiling windows and gazes at the emerald expanse of Central Park, she feels like she could take another step and fall right into the greenery.

LINES

"Welcome, welcome!"

Abby turns around and has trouble finding the source of the voice, as Imogene Beecher, in a white dress and brown heels, almost blends into the environs. White grand piano, white leather couch, brown rug. This living room has got to be twice the size of Abby and Joshua's entire apartment.

"Good afternoon," Abby says.

"Timothy will be here any moment, he's having a late brunch with the mayor. I see you've met Rascal."

"He led me here."

Imogene gives her a wink. "I taught him that. He's quite the butler. He'll even bring us our bedroom slippers. But only if I ask nicely, isn't that right, Rascal."

The dog, his owner, the crystal chandelier above them, the sunlight from the window: Abby's heart beats a little faster.

"I can't wait to start," she says.

"I wanted to wait until Timothy got here to show you, but oh, what the hell," Imogene says. She walks around the back of the sectional and brings out something under a white bedsheet. She stands it up with the sheet intact, as if she's practiced this before.

"Voila!" Imogene yells, and off comes the sheet with a tug. A wooden easel, as white as everything else in this space.

Abby laughs. And as she sets up her sketchpad and takes out her pens in this most beautiful room, all of her upturned life vanishes into the white.

*

The crown jewel of conference rooms in PayRight's Jersey City office is named the Edison, the only one with view a of the Hudson River. It's a truncated glimmer, a band of flowing water sandwiched between two skyscrapers, but late in the day, the sun hits it just right and it's like a golden bracelet. Most of the time, if Joshua is still here that late for work, he's too tired or bitter to enjoy it, but this evening is the opposite. He's pumped, he's excited, and as he paces the length of the carpeted conference room, waiting for Damien and Violet to arrive, he's astonished that everything has gone better than the plan. His dumbass boss Harold was out sick, which meant no review and retrospective meetings, always huge wastes of time, but today it meant Joshua was able to prep for the brother-and-sister graphic novelists. An hour ago he received a text from Abby, who's still at the rich people's house, working on their portrait. That meant serious money, finally, which they could dearly use with the baby on the way; plus, her half of the proceeds from her gallery show came in, too, so for the moment, they were almost solvent. And to top it all off, the last meeting that was held here had food left over! He inhaled a turkey pesto wrap and a Portobello mushroom sandwich that was so good he had to fight himself from eating a second one. Dinner, done.

As much as Joshua complains about his job, at times like this, he's almost proud of it. If nothing else, he's a survivor, managing to keep his position through the bursting of the internet bubble and the cataclysmic Great Recession. Almost a quarter of the company was laid off as Lehman Brothers and Bear Stearns fell, but somehow Joshua managed to stave off the office grim reaper, and now here he is, able to invite his co-conspirators to this posh conference room of wine-red walls and mahogany trim.

The elevator dings. The only thing that would've made this day better is if this meeting could've been held a little earlier, like right around five o'clock, so his co-workers could get a glimpse of Damien and Violet with their goth makeup and ripped jeans. These sibling artists were the kind of people who could bestow Joshua with some cool literary street cred, which he could use because no one around here thought much about his artistic life. The next best thing is to take a photo of them, which is why he has his smartphone's camera at the ready. With the PayRight logo right above the elevator doors, the contrast of corporate staidness and artsy funk is just perfect. Wait until his cubemates took a look at these two tomorrow.

Except when Damien and Violet get off the elevator, he's in a button-down blue shirt and khaki pants and she's unrecognizable in a white power suit from the Hillary Clinton campaign collection. Damien's long, untamed mane from the reading is balled neatly into a man bun.

"Sorry to make you wait," Violet says. "A breakdown on I-78 turned a twenty-minute drive to an hour."

"I thought you guys live in Brooklyn."

Damien laughs. "Like we could afford Brooklyn. I guess if we burrow far enough into the borough, but then it's no better than living in Parsippany."

"You don't live and work in the city?"

"And I bet you thought I worked in some exotic or braindead job, like a welder or a bus driver, while Violet made coin as a graphic designer."

He's not wrong. The last thing Joshua expected was for this artistic duo to be vanilla like him. "You guys are dressed like you work for an insurance company."

A smirking Violet dips her hand into her purse and fishes out a business card.

VIOLETTA MOSCHETTI
Principal Adjuster

Prudential Insurance

"Good guess, Joshua," Violet says.

"I don't have my business card with me, but I'm not too far away from your space. I'm with an online HR startup, writing external press releases and internal communications."

"So your black eyeliner and long hair…and your hoodie and spikes…"

"Mr. and Miss Hyde to our boring Drs. Jekyll," Violet says. "I say we should pat ourselves on our backs, D. Looks like we gave Joshua a convincing show at the Mermaid."

"Now Mr. Kozlov, we'd like for you to leave us for exactly ten minutes so my sis and I can set up and dazzle you some more. Set a timer and come back, okay?"

"Umm…sure." And just like that, he's kicked out of his own conference room.

It's now a minute before seven, which means a minute before two-thirds of the lights turn off…and there they go, the office now officially a moody ghost town. Joshua passes by one vacant cubicle after another, like a warden touring his prison. At the break room, the only Keurig pods remaining are decaffeinated, the least loved. Still, decaf is better than none; he pops one in and waits for the machine to do its thing.

He's fortunate to lid the Styrofoam cup, because when he exits the break room, he almost runs into Marlene.

"Didn't I see you leave like an hour ago?"

"Did I get you? I'm sorry, Joshua."

"No, I'm fine, but you don't look fine. What's going on?"

"My home internet," Marlene says. "Something's up with it."

"You tried what I told you last time, I'm guessing."

LINES

"Oh…yeah, unplugged and replugged and all that, but nothing," she says. "Doesn't matter, I'm here now. You're meeting with your graphic novelists?"

"I am," Joshua says, amazed that even though she's harried and hurried as hell, Marlene still remembered what he told her a week ago. If he were at her place to look at her internet issue, he'd be able find the problem, but it's just her in her house in Bayonne.

"Well, I'll be here for a bit, trying to get my deck ready for senior leadership tomorrow morning. Been working on it all day, and as it turns out, all night."

"I'm not sure what these two have in store for me, but I'll swing by before I leave, okay?"

"All right," Marlene says, and it's the way she utters those two simple words that spikes his heart. A tenderness like this shouldn't be wasted on someone like him; it should go to the one she loves who can love her back the same way.

Now feeling bummed, Joshua returns to the Edison conference room, where the entirety of the table, one long enough to seat twenty people, is wholly covered with large pieces of paper.

"Broadsheet," Damien says, but Joshua is hardly listening. "Eleven by seventeen, two regular print papers put together."

Some broadsheets are broken down into square or rectangular cells like a comic book, while others are full pages. The one nearest to the door, the first one Joshua sees, is a close-up of a face. His face, except his beard is bushier, his eyes brimming with displeasure. Sketched roughly with a black marker, the bold lines make him look downright sinister.

"That's me," Joshua says.

"Sort of," Violet says. "A hyperbolic representation of you, I'd say."

"And this…this is Abby?" he says, pointing at the sheet adjacent to his enormous mug. On this one, Abby is as small as a mouse, literally;

like the old Tom and Jerry cartoons, she's placed inside one of those arched mouse holes at the bottom of a wall. She's got a palette in one hand and a brush in the other, and she's working on a round disc leaning on an easel. "Is she supposed to be tiny?"

"See, sis," Damien says to Violet. "The scale is conveyed, like I said it would."

"For him, but he's the content provider. We need verifications from the unaffiliated."

While the siblings chat amongst themselves in their jargon, Joshua circumscribes the table slowly, starting from the top left corner, the page numbered as 1. There he sits on the full page, hunched over his work desk, the monitor on his screen on the *Game of Thrones* recap site. Then on the next sheet, split into three cells, he's at the water cooler chatting with Walt, who empties the water into his bottle. In the middle cell, there are lightning bolts emanating from Joshua's back as he fumbles with replacing the empty water cooler with a new one. In the last cell, Marlene comes to the rescue.

A month ago, he'd sent Damien and Violet an email detailing his life since the beginning of the year. They'd asked that he not embellish or dramatize any of it. What they requested was journalistic distance, a factual recounting of his days and nothing more. Initially Joshua felt a little hurt, wondering if this was a kind of an indictment against the quality of his writing, but then he realized that the siblings wanted to make their own choices about what to tell without bias. So he complied, and complied and complied, the email becoming overlong that he converted it into a Word document, which, single-spaced, ended up spanning over thirty pages. Frankly, Joshua was astonished. He had no idea he could write about his own boring life in such straightforward detail; he'd enjoyed it immensely.

But now, looking at the table littered with pictorial depictions of his mundane existence, he feels naked, violated. He's written about his friends and family before, though not in exactitude, always mixed and remixed into the stew of fiction, where the innocent and guilty stood equally protected. No such protection here. When the people he wrote about read what he'd written, is this what they felt, too?

"It's all just ideas," Violet says. "We'll be fortunate if ten percent here make the final cut."

"I still don't understand why you think my life is worth telling," Joshua says.

Damien laughs. "That is precisely why."

"What does that mean?"

"Don't worry about it," he says, and brings out his smartphone. "Now that we've wowed you sufficiently, V and I have a bunch of questions to ask. It might look like I'm texting, but I assure you, I'm taking notes. Okay?"

"Yes, okay, I guess."

"Excellent," Violet says. "Take a seat and hold nothing back, that's all we ask."

For the next hour, he feels like a bystander who had witnessed a crime, except the crime was his life and the criminal was him. Joshua has never been interrogated by the police, but this couldn't be far off. The two aren't exactly playing good-cop-bad-cop, but at times it does feel like that, and they take turns being the aggressor, so much that Joshua is kept on his toes the whole time. Holding up the sketches like evidence, the siblings ask about exact locations, the time of day, what the weather was like. Some questions are way personal in nature, such as if Joshua was thinking about Marlene that time he missed Abby's solo show.

"You gotta be kidding me. You seriously expect me to answer that?" Joshua asks.

"Why the hell would we ask you if we didn't want an answer?" Violet says.

"V, let's let that one go."

"This is fucking important!"

At moments like these, Joshua stays silent and repeats a phrase in his head: *This too shall pass.* Everything passes if one remains calm and patient, and sure enough, after all the queries and replies, Damien and Violet pack up their sketches and put the conference room back in order.

Feeling like a heavy bag that's just been beaten up by a pair of dogged boxers, Joshua escapes to the break room and downs two decaf Keurigs in a row. He remembers reading somewhere that decaf actually has caffeine, just not a lot of it, so if he drank enough of it, he might experience a tiny buzz. Because god knows he needs it. He makes one more and takes it over to Marlene's office.

He's about to knock but stops when he sees her head laying sideways over her folded hands, her eyes peacefully closed. He remembers taking naps like this when he was in elementary school.

Joshua puts her coffee down atop the filing cabinet and doesn't know what else to do. Her beige cardigan hangs behind her chair; he could put that over her, he supposes. But no, what she really needs is to wake up and get home, because it's almost nine o'clock and this is no place to sleep.

"Hey," he says, but she doesn't answer. He places a hand on her shoulder.

She's not cold, but she's not warm, either.

He moves his palm from her shoulder to her bare arm. There's something tepid and inelastic about her skin, like he's touching a piece of rubber.

"Marlene," he says, loud enough to attract attention if anyone was around to hear. But there's no one here, no one but him, to see the spittle of saliva and blood dribbling from Marlene's lips when he shakes but fails to wake her.

apart

Big Islands

SEVEN-SEVEN, THE seventh of July. Marlene isn't the superstitious kind, so she calls it her most favorite number instead of her luckiest.

For the last three years they've been on Hawaii on this day. First time they stayed on Oahu, in a Honolulu luxury resort, which was so fantastic that they did it again the following year. But last year they went to Kauai, the least populated of the Hawaiian Islands, which was a nice change of pace but perhaps too much of a change. So this year they're on the largest island, the eponymous Hawaii, in a town called Waimea on the northern coast. It's the middle of summer, but you wouldn't know it from the way it feels. At the warmest the mercury hits a spring-like 68 degrees Fahrenheit. Sitting upstairs in the loft of the A-frame cottage they rented for two weeks, Josh composes the following with a blanket wrapped around his feet.

Passion (I)

"based on a fire I saw while camping in Northern Germany"

She is six years old, and she's watching her father pack his tobacco pipe.

He does this once a day, after dinner, and it is an elaborate affair, a ritual. He unwraps the black velvet cloth one corner at a time, and in the center of that soft blanket lies the wooden pipe, its body the color of dark cherries, the mouthpiece tapered like a comma.

He opens the gold drawstring of the white pouch and dips his thumb and forefinger for a pinch of black tobacco. His thick fingers belie their deftness; not a single particle of tobacco is lost in the transport from the bag to the well.

And now he removes a matchstick from a silver box and places it in the middle of his palm.

"For you, m'lady," he says, and she takes his offering slowly, with gravitas, for this is the only time she is allowed to strike a match.

LINES

The sharp scent of sulfur as the head catches fire, the violence of transformation, the darkness of decay: life, then death.

She holds the burning match for as long as she can. It is never long enough.

"Hey," Marlene calls from below.

Josh rises from his chair and kneels in front of the banisters that enclose the loft. He presses his face between two rungs.

"I didn't do it," he says.

"That's what they all say."

"Should we go for our afternoon meander?"

"I don't want to take you away from your writing."

"I've been waiting for you to call me," Josh says.

Marlene smiles and blows him a kiss.

They don't have to go far for their walk, as there's a nature path that runs parallel to the stream that cuts through the back yard. Waimea is cattle country, and the landscape corresponds to what is asked of it: miles and miles of verdant grass over gentle hills. Their cottage overlooks an enormous expanse of a ranch, midnight black and redwood brown cows with yellow tags on their ears, masticating their cud in that blankly serene way these animals do.

They pause for one more look at the creatures, some sitting, some standing, some so far away that they are mere dots, before the forest begins and their walk becomes a quiet journey for two.

"*Because we don't know when we will die, we get to think of life as an inexhaustible well,*" Josh says.

"*Yet everything happens only a certain number of times, and a very small number really,*" Marlene says.

Josh introduced this Paul Bowles quote to Marlene four years ago, moments before she was being rolled into the OR.

"You're lucky," Josh told her as the operating room lay ahead.

"You gotta be shitting me," Marlene said.

"The luckiest lady in the world," he said, and kissed her forehead, her nose, her lips.

And then she was beyond those huge swinging hospital doors with the circular porthole window, and all he could do was wait while the surgeon cut into Marlene, carved out the cancer that had attached itself to her pancreas, a walnut-sized tumor that took seven hours to extricate, because it wasn't just the walnut but its tendrils that stretched out onto her small intestine, claws dug into the smooth flesh of her vital organ.

As he stood in that cavernous hallway, listening to the fading squeak of the door hinges as they slowed to silence, he did think Marlene, his friend, his lover, his fiancée was indeed lucky, because it was a complete stroke of luck that she got herself tested. A week ago, she and Josh were having dinner with Ian, a college buddy who came into town, and he'd just gone through his mother's fight with pancreatic cancer, a fight that didn't even last two months.

"Back pain," Ian had said. "She complained about it, but how the hell do you know that's cancer?"

On the drive back from the restaurant, Josh mentioned that Marlene herself complained of back pain the night before.

"I had a headache, too. Does that mean I also have a brain tumor?"

Except Josh wouldn't let it go. After failing to convince her to get a checkup, something she hadn't done in almost a decade, he enticed her by scheduling a tandem physical, hers at noon and his an hour later.

Now, as they walk under the shade provided by Hawaiian palm trees that line both sides of this path, Josh says, "Is it wrong for me to think that you were kind of pissed that I was right?"

LINES

"About…?"

"Sometimes I forget that my brain isn't yours," he says. "I was just thinking about the couples physical."

"Ah," Marlene says. "That little thing where you saved my life."

She tucks a long springy curl behind her ear, one of the strands most definitely gray. How happy he is to see gray hair on her — it is indeed a privilege to grow old.

"I don't think I've ever asked you."

A family of chickens, with shiny brown feathers of varying shades, teeter and totter through, parents with two babies in tow. The rooster, with his red regal crown, raises his neck to appear taller and gives the humans a wary eye as he shepherds his wife and his brood across the path.

Marlene takes his hand as they crest the slope together. "It would be terribly ungrateful of me, wouldn't it?"

"Emotions can be a fickle thing, sometimes outside of us."

"I couldn't shake the idea that you made it happen. Because you were sure that I had cancer, and then it turned out I did, it was as if your conviction manifested it. Which of course is ridiculous on all fronts, and yet…"

"You feel what you feel," Josh says.

From here, they can see the blue of the ocean, the white of the sand, the lookout at the end of their forest path like an oval portal to another world.

"I don't think I'll ever tire of seeing that," Marlene says.

"Mind if we just sit here for a bit, admiring our full view to come?"

"I think those two tree stumps were made for us."

They sit with their jean legs touching. In the shadows and with the breeze, it feels like autumn, their favorite season. They lean into each other; Josh extends his right arm around her shoulder and she snakes her left arm around his middle. He squeezes her and she squeezes back. His ear is against her ear and the sound Josh hears could be the faraway waves of the beach below, or the rush of Marlene's blood as it courses through her body.

"In another life, I might already be dead," Marlene says.

"Or I died before you did. Car accident, lightning strike, food poisoning, quicksand…"

"Quicksand?"

"Did you know that kids nowadays don't worry about quicksand? Totally not on their radar because TV shows and movies don't show them anymore, a 94% reduction since the 1960s. Out of sight, out of mind."

"How…why?"

"A fiction writer's thirst for useless knowledge can never be quenched."

The wind picks up and they press even harder into each other, as if to fuse their bodies into one.

"Do we really have to go back home?" Marlene asks.

"We're here another two days."

"I love our tiny little cottage. Two people need so little room — our house is going to feel obscene when we return."

"For a bit. But before you know it, it'll feel like it's always felt."

"Such a realist. Aren't you the guy who makes things up?"

What Josh wishes more than anything to take back in his luggage isn't the weather or the quiet or the fresh air of Hawaii but rather this joviality, this lightness of mood between them. If only.

When he wakes in the middle of the night, Abby is so on his mind that she feels as bright as the full moon floating in the sky. This bed is a queen, which is so much smaller than their king at home; that is one thing he will not miss from this place. He rolls out as quietly, as furtively as possible and tiptoes to the desk on the opposite side of the room. The hardwood floorboards groan with every step, but Marlene is a fairly deep sleeper and continues to snore lightly.

He hasn't thought of Abby this entire trip, and he feels good about that. He wanted this time to be about him and Marlene, and it has been, but the future beckons as it always does. Less than thirty days remain before he gets on the flight to Portland, Oregon, and he's only written six stories. He's not a fast writer, never has been, and this project, even though the scope and scale of the writing has been drastically shrunken, hasn't been any easier than to write than his first novel. Staying under 200 words per piece has been the greatest challenge, to force himself to do more with less. But constraint can work in your favor, the limitation forcing unknown, untapped creativity. Or so Josh hopes.

The moon, now high in the sky and over the roof, can no longer be seen from this window that looks out onto the grass, but its illumination is pervasive. As he keeps staring into the darkness, Josh starts to make out the cows, black dots with pinpricks of glint, the yellow plastic tag on their ears reflecting the lunar glow. Melding with the stars above, Josh's entire vision is overwhelmed with twinkling jewels, a natural and artificial constellation of distant planets and local bovines — but only for a moment, as one by one, the tiny reflectors blink out. The moon, always in motion, is ready to move on.

Josh turns on his laptop and goes to work.

*

On a night like this, with the air as warm as a lover's breath, Abby would like nothing more than to be on her bike. But now that she's seven months deep into her pregnancy, she only rides in her mind. Like the umbilical cord that feeds her child, the memories of her past trips sustain her sanity.

Lately she's been having trouble staying asleep, electric bolts of pain in her lower back shocking her awake around three o'clock. So for the past two weeks, she's gotten used to taking a walk around her neighborhood, which is the best way she's found to alleviate the ache. Even though she now lives in the Upper West Side at Ted's apartment (now *their* apartment since they have been husband and wife for months, Abby reminds herself), the city doesn't exactly feel inviting at this time of night. After the brutality of Giuliani and the money of Bloomberg, New York is nothing like what it used to be, but still, in the wee hours, the streets feel wider, harder, desolate.

Which is why it's absolutely lovely to be here in Cape Cod instead of the concrete city. Since Monday they've been at Ted's family vacation house in Martha's Vineyard, just the two of them on the bigger of the two islands off the coast of Massachusetts. Abby is not a beach person, except she is on two occasions: in the middle of winter or very late like this. Basically, she wants the beach for herself and no one else. *I'm a selfish beach.*

Abby chuckles at her silly wordplay, and for the first time since she's been here, she thinks of Josh, the only wordsmith she personally knows. He'd appreciate her verbal goofiness. Because he's already on her mind, it doesn't surprise her in the least when she feels a buzz in her pocket, her iPhone. It almost seems preordained that she should see an email from him.

LINES

Insomnia (II)

When the moon is full, the moon might as well be the sun. She still considers it a blessing to be able to read text as small as newspaper print by moonlight alone, but not always. Sometimes it feels like a backdoor curse, for when she shuts her eyes inside her tent tonight, it's as if there's a spotlight on her eyelids.

She tries a trick that sometimes works. In one of the backpack's pockets is a stethoscope, a present from her uncle many years ago. She slips the earplugs into her ears and places the chestpiece against her heart.

Ba-dum. Ba-dum. Ba-dum.

One hundred, two hundred...all the way to a thousand beats, but still no slumber. She unzips the door on the tent and steps out onto the chill of the night.

As much as she wants to be angry at the moon, she just can't. Look at it. How can she stay mad at such a scene that has presented itself in front of her? It's as if the moon is a baby and the surrounding clouds are its cradle.

Though if that were the case, shouldn't the moon be going to sleep? Pretty please?

What is he doing up at this ungodly hour? She has an excuse, three pounds of living flesh and seven pounds of amniotic fluid pressing down on her tailbone. He probably got up because he wanted to draw inspiration from the moon, the lucky bastard.

Of course she's bitter. At this point in her pregnancy, she carries a hand towel with her everywhere she goes because sometimes she just breaks out in a massive sweat, especially her face, which also flushes ridiculously red like a cartoon character. Her ankles are swollen all the time, her toes get numb if she stands in one place for more than five minutes, and her belly is stretched so tight that she needs to slather lotion on it constantly. Never has her body been more burdensome.

Still, when she spots a pair of beach chairs left by a good (or lazy) Samaritan, she takes a seat and re-reads his email; after all, it's not his fault that she's mired in corporal misery. With the waves providing the perfect background music, there seems to be no better place to take in Josh's moony fiction. As usual, she finds it initially difficult to separate herself from his story; always her first response is to refute. She has no doctor for an uncle; both of her uncles are in the textiles business. But the sense of the piece is eerily accurate. She can't be exact about this scene's location, but she's fairly certain it was on the border of Switzerland. She stayed up all night sketching as the yellow circle above her ascended into the dark and descended into the light. The breeze carried the moisture of the distant lake, forming droplets of dew onto her windbreaker, the back of her hands, even onto the shiny cylinder of her #1 pencil.

She reads the story a third time. It's not her favorite; so far, what she's liked the best is the one he'd titled *The Unseen*, the one where she is hiding behind the tree. It's funny; now that she has read that story, she can't help but to see herself there, with her shoes off, on the other side. Josh has changed the way she feels about her own work, and it's both disarming and delightful.

LINES

She closes her email and opens her messaging app. He's probably gone to bed by now, but she sends a text anyway, surprised that this is her first since replying to him when he came to see her at her old place, an eon ago when she was neither a wife nor a mother to be.

hey there

Her two black words hang in the clean white background. A trio of seagulls land on the wet sand and peck at things only they can see.

Eleven seconds later, a reply arrives.

Goodness, Abby, what are you still doing up?

Skimming his previous texts in her messaging app, Abby realizes Josh always replies with full sentences and proper punctuation. This is either because he's of the older generation who don't really understand how texting works as a means of casual conversation, or it's because he's a writer who enforces grammar. Now she feels like she should write back in kind, but no, that's bullshit. She'll be her own person and do what feels comfortable to her; they are, after all, her words and not his.

could ask you the same question

It's not late where I am — it's not even eleven.

where?

He sends her a photo from his phone, which is hard to see because even the best smartphones take so-so night pictures, but he's framed it nicely regardless. It's a picture of an open window, its wooden frame distressed with cracked white paint, and outside there's a hill with dark blobs strewn throughout, and above the gentle curve of the earth are stars that shine like lines of Christmas string lights.

Hawaii, the Big Island, is where we are, for a few more days.

She takes a snapshot of her present view with her own phone, of the moon reflected against the ocean, the seagulls walking about, and sends it on.

in marthas vineyard

Peaceful. I've never been to Martha's Vineyard.

ive never been to hawaii

In a week, we'll both be in a place we've never been before.

The Art and Music Festival at Breitenbush Hot Springs, in Detroit, Oregon: it's been on her calendar for months now, and she's fortunate that she'll still be able to travel by air. She is not looking forward to the five-hour flight from JFK to Portland, and to be frank, the event itself unnerves her. Through her talent, she's been invited to similar festivals held in Amsterdam and Nice, so she's no stranger to how they work. Her only responsibility at Breitenbush is to lead a small introductory workshop in miniature painting, a two-hour thing she's taught a dozen times already at museums and colleges. The rest of the time, she'll be able to kick back and soak in the hot springs.

LINES

She's also familiar with doing a show with another artist. In fact, she just had one last year with Roberto, *Enormously Tiny in Chelsea*, where the gallery owner juxtaposed an older set of her small paintings with his sketches that were large enough to be murals. It was a hoot just to see the audience turn into human zooms, walking up close to Abby's two-inch circles and scrambling all the way back for Roberto's wall-covering canvases.

As much of a show of contrasts *Enormously Tiny in Chelsea* was, this feels different, more adversarial, as if Josh's words are pitted against her paintings to expose some essential truth, except of course, there is no such thing. Abby takes liberties to inject a sense of heightened reality into her paintings, no different than the way Josh pushes characters into dire situations to create drama. And yet don't words carry the higher degree of veracity, more so than lines and color? The pen is not only mightier than the sword, it is mightier than the paintbrush, and that pisses her off.

But before she gets too indignant about her woeful fate as a visual artist, she rises from her seat and dusts the sand off her sweatpants. As she makes her way back to the house, she considers where she is, on the coast of an island, philosophizing on the value of artistic truth. If there is a dictionary definition of a first-world problem, here it is. She's so fucking lucky, luckier than millions of people who don't have enough to eat, who have no place to sleep, who are oppressed by their autocratic government or worse. She paints for a living. She has a devoted husband. And she's about to become a mother.

were so lucky, arent we

Half an hour passes by the time Abby returns to the house. There's no reply from Josh, which makes her happy. He's finally asleep in Hawaii, snoozing next to his wife. She wonders if they are there to celebrate something, perhaps their anniversary. It's good to think about Josh with Marlene; often when he crosses her mind, he's by himself, and that feels wrong, like she's trying to see him as someone who isn't loved. He is loved, as is she.

To the moon they all share, she wishes Josh and Marlene, on the opposite side of the country and far beyond into the Pacific, all the best.

together

Bigger Islands

STANDING IN THE middle of their living room, Abby's eyes target objects within her reach: a hardbacked book with a blood-red cover, the cable remote with its litany of buttons, a clear vase that was given to them as a wedding present by…someone. She can't remember.

She has never before hurled anything against a wall in anger.

The vase would be perfect, an appropriate metaphor in action as the symbol of their union smashes into the drywall and splinters into a thousand spectacular shards, but even now, fully immersed in her scalding fury, Abby knows better than to make a mess like that.

For once, she wishes she knew worse.

She snatches the remote in her hand and flings it as hard as she can, the black stick spinning end over end like a tomahawk, and even though it is a piece of molded plastic, the resultant impact is not without flair. The batteries, safely clasped under the hidden back flap, fling open like a jet pilot who'd jammed the eject button; a pair of silver cylinders launch themselves into the air and clatter onto the hardwood floor. The remote itself splits into two — *his and hers*, Abby thinks for a moment, a part of her mind still on the vase, on their wedding those many years ago, that joyous day.

Joshua walks out of their bedroom with his backpack, which is actually her old backpack, which she gifted to him after his cheap rolling suitcase lost one of its wheels. Which trip was that? Seems like she should remember, considering how infrequently they have traveled together in the last couple of years. Is that why this is happening, why their bond as a couple, when it should be at its strongest, is an illusion?

He bends down and picks up the pieces of the broken remote.

"I don't think there's much else I can say at this point," he says.

Abby stays silent.

Joshua places the broken remote on the table by the front door where they toss their keys. He picks up his set, opens the door, and that is that. Thirty-one weeks into her pregnancy, nine weeks from delivery, she is alone.

As she walks, or more accurately, waddles — because that's what she does now, she lurches about like a penguin — to the 28th St. and Broadway subway stop on this still Hades-hot July evening, she pauses in front of an ice cream shop, not because she wants sweet coldness but because there's a bench. She needs to sit down, for she's out of breath from carrying her backpack two blocks. A sign posted on the window front clearly states the bench's intention: FOR CUSTOMERS ONLY.

Abby glares at an aproned worker wiping down the table by the window as she places her backpack onto the bench.

I dare you.

The worker averts her gaze and moves onto the next table, leaving Abby with an empty sense of victory as she sits on the wooden slats. On a night like this, she's going to have to take what she can get, because, if score is being kept, she's already lost.

It was one thing for Joshua to stay late each night for all of last week, but now, abandoning his wife for the weekend to be with Marlene? To take care of her during her sickness? Bullshit. If he had the guts, he'd admit what they both know, that he's fallen in love with her. The way he speaks about her without ever meeting Abby's eyes, the

LINES

gentleness of his tone — it's as clear as a traffic signal. What is worse, that her husband has given his heart to another woman, or his inability to realize his emotions like an adult?

If Abby had another remote in her hand, surely she would chuck it, hard. But all she's got are the straps to her well-traveled backpack, the rubbery part of the grip almost smooth now from all the use. Holding them tighter calms her, makes her feel young and hopeful. She can do this. She can switch to the 7 and take the Queens line all the way to JFK and fly standby to Dusseldorf or Reykjavik, there's always room on those less popular European cities. She's got all the gear she needs except for a bike, but she can rent one, she's done that before, all of this she's done before, so why the fuck does she feel so unsure, so unprepared…so frightened?

Her phone dings.

I'm sorry, Abby. I know the timing of this couldn't have been worse, but I have weighed the consequences of action versus inaction. There are times in one's life when one needs to make the more difficult choice, and this is one such occasion…

And on and on — she's stopped reading. As usual, Joshua doesn't understand what texting is. It is not the place to write a novel, and yet here he goes again, filling up her entire messaging app with his text bubble, so much that she has to scroll another whole fucking screen to get to the end, which is no different than the beginning: she's on her own.

fine, ill see you when i get back

SUNG J. WOO

You are not seriously, truly leaving for Europe? In your present condition? Abby, you are simply being unreasonable. Beyond immature, in the realm of maternal negligence.

and your a fucking asshole

She regrets as she touches Send, but too late, her juvenile, puerile missive is gone. Time to put the phone away and get this journey started.

Except for that to happen, she'll need to rise, but she doesn't want to rise. Maybe she'll just spend the night here, push her backpack to the end of the bench and use it as a pillow. She's done that before, too, in the town of Brno in the Czech Republic, a year after graduating college. It was a balmy summer night not unlike this one, and as a young woman traveling alone, she should've been more careful, but her trust in the universe back then was unassailable. Though really, what she had been was just lucky, lucky as hell, exactly the opposite of Joshua's Marlene, a woman a few years her elder and yet beset with stage four cancer of the pancreas.

She's only met Marlene once, at a company holiday party a few years back. Truth be told, Abby can't recall her face, just her hair, an unwieldy mass of strawberry-blonde curls but the variance of color magnificent, every shade of gold and brown represented within that thicket. If she goes under chemo, all that beauty would fall out, and just like that, Abby really feels for Marlene and hates herself for the rush of jealousy she felt earlier in the evening, before the remote took flight.

The wind kicks up and a paper brochure flutters against her leg. Black letters laser printed against a pink paper stock, it's a plain piece of advertisement, something that must've taken a minute to make with Microsoft Word.

LINES

**OPEN MIC
7-9PM
CHELSEA INTERNATIONAL HOSTEL
CAFETERIA**

Located between 7th and 8th Avenue on 20th Street — that's only seven blocks from where she is. Seven blocks is a whole hell of a lot closer than Dusseldorf, and it would almost be like going away, wouldn't it? She'd even meet the same kind of people she would've if she did go away, or least this is what Abby tells herself as she threads her arms through her backpack's straps and forges ahead with renewed vigor. She still gets the hell away from their apartment, which, post-argument, feels like a place of doom.

Even though she's recommended people she met abroad to this hostel, Abby has never been here herself. It's simple and almost academic in the way it looks from the outside, a blocky three-story building painted in neutral beige with chalky blue doors and trim. A burgundy awning extends over the entrance and she strides through. At reception, she lucks out twice, that there's a single room with a shared hall bath available and that she's brought her passport with her; even American citizens need to bring one to stay here.

Half past seven, the open mic night is in full swing, evidenced by the cluster of people surrounding the makeshift stage by the pair of silver industrial coffee machines. Everybody's young, from the songstress with the pink heart-shaped guitar and the matching pink hair to the trio of scruffy bearded men all wearing identical blue and white striped soccer jerseys. Without a doubt, Abby is the oldest person here (not to mention the most visibly pregnant), the only one without any tattoos, which is why she merely pauses before continuing to the stairs for her second floor room, B11.

She opens the door and smiles. Most people her age would not, because by the time one is thirty, one is supposed to appreciate the finer things and not feel such longing at the gray stack of scratched-up metal lockers at the foot of the twin bed. The nostalgia is so strong, all the ratty hostels she stayed at throughout Europe, the people she met like the fraternal twins in Normandy, Francois and Marie, how they sang their French songs in harmony and shared their never-ending cache of the softest brie.

But that's all in the past. As Abby sits down on the bed with its creaky springs and sagging middle, her present reality rips through the gauze of her memories and she feels worse than ever. Here she is, a mother-to-be measures beyond her youth, with a husband who's disappeared to take care of another woman, a woman he obviously has feelings for. How did her life stray so far from the correct path? Abby leans against the fading yellow wall and hugs the single pillow on this tiny bed and weeps into the white fabric that's as soft as an old t-shirt.

Her phone rings. It's Ted, whom she texted before she left the apartment. She knew she shouldn't have done that, but she did it anyway, so as a form of self-punishment, she lets this call go to voicemail. It's still awkward with him at the office, his High Line confession an unwelcome albatross, but they have agreed not to look at it for now and just keep going with their lives, and it has been working…oh, who the hell is she fooling. It isn't working, nothing's working, she rings up her voicemail and listens to Ted's voice.

"Don't get on a plane, Abby, please. You don't have to do this by yourself. You're not alone. You have people who love you, very much. Even more than you might think you know. Even more than you may have heard."

Is this what she wants, to complicate her life even more? Really?

Abby holds her phone to her chest, thinking. Deciding. Hurting. Dialing.

LINES

"Ted," she says into the phone.

"Abby," he says.

She starts to cry.

"Oh Abby, Abby. Where are you? Please tell me."

"It is ridiculous, where I am."

"No," Ted says. "Wherever you are, you are perfect."

His words are a salve to her bitter, broken heart.

"The Chelsea International Hostel," she says, and after a moment of silence, she hears the sweetest sound: laughter.

"Really? That's where you are?"

And she laughs, too. But as they giggle like children, in the far corner of her mind, she recognizes the danger of this moment. How her fragility could turn into…

I don't care.

"Let me come," Ted says.

"Yes," Abby says. "Yes."

*

"I'm not here to give you false hope, Marlene. Your chances of survival are low, but they are not zero. You can pull through here, but it'll take every ounce of your resolve. Your body may have betrayed you, but your mind — you have control over your mind, and what your mind believes matters more than you think. More than what is scientifically measurable."

Joshua clicks off the recording on Marlene's phone for the third time, this candid conversation of mortality.

He looks up Marlene's oncologist, Dr. Nina Chakrabarti, on Marlene's laptop. The face that pops up on her practice's website displays a woman with enormous brown eyes that would fill any Bollywood actress with envy.

What the doctor foretold has come true: Marlene is sick. Sick enough that under the cloud of pain killers, she hasn't asked Joshua the obvious question: why a man with a very pregnant wife has stayed with her for two nights.

Is Joshua taking advantage of her? Possibly. Though exactly what this advantage is, he is unsure.

Joshua reads through Dr. Chakrabarti's impeccable credentials, Harvard and Cornell in the educational department and legendary hospitals Mount Sinai and Sloan-Kettering for her professional career. She's even given a pair of TED Talks, so it's no wonder she sounds like she could be on the radio. If anybody can help his friend, it's this superstar physician.

When he closes Marlene's laptop screen, he notices the white tape with black letters on the bottom right corner of the case that details the computer's network name and its owner, MARLENE MCNALLY, courtesy PayRight's IT department. His own work laptop is smaller and encased in cheap plastic while Marlene's is brushed aluminum. But none of that matters now, does it? Her laptop could be made of solid gold, and it wouldn't make a bit of difference.

Joshua is upstairs, in her home office, where she has spent more time than she should have. From below, he hears her stirring from sleep, a combination of a moan and a yawn that hurts his heart to hear. It is the involuntary song of primal, human suffering.

He climbs down the back stairs to grab a cup of hot tea and makes his way to the living room, where the beige couch has been transformed to a makeshift daybed. Bocci, her coffee-brown dachshund, has curled himself like a cat on her lap. Joshua has never seen Marlene without makeup, her hair in disarray, in a baggy gray sweatshirt and flannel pajama bottoms. Even though it's summer and the house's thermostat is set to 78 degrees, she dresses like it's winter because she's cold all the time.

"Hey," he says, putting a hand on her back. "Let's put a nice dollop of honey in there, yeah?"

"Sounds good," she says, her voice thick from sleep. "That and another pill will help."

The dog lifts his head and looks up at Joshua with an expression of approval.

He spoons up a scoop of honey from the jar on the coffee table, a pale yellow glob with the texture of tomato paste, unprocessed honey he's never seen before until he got here. THE HEALTHIEST HONEY IN THE WORLD, the label prominently displays, the words in a spoken bubble from a grinning bee wearing glasses and a graduation cap. Did Marlene purchase this after receiving her terrifying diagnosis? If so, more power to her. She is going to need every bit of help she can muster.

As he watches her stir her cup and listens to her slurp up the tea, he recalls something he's read before, how instead of a burden, how much of a privilege it is to take care of someone in need. Why this feels so true with Marlene but almost nonexistent with Abby, Joshua does not fully understand. Is it the grass-is-greener syndrome? Or is it because with Marlene, it's a choice he's making while with Abby, it's a requirement? Or is it just that he's a fucking asshole, as declared by his spouse?

Abby. Goodness, what a mess that is now. As long as he's known her, she's never thrown as much as a pillow in anger, and now she's off to somewhere in Europe, swollen belly and all. Or is she? She could've found her senses and never left home, just ignoring his texts. That's what Joshua desperately hopes for when he returns to their apartment tomorrow evening, which is when Marlene's older sister Stacy is due to arrive from Pittsburgh.

Feeling awkward hovering over her, Joshua joins Marlene on the three-seater sofa, taking up one end while she's spread out on the other two, though the specific demarcations of the cushions has been lost due to the flower-patterned bedsheet covering the furniture.

"You're still here," Marlene says, the drowsy smile in her voice signaling that the Tylenol with codeine has kicked in.

"Of course. Is there anything else you'd like?"

"No."

"What?" he asks, laughing at her goofy-sounding response.

"It's weird seeing you here, in my house. You wanna know why?"

"Tell me why, Marlene."

Prefaced with a girlish giggle, she says, "Because I've thought about it, a lot. About you being here. Like I'd get home after work and I'd sit here and I could almost see you here, if I thought hard enough. And I thought hard, a lot. I'm saying *a lot* a lot. This is stupid. I shouldn't have said anything."

"No, no," Joshua says, trying his best to hide his embarrassment, or embarrassment he's feeling in her place. "It's fine. It's all good."

"Good," she says. "I think I'm going to close my eyes for a bit now."

"I'll rub your feet?"

"No woman has ever turned down a foot massage in the history of humanity."

Bocci, ever the sage canine, leaves her lap and saunters away to his bed in the corner of the room. Marlene stretches her legs and reveals her ankle-length pink socks that feel like soft terry cloth. He's never seen her feet this close up, and they are tiny little things, smaller than Abby's even though Marlene is a good five inches taller. How amazing that

LINES

people can balance on such a tiny surface. Everybody's a pencil standing and walking on its eraser end, doing it without a second thought.

Within minutes she's asleep, snoring away. Once Joshua pries himself off as surreptitiously as possible, he takes the small down blanket draped over the couch's back and places it over Marlene. With her eyes closed and her hands together by her face, she looks impossibly young, like a toddler, and he turns away before his tears fall on her face.

Joshua climbs the main stairs, passing by framed photographs of soaring sunrises and soothing sunsets, faraway birds dotting the horizon like an unfinished thought. The bed in the guest bedroom where he's staying had seven pillows on it; now it just has one because he's tossed them all down onto the floor. Marlene's house is decorated so tastefully, so professionally, to a point where it could be a model home used by a real estate agent: there's so little of herself in this three-bedroom colonial. Is this by design, or is it just a natural outgrowth of her desolate life?

It's wrong of him to enter her bedroom, but he does, not out of curiosity of her belongings but because Joshua wants to know what it feels like to be her love, to be her special person, because that's who he is. Whether her drugs pushed to the surface a fantasy or the latent truth, it doesn't matter. He's always liked Marlene, and Marlene has always liked him, and in another lifetime, another universe, they would be together, of this Joshua is sure.

Her bed is flawlessly made, the corners as sharp as a box, the end of the mustard-colored duvet lined up with the top of the beige bed skirt with the precision of a ruler. He'll ruin its perfection by lying on it, but ruin it he must. This is what he does — he ruins things. Joshua lies horizontally, parallel to the bottom of Marlene's king-sized bed, and draws his legs into him into a fetal position. He stares at the mirror across the room, at his odd reflection. *Who the fuck are you? What are you doing here, in the bed of your cancer-ridden co-worker, while your super pregnant wife is flying over the Atlantic Ocean, running the hell away from you?*

When he wakes from his unplanned nap, he almost screams because there's someone staring right at him.

"Stacy," she says. "Hi."

There's no doubt she's Marlene's sister — they have identical eyes, slightly curved up at the edges, as if in permanent playfulness. Her features are more masculine, though that just might be because unlike Marlene, Stacy wears her hair as short as Annie Lennox.

"I'm sorry," Joshua says, trying to figure out a way to explain what he's doing in her sister's bed, but he's got nothing to worry about because Stacy, like Marlene, assumes the best in people.

"You must be exhausted," she says. "I'm the one who's sorry. I should've been quieter and just let you sleep."

If the lie is set, the less said, the better. Joshua heaves himself off the bed and smooths down his shirt.

"When did you arrive?" he asks.

"Like half an hour ago? Cancelled my flight and drove instead, which is why I got here early. Listen, I can't thank you enough for doing this, being with her. I know it wasn't easy for you. Please, take this to your wife. Marlene told me she's seven months pregnant and she's an angel just like you."

He takes the pink paper bag and sees a tiny black baseball cap with a gold P logo, the Pittsburgh Pirates.

"It's nice to think about a baby at a time like this, so full of life and…future," she says.

Joshua takes out the cap and runs a finger around the inside rim. So small, the size of his fist, and seeing it and holding it makes the child that's coming more real than ever, but it also reminds him of the fiasco that is his strained relationship.

LINES

"You didn't have to, but thank you, we'll cherish it," he says.

The cap is the final item in his backpack, carefully stored in the top compartment with a balled-up towel in its head space so it doesn't get crushed. From the foyer, he sees Marlene still asleep.

"I'll just go," he tells Stacy.

They both look over to the couch, and Joshua isn't imagining the grimness that passes between them, the reality of this moment: that he may never see Marlene alive again.

It's half past eight by the time Joshua returns to their apartment. The bottom shelf of the hall closet, where Abby's backpack would be, is a black hole.

He crashes onto the couch, arms and legs splayed open. Marlene's sickness, Abby's absence, this is all too much to take. If he were a drinking man, he would drink, but no, he's never found solace in a bottle, or anything else for that matter.

I think you like to suffer, Abby has accused him on more than one occasion.

There is a certain sweetness to pain, to surrender yourself to all that is wrong, to take it and take it, let circumstances overwhelm you. That's what he does now, opens his arms up as wide as they'll stretch, to embrace every inch of this darkness.

apart

Barely Novel

JOSH TRIES IT both ways, with the windows of his cabin left open for cross-ventilation cooling, then closed with the blackout shades down to block the broiling sunlight. Neither works. This tiny cabin with its twin bed and desk remains his personal sauna, sweat dripping off him even as he just sits here in his chair with his laptop somehow not overheating. The best he can do is to be stripped down to his boxers with the fan blowing on his face and chest.

According to the forecast, which he only knows about because of the blackboard at the lodge — there's no cell service out here in Breitenbush Hot Springs — it hit a hundred degrees at three o'clock this afternoon. Now that the sun has almost set on this godforsaken day, it's supposed to have gotten cooler, but Josh doesn't feel it. After having an early dinner with Abby and the Art of Letters Festival's director, he thought he'd be able to sit and crank out the rest of his pieces, but the heat has made concentration almost impossible. It has taken every ounce of his discipline to have come up with this.

The Path (III)

There's something about dusk that gets her mind to wander. Like where she's going to spend the night. Like those clouds over there portending rain, which means she'll need to dig through her backpack and pull out her windbreaker.

She slows down, tries to realign with all that surrounds her. She passes by tendrils of honeysuckle, their sweetness lingering in the air. She breathes in deep, breathes out even deeper.

No. Her thoughts are a scramble — her bank account, which has enough but never *feels* like there's enough. Her parents, with whom she hasn't spoken since Easter, not out of malice but perhaps a more insidious reason, complacence. It's been even longer with her brother. She can't even remember when they last talked on the phone. Yes, they exchange texts every now and then, but it's not the same. She needs to be a better big sister.

And what about him? Yes, him. She knows he misses her, and she misses him just as much, even if he has trouble believing it. But this trip, this journey — it's hers and hers alone. He understands it in his head, but in his heart...

LINES

Oh, Night. Fall on me.

It's not bad, but he can't help feeling disappointed. At the outset of this project, gazing at these path scenes Abby had painted, Josh knew they would serve as the backbone of the story he was trying to tell. What better metaphor for a character's journey than the open road? And yet here he is, having completed just the third in the series, and frankly, tapped out. What he needs to do is cool down, dip into those pools located in the southwest corner at the bottom of the hill, but what he didn't know about Breitenbush was that it was a bit of a haven for nudists.

That's not exactly true: he did know, but knowing it and being confronted by it were two different things. The words on the hot spring's website were "clothing optional," which made it sound like there was an option, but it simply isn't true. Everywhere water exists — whether it be the natural springs, the spiral tubs, or the river itself — people are buck naked. At first Josh found this almost comical, like if he took a glass of water and dumped it on a person, would they strip right then and there?

Abby laughed at that when he told her; she, too, felt uncomfortable by the hair-trigger clothing removal tendency of the festival presenters and participants, but perhaps it goes with the territory. As it turns out, he and Abby are the only representing painter and writer; the rest of the lineup at the festival consists of performance artists and musicians, definitely the wilder wing of the artistic branch.

What is the big deal, though? If everybody is naked, why couldn't he be? Is it vanity that's preventing him from joining in on this orgy of human nudity? It's not like he's a prude or anything — or is he?

Josh does not know, but what he does know is that he's cooking in this cabin like a bird in the oven. And now that the sun has set, under the cover of semi-darkness, he feels a bit braver.

As wacky as this place is, it's also achingly beautiful. The path from his cabin to the Middle Pool is as impressive as a national park, ancient evergreens lining both sides of the wide road to form a natural tunnel. The birdsongs of the day are replaced with the night concert of crickets, the buzz loud enough to sound like a machine. But when the pool comes into view, the tranquility and oneness vanish, because thanks to the almost-full moonlight, all Josh sees now is a mass of human flesh, a gaggle of legs and arms and butts and breasts, just too much of it in one place. Grabbing his towel tighter, he makes a hard right, toward the sauna with even more naked people congregated around it, including the director he had dinner with.

"Josh!" Chris says.

"Hello, Chris," Josh says, doing his best to not look down there but how can he not? Curse his excellent peripheral vision: poking out of Chris's scraggly black bush is his one-eyed snake, pink and proud, a pig in a blanket.

"Sauna's really excellent. So hot that when you come out to this balmy night, it feels positively frigid."

"That's great." Two others exit through the pair of saloon-like swinging doors, a couple with perfect youthful bodies, and being the only one in shirt and shorts, Josh feels more like a Peeping Tom than ever.

"How's the writing going? Breitenbush working its magic on you?" Chris asks.

"Oh, it's going, you know," Josh says. A woman wearing nothing but a gold chain emerges from the sauna door to stand next to Chris.

"You haven't met my wife, Christine," Chris says.

"Hope you're enjoying our zany little paradise," Christine says, and Josh looks right into her eyes and not her ample breasts with dollar-coin areolas or the wild jungle of her pubic hair. Chris and Christine must

LINES

be at least ten years older than he is, but they are in far better shape, taking advantage of the outdoors more than he ever does.

"You know, I think I'll try the Spiral Tubs. They're like different temperatures, right?"

"Exactly, work your way up from lukewarm to toasty to hot, then dip into the cold," Christine says.

"Does wonders for your circulation," Chris says. "You'll feel the tingle run from your toenails to the tip of your head."

"Sold," Josh says, and finally, he's able to get away. When he looks back to give the two a wave goodbye, he sees a scene he'll never forget, a continuous stream of bare human skin flowing around the Chrises, a night parade of fellow nudists. To them it must feel like heaven, but to Josh it's like a procession of ghostly zombies.

Whether due to his uneasy encounter with the Chrises or the vagaries of this steaming weather, as he passes the Main Lodge to his right and makes his way down to the tubs, Josh swears it's getting hotter. If he were to veer left on the paved path, he could visit the Sweat Lodge (no thanks), the octagonal River Yurt where they hold meditation and yoga classes, the stone Labyrinth for circular solo ruminations, and the Fire Circle with its stony pit and surrounding benches. Even in this heat, there are people who aren't afraid of a little fire, as a trio of brave souls are stoking the flames with pokers and reveling in the primal act of burning wood. As Josh breathes in a noseful of the charring lumber, he's reminded of the campfires of his youth, the two years when he was a Boy Scout in a quest to earn those precious merit badges. Goodness, how he pined for them! The one he wanted more than any other was the Lawful one, with its old-school golden weighing scale on a purple background.

His mind sweetly stuck in the past, Josh hardly notices he's arrived at the Spiral Tubs, four large hot tubs set in a square, plus a smaller metallic tub in the corner, the "cold soak" according to the signage. In the canopied area off the side with hooks for clothes, Josh comes face to face with the only other person here, Abby, who stands before him with not even a necklace or a bracelet, her immense belly glowing like a spherical orb under the Oregon moon.

What could he possibly say at this point, *I'm sorry? Excuse me?* Abby instinctively crosses her arms across her bare breasts and looks away, and the two of them stand locked in place for what feels like an eternity.

"Okay," Josh says. "Let's make this fair."

As he pulls his t-shirt over his head, the night becomes momentarily darker, and he flashes through the three women who have seen him fully naked: Rosemary Willis, the girl he dated for a year in college, his first sexual encounter; Julie Bauer, a woman he didn't really love and who didn't really love him, and yet they stayed together for three years; and of course, Marlene. Just a trio, which he figures isn't many, but that's the kind of careful person he's always been. How anybody could ever take part in a one-night stand, he'd never understand. Touching a woman he hardly knows, let alone putting a part of his body inside her — it's inconceivable.

And now here he is, pulling down his shorts and boxers in one quick motion. He stands fully bare in front of his fourth woman, but this is an utterly different situation, so strange that he doesn't know what to make of it. For more than half a year, he's been living with her artwork, connecting with her real-life adventures through his imagination, living the world from her point of view as much as possible. In a way, he's never been closer to anyone else, and yet it's entirely in his realm of make-believe. This is what crazy people do, but then again, the act of writing is a kind of controlled madness, isn't it? Creating realistic characters, making them do and say things that made sense, placing them in cities or entirely made-up worlds...it's all nuts.

Another truth: the woman he's been dreaming of, dreaming with — here she stands, in reality, in her all fertility.

LINES

"Good evening, I guess?" he says, and she laughs.

"Good evening."

"This is supremely weird."

"The same," Abby says.

But there's something else here, too, something closer to whimsy, two grownups facing each other in their birthday suits.

"Innocence," he says.

"Innocence," she repeats.

"I was just thinking of the women I've been naked with, and all those cases were for…coupling, or copulating, I guess, is the more accurate if blunt phrase. But this is most definitely not that, and as odd as this may sound, I feel like a child here with you."

Abby smiles and extends a hand to him.

"This first tub is good for me, I'm not supposed to go into the warmer ones, with my pregnancy."

"Of course."

"Shall we?"

He takes her hand into his, and they walk together down to the tub and wade into the water.

*

Like the way she gets quiet when she's confronted with awkwardness, Josh uses words to barricade himself. Which is why since they've set foot into this tub, he hasn't stopped talking. Somehow they've gotten onto the subject of Lyndon Johnson, a name Abby doesn't recognize but knows she's supposed to and therefore is unable to ask. While Josh prattles on, she pieces together ancient memories of history class from eons ago. President, of course, the guy who took over after Kennedy was assassinated. Right now Josh is in the middle of reading a biography of Johnson, but it's just the first volume of four enormous tomes.

"A fifth one is on the way, but Robert Caro, this amazing biographer, is in his eighties now and even though he knows as well as anyone that time is growing short, he's still doing the same type of meticulous research…"

Of course, she thinks.

Abby sees it as clear as glass, this thing between her and Josh, what it means, how it's come to be. The sensation of understanding something in its entirety is not unfamiliar to her. It's how she conceives her paintings, the complete scene formed in her mind; easier said than done, but all she needs to do is grab a brush and execute what she's already seen. It's a kind of possession, the art inside her directing her fingers and limbs to do its bidding. The difference here is that this urgency to share a vision has never been something spoken; maybe it's this water and the freedom she feels within, naked not only of her body but of her mind's usual constrictions. Or after being immersed with his tiny stories for all these months, this is Josh's serendipitous gift to her.

"Josh," she says. "May I say something?"

Josh cups his hands together and throws a shovelful of water onto his face. He then wipes it down forcefully with his palms, as if to cleanse himself.

"I'm sorry," he says. "I really need to shut the hell up."

"No, please, I like hearing your voice. This is not what I mean."

The tub is big enough to fit ten people comfortably, and the water is thick and viscous, full of minerals and nutrients right from the hot springs, according to the brochure she read in her cabin. It feels like a warm, inviting hug. Abby slides over until she's sitting almost next to him, her back leaning against the smooth curved surface.

"Thank you for bringing me here," she says.

LINES

Only a cloud-obscured moon provides any light, but it's enough for her to make out the outline of his smile.

"You don't have to say that. Besides, it's your generosity that brought us here. You could've just as easily have said *No, you cannot write about my paintings, who the fuck are you?*"

"True. There is this easiness between us, don't you think? Like we know each other more than we should."

Josh says nothing for what feels like a long time, then expels a long, grateful sigh of relief.

"All this time I thought it was just me."

"It was just you, at the beginning, but then you sent me your stories, and I read them. They're frightening, if I am honest. They are lovely, of course, but sometimes they are so accurate, like this last one you sent me this afternoon. I have had some of those very thoughts you wrote, and I think, how does he know? How does he know what was in my mind at that time, when he was nowhere near and I did not even know him?"

"I look at your work and pretend to be you. Just lucky guesses."

"And am I correct in guessing that what you send me is not the first — what is that word, the first attempt…"

"Draft."

"Yes, draft. Like a cold wind."

Josh laughs. "And despised just as much. You are absolutely correct. That was not only my fifth attempt, but the fourth version of that fifth attempt. Technically you read the eighth revision."

Others join them in the tub, two tall older ladies who must be identical twins, their generous breasts like teardrops, floating up like buoys in the water. They all exchange nods and smiles.

"Do you see why we find it easy, Josh?" Abby asks.

"Sorry," he whispers. "I still find this whole naked thing quite distracting. You were saying about this easiness of ours."

"Attraction, too, if we continue to be honest."

"You are such an incredible person, Abby," he says quietly, "so talented and a beautiful human being, if you'd allow me to say so."

Unknowingly, they have drifted closer to each other, close enough that Abby now sees a faint horizontal scar just below Josh's right eyebrow. As a bead of water runs down the length of the groove in his skin, Abby revels in her revelation: we all contain multiple drafts of ourselves, and as someone approaches us, physically or spiritually, the layers reveal themselves in succession.

"I find you incredible as well, Josh, but it is fake, not real. What we show to each other through our carefully curated, carefully worked and re-worked art are the final drafts of us. We share our best with each other, only our best, while the ones that put up with our rougher selves, our worse selves, are your Marlene. My Ted."

They both lean back against the tub, side by side, not facing each other. Even though the wraparound seat is hard like marble, it's shaped just right, caressing Abby's back. Josh's right hand emerges from the water's surface, palm side up. It's an invitation; she grabs it and their hands sink under, clasped and sealed, this special moment forged forever in liquid. He squeezes; she squeezes back.

"Aren't we the luckiest," Josh says.

She closes her eyes and opens up her heart a little more.

"There's a word in Korean, *jung*. I do not believe the same translation lives in English. It isn't love, *sa-raang*. This is a deeper caring, more than friendship. Anyway, that is what I feel for you, Josh. *Jung*."

Silence. Sitting across from them on the opposite side of the tub, the twin sisters have wet their hair, making them even more alike than before, almost to the level of illusion. The evening has never felt more dreamlike than now; the moon, hidden behind a skein of clouds, presents itself in full, turning the surface of the water into a dance of light.

"Such a simple-sounding word," Josh says. "Yet it holds so much."

Abby lifts their clasped hands out of the water and writes on the back of Josh's hand with a fingertip of her other hand. The characters of the Korean alphabet, the *j*, the *uh*, the *ong*, are simple to trace: a trio of angled slashes, a pair of perpendicular lines, a circle. Josh stares intensely, as if to tattoo the word permanently in his brain.

"I'm going to write a novel, about this," Josh says. "About us."

"Really?"

"I've been wrestling with it for a while now. It'll start with your locket, that much I know. And I also know how it'll end. But of course, the middle part is murky."

"Grunt work."

"You know the drill as well as I do. Something else: in the fictional version, you'll be the Belarusian, and I'll be the Korean."

She nods approvingly. "To protect the innocent."

"And the guilty."

"They may be the same," she says.

And with that, their hands finally part.

When she wakes in the morning, her breasts are sore and her nipples are coated with a yellow liquid. Before her pregnancy, something like this would have freaked her out, but after her body has gone through so many changes so quickly, she knows better. She brings up the document she found on the internet, her baby bible, and looks at the chart. So this is colostrum, milk that her breasts are manufacturing. In a way, this journey to babyhood has been like a ride on a train; all Abby has to do is just be on it and come to each stop with acceptance, and frankly, gratitude. Because not everyone has it this easy.

After she stretches her arms and slowly rises from the bed, creaky back and all, she finds a piece of lined paper slid under her cabin door. It's folded into a square, and when she unwraps it like a present, a handwritten story presents itself. His penmanship is dense and chaotic, letters elbowing for space, the g's and y's dipping wildly, but it's all legible.

Dream (I)
"vaguely based on a sunrise somewhere between Kiel and Lubeck, Germany"

In her dream, she's a lion and sitting in an airplane seat. The plane is descending, a minute from touching ground. Out her window, the sky is the color of sand. A few rays of the early morning sun peek through the leaves of a cluster of trees.

Africa, she thinks. *I'm in Africa.*

She's unsure whether she is indeed a lion or if she is wearing a costume, and this unnerves her. She looks down at her paws. They feel like hands. How would she know what paws feel like? She's frustrated, angry. There's a word at the tip of her tongue. She looks to her seatmate, but there is no one there. Across the aisle, those two seats are empty, too.

The plane does not land; it just stops.

"You're not home," her brother says. He's not a lion, he's the boy she's always known. He stands where the stewardess would stand to instruct about the emergency exits, the floats beneath the seats.

She wants to be where he is, but the captain still hasn't released the aircraft. Her seatbelt remains tight against her belly. Her brother watches as she fumbles with the clasp. She scratches the metal. It just won't open.

As soon as she finishes reading it, she reads it again. As much as she enjoys seeing Josh perform his Jedi mind trick and pick something eerily accurate about her trip, she likes this even more, a completely creative endeavor that has no bearing whatsoever with her actual life. She has no brother, rather a younger sister, and as far as she can remember, she's never dreamed about the continent of Africa. And yet she could have, which is delightful. There's nothing more satisfying than options, alternate possibilities, the open paths of a person's existence.

It's half past six in the morning, Sunday, the day of their presentation, though she really sees it as the day of Josh's reading. After holding an hour-long drawing workshop at ten for the dozen people who have signed up, she'll head over to the Main Lodge, where the festivalgoers will listen to Josh while her paintings will be projected behind him on the stage. He's looking forward to delivering their collaboration to an audience; she knows this not only because he's told her, but because that's the kind of person he is, someone who enjoys addressing a group of people while everyone looks and listens. Thank goodness, because there are few things in the world she despises more than public speaking. Abby doesn't fear it, exactly; she's done it enough times at gallery openings and art conferences but being the center of attention has never agreed with her. What's funny is that she absolutely does want all the attention when it comes to her work; in fact, she'd be the first to admit that her hunger for a wider fandom of her paintings will never be sated. What does this make her, an artistic exhibitionist?

She supposes it just makes her human, in all the glory and fallibility that comes with being in this body, trapped inside this brain.

Abby gathers her toiletries for the shared bathroom located two cabins over. It's been like being back in the dorms, these past few days, waiting for the shower, going to the dining hall to eat. She hears an odd sound by her door, like an animal scratching against the wood. It's another piece of paper sliding underneath.

"Hey," she says through the door.

"I wasn't sure you were up yet. Good morning, Abby."

"Good morning, Josh. I loved what you wrote, the dream one. You wrote it last night?"

"I did."

"Why are we talking with a door between us?"

"I don't know," Josh says, then laughs, and she laughs, too. "I kind of like it."

"Me too," she says. "So you wrote yet another one?"

"The tenth and final one. I know you have to get ready for your workshop, and I gotta get ready for the reading, so I'll leave you to it, okay?"

"Okay."

She draws the small curtain by the door and watches him as he walks away, his hands in his pockets, a blue baseball cap on his head. She'd heard that the heat wave was to break today, and it must be true because when she opens her window, the breeze is sharp and crisp. She sits down on her chair and unfolds Josh's story.

Last one, she thinks to herself. She'll read it slowly, savor it. The included photo is one of her favorites in the series, of Lorelei castle. She's done a bigger version of this scene, on an eight-inch Plexiglas disc that took her two months to complete, and yet this one, which took only a week and is far less detailed, is in her opinion the superior rendition. The smaller scale feels more accurate, for when she woke up that glorious summer morning, that's exactly what she saw, the castle no bigger than her thumbnail.

Dream (II)
"from the night I spent camping above Lorelei castle in Germany because the Rhine was too flooded to keep cycling"

In her dream, she's bicycling as fast as she can because there's a wave of water behind her. For a split second, she realizes she's dreaming and thinks: *that's kind of on the nose, isn't it?* And it's funny. And she laughs. And now she's in the castle, sitting on a throne of thorns with her feet up on the back of a crouched man. The walls are leaking, water pushing through the seams, and if the man does not rise, he'll drown. She prods him with her feet, gently at first, but when he does not move, she kicks him. Which is when she realizes he isn't a man at all but made of stone, and it is she who is in trouble. She tries to rise, but the throne of thorns keeps her in its pointy grasp, and she closes her eyes and braces herself for the coldness. Except the water is warm and she's buoyed up, past the ceiling as if she's a ghost, past the touch of fog, offered to a powder blue sky like a gift. She turns mid-air, glances down at the castle below, so tiny. *I ruled in that little place,* she thinks. *I was a good queen.*

Her baby twists inside her, a shift right, then left, then back again. It does this when it's happy, a primitive dance of sorts. Now thirty-five weeks old, it is as large as a honeydew melon. As Abby reads the story again from the beginning, she hums the first song she ever learned, the Korean "Arirang," a plaintive folk tune her mother sung to her as a lullaby. Abby imagines each resonant note carrying from her throat to the amniotic sac, enveloping her unborn child with its soundwaves.

together

Points of No Return

ABBY'S RIDING THE N train, on her way to Queens to meet a real estate agent named Hamid. To be more exact, she's headed to Astoria, to a red-bricked two-story building off 36th Street, three subway stops from Manhattan.

"Owww," she mutters, her baby giving her a sharp karate kick to her right kidney. That made her leak a little pee, but thankfully, she's wearing a maxi pad.

"You all right there, miss?"

The young man sitting next to her on this bumpy journey out to the borough is so not from here, with his pressed white button-down shirt, white slacks, and a thick Southern accent. As her belly has increased its girth, the concern of strangers has increased in lockstep, about the only thing that she considers a positive.

"Yes, thank you," she says.

When she rises from her seat at her subway stop, he asks if she needs any assistance to where she needs to go. She gratefully declines, letting the escalator and elevator do the heavy lifting instead to bring her back up to street level.

It is not much to look at, this road. Every building as far as her eyes can see is laid with red bricks, from the row of the apartment complex to her left to the cubes of commercial establishments to her right. It almost feels communist, this crimson-hued conformity. Queens may be adjacent to Manhattan, but this far from the island, Queens might as well be New Jersey or Connecticut.

If she had more time, Abby feels like she could find another office space like the one she had with Ted, but she doesn't. She's already made plans for tonight to pick up her rental car, to get all her shit out of there after Ted has left the office. Ten p.m. should be late enough to ensure that he'll be gone.

No one else than Elizabeth. Never. Not until you.

She only heard those three short sentences once on her voicemail, but once was more than enough for her to never forget Ted's words, more accusation than confession. She deleted the recording before it was even over, cutting him off mid-word, wanting to be rid of its radioactive contents. He'd never once referred to his wife by her full name to her. It was a queen's name, a name not to be sullied, but she'd done exactly that by sleeping with him. Yes, he had professed his feelings to her. Yes, his marriage was in trouble. So yes, this was not some hoary enticement by a manipulative vixen but rather two lost people finding carnal comfort, but the last thing Abby had expected was for Ted to become this monster of remorse, hell bent on decaying both of their orbits into the blazing sun of his suddenly reclaimed wifely devotion. How could this man she's known for this long turn into someone she did not recognize at all?

Sex, of course. Sex wasn't poison, no, poison would be easier. Sex was a hideous transformer, a chemically reactive agent that rendered the familiar into the foreign, the inscrutable, the untenable. How was she to know that Ted had physical relations with no other woman than Beth until her? That was the trouble, that by shoving his penis into another woman, he was now stricken with guilt and grief, and Abby became the unfortunate receptacle of his self-loathing.

Which is why she has arrived here, in Astoria, to right this wrong the only way she knows how: run away. She has to run away from Ted,

LINES

but after she walks past a sign on the sidewalk of a four-story apartment building, she stops and doubles back.

OPEN HOUSE
TODAY ONLY
9AM-1PM

It is five before one, five minutes before she's supposed to meet Hamid, but Abby stands before a brass sign affixed on the outer brick wall, ASTORIA MANOR, the monospaced sans serif font reminding her of the nameplate on her old apartment, JAMESON REHNQUIST, DOCTOR OF PSYCHIATRY. That was her place before she met Joshua, her one-bedroom apartment that served both as a studio and a living space. Could she do this again, by herself?

She leans against the apartment building, the brick surface singeing her bare arms. She's stifled this undeniable truth long enough, hasn't she? Willfully ignored it, but time is running out.

This is not going to work, her and Joshua.

Except it'll be a million times harder because it won't be just her, but her baby who'll test every last inch of her. Yet what good is a husband if he's not there to help? In fact, he's been an impediment in just about every way so far, so why would that change for the better once the baby is born? He may not have said it out loud, but his actions have spoken plenty, the last one especially, his thorough abandonment.

Abby pushes the door open wide to the office of Astoria Manor.

"Hello?" she says.

It isn't the office but rather a model apartment, an aged one at that. Across the cramped living room with its fake plastic flowers in a chipped vase and an enormous freestanding old-school television, a woman sitting at the dining room table looks up.

She glances at her watch, then sighs. "Come on in," she says, not even bothering to hold back her annoyance.

"I am sorry, you are about to close," Abby says.

"It's fine." She's a tall Black woman with queenly cheekbones; in better times, Abby would ask to sketch her. "Shaniqua Merriweather," she says, and they shake hands. "You're the first one to stop in today, so if you can just sign this ledger, it'll justify my existence to my boss."

Abby writes her full name, Abigail Kim, and there's something both liberating and frightening about this action, as if she's signing some legally binding document that imbues permanence to her vague intentions. Shaniqua, noticing Abby's pregnancy close up, asks in a softer voice, "How far along are you?"

"Seven months."

"And you're looking for a place for…"

"Me," Abby says. The agent's high cheekbones carve deeper as she frowns in sympathy.

"Well," Shaniqua says, "you'll have everything you need here. This is the one-bedroom model, but we also have a studio and a two-bedroom version. This one costs more than the studio but less than the two, obviously."

"That makes sense," Abby says, and it's true, it does make sense. All of this makes sense, because ever since the home pregnancy test signaled her maculate inception, she's been living a lie. Hoping her hirsute Joshua would mature into a loving husband, a loving father, even though she knows full well that no one really changes.

As she sidesteps the coffee-colored stain on the worn beige carpet and walks into the bedroom, she stares at the wooden bed with its plain brown headboard and the white duvet with yellowed edges — and tries to feel this place as her new home, her new studio. That is the only way she'd be able to make it on her own, by once again combining her living space with her working space. She did it before; she can do it again,

LINES

though she's forgetting that in the old days, her focus was her miniatures, which required hardly any real estate at all. On her own, she'd need to take on bigger works requiring bigger areas, at least as large as baby Cecilia and the portrait of the Beechers.

She'd turn this bedroom into her studio. That makes more sense anyway, since she'd want to keep the baby away from the oils. Since she's been with child, she's been using water-soluble paints to avoid toxicity, but she misses her Vasari and especially Winsor & Newton's Cadmium Red, the depth and fidelity of those colors.

She catches Shaniqua checking her watch.

"What is the deposit policy?" Abby asks.

She rides the W train on her return, seven stops to Times Square. She always switches to the 1 downtown for the 28th Street station, but what's the hurry? The deed is done, literally and figuratively. Her day is done. The life she has known is done.

As a New Yorker, she assiduously avoids Times Square, but not today. Today she takes the elevator up from the bowels of this gorgeous and filthy city to join the throng of natives and tourists on 42nd Street. She disappears into the anonymity of human traffic, content to be a foot soldier in her continuing war of existence and walks a block to Bryant Park. There are a few empty seats around the fountain, one almost entirely in shade, so Abby sits in the relative coolness of this balmy August afternoon, takes a sip of water from her bottle, and brings out her Koval sketchbook and her Zebra pen. How many pages has she filled with drawings of buildings and people and trees and animals? Too many to count. These thin hardcovered volumes are scattered everywhere back in her apartment, in between the books she's reading, on her nightstand, atop the toilet tank, inside the bottommost kitchen cabinet where the frying pan sleeps. It used to drive Joshua nuts, but now he's become inured to their perpetual presence.

She'd be the first to admit that too often, her deployed sketchbooks become idle distractions, a way for her to revel in pointless nostalgia when she picks one up and loses herself in the space-time of her work, but they serve as faithful reminders, too, of her chosen purpose on this planet. Sketching is both prayer and meditation, a space for her to empty her mind and carry out the most basic duty that binds all artists together: see, draw.

Now she sees: the humble lamppost with its two domed lights and curlicue wrought-iron framework, how elegant its curves, how pure its colors. Attached to the beam are street signs, Avenue of the Americas and West 40th St, also known as Nikola Tesla Corner, three green rectangular slabs competing for her attention like eager hands raised in the air.

Now she draws: a straight line. And another. And then crosshatches a rectangular plane, like she's weaving the tiniest of baskets. Abby sees, Abby draws: even in the worst of times, she is saved.

*

Is there anything sadder than the cafeteria of a hospital? Even here at Hackensack University Medical Center, one of the best teaching hospitals in the entire country, this is no place to eat. And yet eat Joshua must, because despite what's happening on the third floor in the palliative care unit, the fourth room from the elevator where Marlene swims in and out of consciousness in her pool of morphine, his stomach emits its beasty growls. Hunger means you're alive, doesn't it? The body machine must be fed, because to not eat is to die. According to her sister Stacy, the last meal Marlene had was two days ago, breakfast in bed. A short stack of round blueberry pancakes, genuine maple syrup, and lemon Jell-O, all of which she vomited half an hour later into an

LINES

aluminum pan. *But she'd eaten*, Stacy told him with such conviction, unable to see the Pyrrhic nature of her sibling's victory.

Second Street Café is what this eatery is called, as if giving it a restaurant-like name shrouds its basic nature. It fools no one, not when there are trays to pick up, utensils to fish out of their cylindrical bins, and stations to push the said tray on wraparound chrome rails. Today's specials are fish tacos and spinach lasagna, but Joshua opts for two slices of pepperoni pizza and an empty cup for his choice of fountain drinks at the end of the checkout line.

It's ten past nine at night, which explains the dearth of diners. Joshua has never been fond of eating alone, so he chooses a two-person table that's a table away from a Black woman and a white man sharing a meal. Both about in their sixties, the man severely overweight, his butt spilling over the chair on all sides, while the woman is as thin as a pretzel stick. If they are a couple, they are as opposite-looking as can be.

"That security guard," the man says, his voice gruff.

"I thought it *was* Joey," the woman says.

They laugh, hers louder than his. It peters out into a chuckle, then silence.

I'll write it, and you'll paint it.

As Joshua eavesdrops while biting into the greasy, cheesy, bready saltiness of his meal, he recalls one of his first dinner dates with Abby, sitting at one of the many small pizza joints in the city after walking around Bleecker Street. That's what he told her, and she smiled, of course. He's sure he smiled, too, telling her. There was a lot of smiling in the beginning, no different than all his smiles while banging out the first thirty pages of a working novel; there's nothing but hope and bliss at the start, so much promise and potential that leave no room for the future failures to come.

In that restaurant, just like here, he and Abby had sat one table away from an ancient cotton-headed couple, the woman wrapped in a red shawl, the man with a cane. Watching them, Joshua had made his proclamation, that he would make up a story while Abby would paint the scene. And yet a collaboration like this never came to pass, not then, not ever.

That was what their union was supposed to be, the marriage of not only themselves but their art. Even when they themselves weren't working, they'd banked on their passions to protect them, something bigger than themselves to anchor their relationship. It was a beautiful notion in theory, terrible in actual execution. Worse than terrible: nonexistent.

Marinating in his malaise, Joshua finally notices that the couple has left, and now he is alone in this shiny, coldly lit cafeteria, the second piece of his pizza gone stiff and waxy. His wife, carrying his child, is lost to him. His co-worker and friend, his more-than-friend, his some kind of love if he's being truthful to himself, is dying three flights up. His debut novel has come and gone, its Amazon sales rank well over two million, which means no one has bought it in months. Without Marlene, his job at PayRight has degraded from the usual dirge to a font of melancholy. There is not a single thing that is working for him right now.

"Dude."

Damien and Violet, who must always travel together like conjoined twins, take their seats at the table. Seeing them here in full, Joshua feels a tenderness toward them that constricts his throat and moistens his eyes.

"You guys came," he says.

"A little offended that you doubted," Violet says.

"Sorry."

"Pay no attention to my hard-ass sister," Damien says. "We just saw Marlene and figured you were down here."

"I came after work," Joshua says. "She was asleep then."

LINES

"Still asleep now," Violet says. She takes out her sketchbook and shows him, as if she's presenting corroborating evidence. It's a quick pencil drawing of Marlene's serene face, which if not for the breathing tubes attached to her nose would seem normal. After a glimpse, Joshua turns away from the sketch. Is this the real reason they came, to add to their storyboards, fucking fiction vampires to suck out the story of a dying woman's life? No, he's being too harsh. They are here because they were there when it happened, when Joshua screamed out in horror at the blood pooling in front of Marlene's lips on her desk, that horror-movie evening in the offices of PayRight. Damien and Violet had run in to help, and help they did, sister calming him down while brother dialed 911. They drove Joshua to the hospital and stayed with him until midnight, when Marlene's signs had stabilized. This is the first time he's seen them in person since that awful night, but Joshua has been in constant communication with Violet, who has emailed him a drawing at least once a day.

She rips the sketch then slips it into a folder and hands it to him.

"All the ones I've sent you thus far are here, plus a few I haven't, and of course, this latest one. I know you've been blocked, which I understand, but you know, just pushing through, just getting some words on paper, that might prove therapeutic."

"I'll keep trying," Joshua says, but that's a lie. The fact is, though his personal life is in ruins, he's never been sharper in his writing. The work he's doing with Violet is like nothing he's ever done before, supplying internal monologues and dialogue for her storyboards. Except he's hardly shown her any of it, instead pretending to be having trouble, because the truth is just too shameful: it is he who is the fiction vampire. Now with Marlene getting worse each day, approaching the obvious, inevitable end, Joshua has reached peak performance. Even though he only glanced at that last sketch of Marlene's face, he already knows exactly what he'll write: she dreams of her childhood home in Charleston, South Carolina. While keeping vigil in Marlene's hospital room, her sister Stacy has been telling him about their silly girl adventures, chasing fireflies and singing with frogs in summer evenings, and Joshua has forgotten nothing.

He tells himself that this is his gift to her, that she'll be honored and remembered through his words, which isn't entirely untrue but isn't the whole truth, either.

Oh Jesus, Joshua thinks, his lower belly suddenly cramping. He tries his best to let the gas out as quietly as possible, but he fails, a long whistle like that of a leaking balloon making itself heard. Normal people would ignore it, but not these two.

"Did you just fart?" Damien asks.

"He definitely cut one," Violet says.

"I have a *condition*," Joshua says.

"Well, I have a condition, too," Damien says, and lets out a raspberry-sounding ass boom so loud that the threesome who are dining almost on the other side turn to look at them.

"My condition's even worse," Violet says, but her flatulence is a mouse's squeal. "Fuck. Oh, but wait, just you wait…"

"Oh Jesus," Joshua says, the stench almost unbearable.

"What the fuck!" Damien says. "What in hell's name did you eat?"

When did he last laugh as hard as he does now? The kind that makes your eyes water, that makes your stomach hurt, that leaves you almost unable to breathe?

Joshua's shared juvenile laughter is but a memory when he returns to the subtle beeps and blinking status lights of Marlene's room.

"The morphine drip," Stacy says. "It might be set a little too high. I've asked the doctor to reassess."

She is as Joshua left her an hour ago, eyes closed, lips set in a neutral line. She looks at peace, which is the best they can hope for at this point.

LINES

Two days ago is when he last spoke to her, when she was conscious enough to carry on a conversation. What did he say to her? What did she say to him? He can't remember, which means it wasn't anything worth remembering. But maybe that's fine, that their last exchange was easy and domestic, just words to pass the time.

"It's late," Stacy says. "Of course you guys can stick around, but I don't think anything's going to change."

She's probably right, but Joshua also feels that she's wrong, that sometime in the wee hours of the night, Marlene's breath will shallow out until it just ceases. Does it matter that he's here when she takes her final leave? Only to him, and what Joshua wants to do more than anything else right now is return to his apartment and write. Write Marlene back to health, step into his imaginary time machine to make everything good again.

He kisses Marlene on her forehead, which is as dry as paper. He turns and looks back once more, to the white sheets, the white railings, to the ghostly white woman on her deathbed.

apart

Presentation

WHITE, WHITE, EVERYWHERE, here on this bright shiny morning at Breitenbush Hot Springs. Chris, the director of the festival, is in a one-piece tunic that is so white that it's blinding, but that isn't the reason why Josh waves hello and hurries away. No, it's because all Josh can see is Chris's penis that lies beneath that loose tube of cotton, pink and shiny like a New York City hot dog bathing in the cart's dirty water.

Oh, if only he could unsee what he saw last night!

The tent is white, the chairs are white, the name tags are white. Perhaps Chris prefers this color because nothing reflects away the heat like white, and it's another hot day in this Pacific Northwest paradise, Josh's forehead already dripping with sweat.

Because he'll be giving a reading in the main festival tent, Josh is wearing more than he has the whole time he's been here, a white button-down shirt with rolled-up sleeves and the thinnest pants he owns, a pair of khakis so old that the cuffs have frayed into a fine bristle of hair.

"Good morning, Josh," Abby says.

In a lacey white summer dress that hugs her pregnant belly and ends at her knees, she looks impossibly delicate and powerful at once, like a fragile flower at the height of its bloom. He wishes to tell her this, but it's not his place to say such a thing, and it never will be.

"Great to see you," he says.

"Are you okay?"

Standing near the tent flaps that serve as the entrance, attendees stream by, many of them giving him and Abby a double-take, recognizing them from the printed program.

"Nervous, I suppose," he says.

"Let's walk?"

They cross a foot bridge over a stream. It only takes a few steps for the rushing water to overtake the din of chatter.

"Have you enjoyed it, your time here?" he asks.

"Nothing not to like," she says. "Except the weather."

As they approach the river's edge, they see a trio of nude sunbathers on the grass, two men and a woman.

"And that," Josh whispers to her, which makes Abby chuckle.

"To see people again in clothing after nudity…it is like you have x-ray eyes," Abby says, and then she blushes, realizing this includes them, too. And now it is Josh's turn to laugh.

"It feels like a secret code, too. Or possibly post-traumatic stress disorder."

It must've rained overnight because the river is higher than Josh remembers. Yesterday some of the underwater rocks came up for momentary air, but today it's all a smooth flow, as if there was nothing jagged hiding beneath the surface.

"It was lovely, our talk last night," she says. "I shall never forget it."

"It's almost over," Josh says, and doesn't know to what he's attributing that statement: the festival, their time here, their artistic collaboration…or something more. Whatever the case, Abby understands all the myriad permutations of his declaration with a single forlorn response.

"Yes."

LINES

He certainly is reading a lot from that single word, isn't he? Standing here, as he watches the quicksilver current, Josh marvels at the ridiculousness of his own mind, how easily it applies such wish fulfillment to a lone syllable. And yet when he steals a glance at his co-conspirator, his muse, his — what was it that Abby said? *Jung*. His *jung* — he's not mistaking her wistful smile, nor her arms wrapped tightly around herself, as if to safeguard her emotions.

"I wrote two more," Josh says. "Stories."

"More than the two you already gave me this morning?"

"I guess you can say I was inspired."

A pair of large white birds with long spindly legs land on the other side of the river, take a quick sip, then are off again.

"You will read them, too, at the reading?" Abby asks.

"They're kind of downers, so I thought I'd start with them."

She laughs. "I inspire you to be sad."

"Inspiration comes in multiple flavors. They all taste great."

His smartphone sounds an alarm.

"It's time?" she asks.

He nods. As they make their way back to the tent, there's so much more he wants to tell her. Like how he feels he's failed her, that despite all the care and effort he's put into these pieces, he knows he's falling short, for there are no words he can string together to measure up to her artistry.

Like how he wishes to hold her hand, hold her entirely, not so much out of bodily desire but to be closer to the person with the ability to create such visual splendor. What does this make him, exactly, a fanboy, a thief, a wishmonger? Or just a shallow person.

She made him feel things he's never felt before. More than anything, that's been her gift to him, that now firmly in his middle age, there was something new inside him, someone he didn't know existed until he saw her works. He's always had an attraction to the visual arts, eager to visit museums whenever he and Marlene traveled to new cities, but never to the point of passion like this, not until Abby. And there's no doubt it is a combination of the paintings and the person who has brought him such intensity, and such sadness, too, because it's never for long, is it? Because ardor is limited in both time and capacity; the fire can only burn for so long, until all that's left are the expiring embers of nostalgia.

"You are thinking so hard," Abby says. "I imagine air coming out of your ears."

"Very hot air," Josh says. "If there's one thing I wish to change about myself, it's being more in the present. Just now I was thinking how bummed I'll be when all of this is over, instead of enjoying the here and the now. We are here, you and I, now. I'll be reading my stories in front of your paintings to a receptive audience. Why can't I just enjoy that?"

She grabs his arm, and they stop their walk.

"A pause for appreciation," she says.

He stares into her eyes, which means she's staring into his. In the middle of this very green grassy field, it feels like they are the last two people on Earth.

"This is just who you are," Abby says. "You think about the future before it is here. You are not alone."

No, he is not alone. He's with her, at this moment in this space, in this time.

The tent is full, everyone in attendance for the final day of the festival. Josh and Abby are the opening acts. On stage is a lectern, and behind it a wide standalone white screen for the projector, which is on, displaying the first story Josh plans to read. Entitled *Flow (I)* with a subtitle, "flooded rhine river, germany," it depicts a quiet landscape of trees, water, and sky.

LINES

"Never have I seen one of my paintings so large," Abby whispers. "I see many mistakes!"

"Don't mean to sound like a greeting card," Josh whispers back, "but what you call mistakes make it truly yours."

After a brief introduction by Chris, Abby takes her designated front seat, and Josh stands behind the lectern. After a polite barrage of applause, he speaks.

"Thank you, everyone — what an honor it is to be here. Thanks to Chris and the festival volunteers, we all get to enjoy this" — and here he gestures to Abby's painting behind him. "Abby Kim is a realist, a representational artist whose technical mastery is plainly evident. One of her projects this year is called *Cycling Guide to Lilliput*. Abby's round landscapes, witnessed during her long-distance bicycling trips, are painted with oil on Plexiglas and just two inches in diameter—small enough to be held in the palm of my hand. I know it looks huge up there, but believe me, they are miraculously tiny.

"By nature, there is a gap between the painting and the viewer. We are told time and again that paintings are untouchable ("Stand behind the line, do not touch!"), further reinforcing the expanse between artist and the audience. By scaling down her scenic vistas into tiny circles that ask to be held and scrutinized in the well of one's hand, Abby draws us into her private world in a way no standard-sized painting ever could. This encounter can feel antiquated, like gazing at an illuminated Bible from the Middle Ages, but also very modern, like staring into our smartphones. I process so much of my life through a five-inch screen nowadays that Abby's miniature paintings feel oddly normal in my hand. But not entirely normal. The more I look, the more I discern the power in the smallness of her brushstrokes, as if she has reduced the experience of a depicted scene down to its most concentrated essence.

"So now I'll read a dozen stories that have been inspired by Abby's paintings. I don't believe I've done them justice, but I gave it my best."

Flow (I)
"flooded rhine river, germany"

She did not see him because she'd been preoccupied with the state of her tires, which had sunk into the mud so deeply that she could not lift her bike away from the muck. The day before, she'd met a pair of bicyclists who suggested she wait a day to continue, because they estimated the Rhine to be impassable by the time she'd arrive.

She should've listened to their advice, but she hadn't, because...why? A day's delay wouldn't have upset her schedule. The two men hadn't been patronizing, either, like the way some were with her. No, the reason why she'd kept going was because even as a grown-up woman in her thirties who should've known better, she still trusted in the benevolence of the universe. Whatever she came across, she believed that she would be all right.

Foolish — that's what she was thinking when a bearded man, with just his left arm, unstuck her bicycle and hoisted it onto his shoulder. On his other shoulder was his own bike. He wasn't tall, nor did he look particularly strong, but obviously he was strong enough to carry two bikes through knee-deep mud.

"I carry your bike, okay," he said, not exactly a question.
He did not introduce himself and she did not ask.

Flow (II)

She named him Hans because as she followed his swift steps up the hill, that was what came to her. She'd never known a Hans, personally. She'd known a Günther and a Ludwig in college, a pair of German exchange students who got excited whenever bratwurst was served in the dining hall, but this man looked neither like either of those names. She'd initially thought him older, but it was his mountainous red beard that had lent him a false degree of maturity.

At the summit of the hill, he dismounted both bikes from his shoulders and pushed hers to her.

"You are good now, okay," he said.

His words had come out with difficulty, but not because he was out of breath. Droplets of tears were caught in his beard, glistening like jewels as the temperamental sunlight peeked through the clouds and the trees.

Watching him standing there, his hands clasping the frame of his bicycle for support, she recalled her father, the first time she saw him crying. Their cat Vaska had passed away, and he was burying him in their back yard. His hands were black with dirt, and his tears dropped into the earth.

"Thank you," she said, but Hans was already out of earshot, melding into the trees.

*

"Such a great time," Chris, the program director, says behind the steering wheel of his Prius, waking Abby from a light doze.

"I wish it could go on for another month," Christine says, his wife, from the passenger seat.

Josh sits behind Chris, Abby sits behind Christine, and according to the signage on I-5 North, Portland International Airport is the next exit. Abby and Josh took separate flights on the inbound to Portland, Oregon, but on the way out, they're on the same redeye, as he needs to attend a work meeting in the city in the morning.

"Really can't thank you both enough," Josh says. "We could've taken the van."

"Nonsense," Chris says. "Just between us, you were the biggest hit of the festival."

In the near darkness of the backseats, Josh and Abby exchange bemused looks: *I bet he says that to every presenter.*

Chris and Christine park the car curbside outside the terminal and both get out to help with the luggage, though they don't need to. She and Josh packed lightly since it wasn't that long of a trip, but Chris insists on unloading the carry-on sized suitcases from his hatchback and pull up the handles, as if he's a full-service driver ready to see off his clients.

Josh thrusts his hand, but Chris will have none of it. "Come here, you," he says, and yanks Josh into his arms for a bear hug. Abby gets off easier due to her protruding belly, but Chris still manages to plunk a damp kiss on her cheek.

"Here's to hoping our paths will cross again," Christine says, and then they are gone, and the Art and Music Festival which Abby has had on her calendar for all these months is officially over.

"I can get us into a lounge, I think," Josh says.

"A lounge?"

"Yeah, you can get a drink, well, the non-pregnant people can get a drink, and if it's a nice one, they may even have decent food."

"These are also called airline clubs?"

"Yup. An effort to make it feel exclusive, I suppose, though some of them are legit dumps."

She has seen signs of these lounges and clubs for years during her travels but has never entered one. She is certain Ted has a membership or whatever it is that is required for entry, but they have yet to fly together, as their honeymoon was a curtailed, local affair at Mohonk, a fancy lodge upstate, due to their collective busyness.

"That sounds great," Abby says.

Josh takes each suitcase in hand and rolls them to the revolving door.

"Follow me, m'lady."

They're not flying on Alaska Airlines, but the lounge they find is Alaska's. The company's logo is navy blue and gray, the solemn face of an aged Native American man staring down at them from the sign behind the counter. Josh presents a plastic card at the desk and the agent is grateful.

"It takes twice as long to check you in with the app," the lady in uniform tells him.

"Yeah, I learned that lesson a couple months ago when my wife and I were in Hawaii."

"Oh, how lovely. Of course you had a fabulous time?"

The agent addresses Abby.

"Of course," she says.

After Josh signs the paper slip and they make their way to their seats, she says, "I thought it'd be easier."

"Totally. No harm, no foul."

"Is that a sports saying?"

He laughs. "Could be — I don't know its etymology, but basically it means everything is good."

"Everything *is* good. This is really lovely."

They decide on a pair of brown leather chairs by the window, a curvy, cushioned seat that cocoons her. A little wooden table next to her has a lamp and power ports; it almost feels like a hotel. As Abby gazes at the airplanes on the tarmac, she marvels at how far removed she is from her bicycle and backpack days, when an establishment as refined as this would call security on her if she tried to enter. She feels old, but it doesn't feel bad; instead it feels appropriate, even comfortable.

"At Breitenbush, a number of people mistook you for my wife."

"That happened once for me in the dining hall."

He doesn't say anything more and neither does she, but it's not awkward. It's as if they are letting their exchanged words be what they are, without any additional weight or purpose. She feels at ease with him, lived-in.

Here is a man I could be with for the rest of my life, she thinks.

She has never been a romantic, considering the concept of "the one" not so much ridiculous but rather impractical. It just made sense

LINES

that human beings, as adaptable as they are, could spend their lives quite happily with a number of different people. In this airport, there were at least a dozen men with whom she could marry and lead a fine life, and the same would apply for Josh. All it took to mate was the willingness to understand the other; most people possessed that capacity.

"You look like you're a million miles away," Josh says.

"Zoning out is my favorite hobby."

"Would you like some pancakes? I've been to this lounge before, and I know they have a neat pancake machine."

The machine, all chrome and shiny dark blue, is indeed neat in both definitions of the word, in its spotless cleanliness and ingenious mechanics. It's almost like a printer, thin and round brown pancakes that feed out the right side and slide onto the plate.

"Marlene brought me here years ago, when we visited Powell's Books and the rest of Portland," Josh says. "Incredible food carts around that building."

She feels a pang of what might be jealousy, though if that's what it is, it isn't for Marlene, whom she's still never met. This is Abby's first time in Portland, if you can call it that, as it is just an airport stop. She has heard of Powell's Books, a bookstore that rivals New York City's Strand in size and reputation, though she's never seen a picture of it.

No, it's not jealousy or envy she feels but rather an emptiness, a void of limitation. That there's just one life for one person, that time moves only forward, that all we have to supplant our shared shortcomings are our imaginations, and though they wage fair battle against the constrictions of the universe's physical rules, sometimes they fall short.

"There you go again, off in your own space," Josh says.

They're back in their seats, and without even registering a single bite, Abby sees that her plate is empty. It's a miracle she's not three hundred pounds, though right now, she kind of feels like it, with her baby just a month away.

"Does it ever bother you that we only get to live one life?" Abby asks.

"Disheartening might be the more accurate word for me. I do think it's why I write, to be someone else for a while. You don't get that kind of a vibe when you're painting?"

Not really, but before answering, she considers the question some more. When she paints, it is not to become someone else but to become no one at all. It is to disappear, but even deeper than that, to not exist at all, to have never existed. She wants the paintbrush to move on its own, like a ghost.

"No," she replies. Why she doesn't share her thoughts with him, she doesn't know. Are they too personal? Or is she just selfish, afraid that if she were to utter them aloud to another person, they will no longer be true?

They take turns snoozing on the flight back, first Josh, then Abby. There's an empty seat between them, which is convenient because they can both put their flight-necessary belongings there, like Josh's iPad and Abby's water bottle. But a part of her wished they'd been situated together, so her head could've accidentally rested on his shoulder when she fell asleep, or his foot could've drifted over to her foot while he lightly snored. Innocent, incidental touches: that's what she dreamed of, it's all that she allows, because they are bound to their respective spouses, and happily so. She is happy to be with Ted, and it's obvious Josh is quite content with Marlene, so why does she still desire the inadvertent stroke of another man?

While she has conducted this impractical self-debate, she's failed to notice that the cabin lights have completely brightened. A stewardess with heavy makeup and bright red lipstick places the world's saddest

LINES

croissant in a clear cellophane bag on her tray then asks in a quiet tone, "Would your husband like one, too?"

Josh, wearing a sleep mask over his eyes and with his mouth unfortunately open like that of the village idiot, makes a sound that's half slurping, half throat-clearing.

"Yes," she says, once again not bothering to correct the stranger's assumption. "Thank you."

Many passengers are opening the side windows, the glare of the sun even more piercingly brilliant, reflected by the fluffy white clouds beneath the wing.

Abby leans over and pries a corner of Josh's mask.

"Oh Jesus," he mutters.

"I'm sorry, but I believe it is time to arise."

He squints then blinks his very blue eyes. "I can't believe I slept."

"I was able to sleep earlier, but I've been up for a while."

She hands his croissant to him.

"And this is what I wake up for."

They open up their breakfast and agree it tastes better than it looks.

"I have one more for you," Josh says.

"One more?"

"Lilliput story."

"But we're done with our project."

"Oh yeah?" he says as hands his iPad over to her. "Says who?"

35,000 ft.

The game was called SimCity. Her brother had played it on their father's computer, and it was a monochromatic experience, the bird's-eye view of the land laid out in black and white. The point of the game was to build a city from scratch, lay down roads and buildings, a power plant to give electricity to the masses, a police station to keep the peace.

She was too young to play the game herself, not that she'd wanted to. She was content to watch her big brother at it, his brows furrowed as he figured out how to keep the city growing, moving and clicking the white mouse corded to the computer with measured precision, a skill that would lend itself later to his profession as a graphic artist.

After working on his city for weeks, he got to a point where there was no more land to develop. Every square of this fantasy real estate had been turned into a house, a hospital, a park.

You won, she told him.

He clicked on an option on the menu of the game, and disasters popped up everywhere. Fire, flood, a skyscraper-tall monster that brought ruin to his city.

Now, he said. *Now we see what we're made of.*

"I don't understand," she says. "Why does the brother want to destroy his creation?"

LINES

"Don't ask me what it means," Josh says. "I just write the thing."

"You wrote this on the plane? Last night?"

"While you were asleep next to me, yes. Seemed appropriate. That's what the scene is, right? You looking out a plane's window?"

The tenderness she feels is not for the story but the circumstance: her eyes closed, her breathing slowed, a false night descending on the plane as the cabin lights dim to blackness. And Josh, one seat over from her dreaming body, scrutinizing her painting on his iPad, staring at it until it gives him what he needs: a story. She knows he did not intend any of this as a romantic gesture, but it's no use for her to deny it. As goofy as it sounds, she feels like a sleeping princess who has been awaken by the kiss of her prince.

together

Dues and Respects

BY SCALING DOWN her scenic vistas into tiny circles that ask to be held and scrutinized in the well of one's hand, Kim draws us into her private world in a way no standard-sized painting ever could. This encounter can feel antiquated, like gazing at an illuminated manuscript such as the Book of Kells, but also very modern, like staring into our smartphones. The more one looks, the more one discerns the power in the smallness of her brushstrokes, as if she has distilled the scene to its essence.

She's now read the story three times, yet it still doesn't feel real. Yes, it is here in front of her, today's edition of *The New York Times*, the newspaper of record. Not on the ephemeral app or the browser but touchable, evidentiary paper, the front page of the Arts section. *Any Size You Like*, the headline reads, and below the bold Times Roman font are two color photographs, both featuring the Beechers, Imogene and Timothy, whose portrait with their Irish Setter Rascal that Abby completed last week. The trio stand tall by their likenesses, letting the viewer know the painting is larger than scale. Under that photo shows two human palms, and in the middle of each is one of Abby's Lilliput paintings that the Beechers bought from her on a whim at the end of their sitting session, forest scenes depicting the flooded Rhine on a cycling trip from a couple of years ago. The portrait may be impressive, but it must be the tiny circles that grabbed the readers' attentions because in the last two hours, she's gained twenty thousand followers on Instagram, and all the comments she's gotten are for her miniatures.

Her phone dings, a text from Franny:

BLOWING UP, that's what u are, my little kpop painting goddess, breaker of the interweb

Her best friend is being facetious, of course. There was once a time when artists could impact the culture in significant ways, but those days are long gone, ceding to the likes of the vacuous Kardashians and omnipresent Beyoncé. Still, it is something to be featured in the most well-known newspaper in the world, and as Abby sits back on her couch, despite the downward spiral of her relationship with Joshua, she wishes she could share this moment with him.

But she can't because he's not here. His co-worker, his friend, possibly his lover Marlene passed away three days ago and he's at the funeral home with her sister for the service. *Just call me if anything comes up*, he told her before leaving this morning. She'd laughed because it was genuinely funny. You know what could come up? The creature brewing in my belly, your creature. Yes, there's still a week to go before the jettisoning of their child into the world, so the likelihood of an early birth is low, especially because her pregnancy has been like clockwork in every way.

What he should've done is invite her to accompany him, that he cared enough to keep his very pregnant wife within eyesight while grieving the loss of his friend; those actions, after all, are not mutually exclusive. But since Marlene's passing, Joshua has been even more shut in, sealed off, his emotions only accessible to himself. He's taken a vow of wretchedness, and there's no room in that thorny heart but his own pure suffering.

How did she ever love this selfish statue of a person?

LINES

Their marriage is kaput, but her swollen, ready-to-burst baby has no misgivings about entering this world, once again reaffirming the power of procreation. People have so many ideas about what they want their lives to be, or question the purpose of their own existence, but all that is an illusion because the answer is simple: to make babies. That's it, the only true human requirement.

"Oh," Abby blurts out loud at the sudden wave of a uterine contraction, a cramp that runs down from her belly button to her buttocks. These have been happening more frequently lately, but they are of the Braxton Hicks variety, false labor pains that stop once she sits up straighter instead of sinking into the cushions like a sloth. They are dry runs, her gynecologist has informed her, readying her body for the real thing.

Except now, no amount of shifting her sitting position alleviates the rhythmic radiation of pain that turns her torso into solid rock. It's frightening, how tight and hard her abdomen becomes; during these contractions, it's like some external force has taken hold, turning her into a bystander of her own body.

And then, just like that, the invasion is over and she can breathe again.

As she rises from the couch, she says, "That was a lot." She's been doing that lately, chatting with her growing mound, having extended conversations, even. She's read articles that say talking to your unborn baby is good for it, possibly leading to higher verbal skills later in life. With her future child in mind, Abby walks over to the fridge because she's always in the mood to eat, but she stops mid-way, clutching the back of a dining chair as another contraction hits. And this one is a whopper, much stronger than the one before it. When she manages to slide onto the chair, she feels a slight wetness down her leg. In the movies, when the water breaks, it's like a gusher, but as an informed pregnant person Abby knows full well that it could be a trickle or none at all. Maybe she's just sweating from all the cramps?

And as sudden as it has come, off it goes; her belly turns soft, her back stops seizing, silver stars recede from her vision. It almost feels like a joke is being played on her. How is it possible that just seconds ago, she could hardly breathe and now it's like any ordinary day? She hears the cooing of a pair of gray doves from the open window in the kitchen, two bird perched on the edge of the rectangular planter that's just got dirt in it because neither she nor Joshua have bothered to cultivate flowers or herbs or whatever it is that regular people do.

Abby picks up her phone. Her finger hovers over Joshua's icon on her contact list, his bearded face inside the tiny circle. That is a smile peeking through his bristly bush, is it not? Hard to believe, but it wasn't even that long ago, just last year, they'd been walking and talking after watching a movie at the IFC, whose title she can no longer remember but the actors — she can't recall the two leads, either, but she's never been good with names — the actors were excellent, both well into their elder years. It was a story about their wedding anniversary, but it was really about their relationship and how she never really knew him, even though they'd been married for many decades. Not a happy story in the least, but oh, how pumped they both were when they left the theater, and when they stopped at the falafel food truck on Bleecker Street, the rich scent of meat permeating the air with the most delicious perfume, and she snapped that photo —

Abby clenches her smartphone as the next contraction hits, and now all doubt is gone. An image of her future child blooms in her mind, its tiny hands and feet pushing against the membrane of its prison. He or she — in a retro nod, Abby and Joshua have agreed to keep the gender a mystery — is ready to meet the world. Abby takes and expels short puffs of breath the way she's been practicing, and the pain becomes more bearable until it fades away.

She dials Franny.

"I can only imagine one reason why you'd call instead of text," Franny says.

LINES

"Can you get here in the next half hour?"

"I can be there in fifteen minutes, my sweet," she says. "You have your pack ready, right? And Joshua will…"

"Joshua isn't here."

"Did you call him?"

"No."

A pause, as Franny realizes what this means. "I know this has been hard on the both of you —"

"No," Abby says again.

So is this how she was going to take her revenge? It was a secret so secret that Abby herself did not know until just now, her terrible admission lingering in the air like a rotten smell. This is his ultimate punishment, doled out by his ultimate enemy. She knows it's too harsh, but she doesn't care. If this makes her a bad person, so be it. She'll take her badge of evil and wear it proudly over her heart.

"You don't mean that," Franny says.

"When he returns and sees me gone, he'll figure it out. Now please, when you get here, text me and I'll come down. Please?"

A sustained honk on the street below momentarily drowns out all the noise, but when it stops, all that's left is the sweet trilling of the doves. Or dove, because there's just one now, which seems not only fitting but a sign of her chosen future.

*

Joshua, pamphlet in hand, can't decide where to sit, on the left pews or the right, but then he remembers this isn't a wedding. There are no sides to a funeral.

His pants are too tight at the waist, an unfortunate discovery at the last minute as he hasn't worn his black suit in a couple of years. He left the trousers unbuttoned at the top, but now he's sure the zipper is slowly making its way down with every step. Having his barn door open at a funeral should not be a source of worry, but there it is, and here he is. He slides into an open wooden bench not quite in the back.

In front of the altar lies Marlene, a closed rectangular black casket half covered with what looks like a blanket of white flowers. It's beautiful and serene, a perfect combination of darkness and light. Joshua is sure Marlene would've been happy with it, though now that he thinks through that thought, it seems really stupid.

A Celebration of Marlene Elizabeth McNally, the cover of the pamphlet reads, and inside is a simple breakdown of the service, words delivered by the priest and family, songs to be sung by the chorus.

It hits Joshua that this will be the last anything he'll do that is related to Marlene. Once the church's organ plays the exit music and he walks out back to his car, that'll be it. He's not a close friend, he's not family. He's just a co-worker.

On the back cover, two color photos of Marlene stare out at him, a tiny one of her as a toddler in a pink tutu with her arms arched over her head in the classic ballerina pose, and the other he recognizes right away. This was taken when she was in Chicago four years ago, bringing the Zabriskie account to PayRight that basically saved the company from bankruptcy. This picture of her in a dark blue pantsuit shaking the hand of Peter Zabriskie, the CEO of the international pharma corporation, was sent around the company email like a chain letter.

Joshua blinks away his tears, tears not of sadness but indignant fury. Is this her crowning achievement we're supposed to celebrate as the title of the pamphlet suggests, to have slaved for a mid-sized payroll company? If so, then it isn't much of a celebration. This is not what Marlene's life was supposed to be.

LINES

A family of four enters his pew, a couple and their two teenage children. As the wife sits next to Joshua, she flashes him a melancholy smile, the default expression of strangers gathered together for mourning. This, this family, this is what Marlene's life should've been, married to a loving husband, two darling kids who adore their mom. The topic of family used to come up a lot in those first couple of years at PayRight, their early thirties.

If at some point she'd considered Joshua as a potential mate, he's sure it never would've worked out. Just the prospect of his own baby's birth has kept him tossing and turning the last two nights. It could be his body's way of readying him for the sleeplessness to come; all he remembers from his friends with newborns is their craving for a good night's sleep.

He can't even remember when Marlene had last spoken of her desire for children, that particular dream ebbed away by one failed relationship after another, the bad relationships soothed by her higher promotions and greater corporate duties, but motherhood wasn't meant to be for her, either, as according to her sister Stacy, not only was her pancreas riddled with cancer cells but her uterus, too.

"Excuse us," Joshua hears from the end of the pew, and the family of four all rise and make room for Violet and Damien to walk over and take their seats next to Joshua. Funerals are where these twins belong, apparently, Violet with her black-everything makeup, her raccoon eyes in concert with her midnight lipstick and her black dress. Damien is entirely in black, too, even the shirt underneath the three-piece black suit, even his tie.

Is it Joshua's imagination or are these two happy? It's not anything overt, just a lightness about the way they have slotted next to him, a friendly shoulder bump from Violet. Joshua supposes it makes sense, in a twisted way. The twins dwell in darkness, and what is darker than the ritual of death? Why he isn't offended by their possibly callous reaction, he does not know. Since Marlene's passing, Joshua feels like he understands more, sympathizes more, with everyone. If Violet and Damien derive pleasure from death, so what? Live and let live.

"Glad you made it," Joshua whispers to Violet.

"Full circle," she says. "Ashes to ashes, dust to dust. We'll all end up here sooner or later."

"Doesn't matter how rich, how famous, how smart you are — in the end, we're all just flesh and bone for the time blood courses through our veins," Damien says.

Violet, ever the industrious sketcher, opens up her pocket-sized blank book and starts slashing away with her pen. Sitting next to her as she applies her skill, Joshua marvels at her speed and accuracy, how the coffin and altar take shape on paper as if by magic.

"More fodder for the project," Joshua says, but looking at Violet's expression makes him shrink a little.

"Excuse me?"

"I just thought…"

"No," she says. "As the pamphlet states, this is a celebration of Marlene's life, and this is how I'm celebrating it. This has nothing at all to do with you and I and Damien. Not today."

Joshua nods, but her righteous act can't fool him. Sure, what she's doing now may not be directly for the project, but as artists, they are witting or unwitting witnesses to their stories. What was that quote from Nora Ephron? *Everything is copy.* Everything encountered becomes a part of the novel, the screenplay, the poem, the drawing. That is the true tragedy of an artist's life, that it becomes impossible to divorce the experience of life and the constant mental transcription of that life. The job never ends. Not only does Joshua disbelieve Violet and her noble sketching, but he finds her indignant viewpoint offensive. He's trying to craft a nasty little bitter retort when he feels a vibration from the pocket of his trousers. The priest is now addressing the audience, expounding upon God's love and the mystery of His ways, so Joshua

LINES

slides his phone out and glances at the notification from the corner of his eye. Four words and a litany of exclamation points from Franny fill his vision:

BABY ON THE WAY!!!!!!!!!!!!!!!!!!!!!!!!!!!!!!!!!!!

Joshua flicks off the phone's screen and draws in air through his mouth and out his nostrils, or nostril, because his right one is stuffed up as usual. Always the right, never the left, which means he has a deviated septum or some other kind of nasal deformity, though why he's ruminating on the origin of his frequent airway occlusion at this particular time makes no sense. Just distractions, his mind not wanting to realize the enormity of his impending fatherhood.

A pair of sopranos breaks through Joshua's thoughts, a stanza of the hymn being sung by the chorus:

Yea, though I walk through death's dark vale
yet will I fear none ill
for thou art with me; and thy rod
and staff comfort me still.

The voices of the two women are so high and airy that Joshua feels lifted, like he's levitating off the pew. Maybe it's the confluence of the high emotions he's experiencing — death, life — but as hot tears run off his cheeks, he desperately wants to believe that these words are a key that turns the rusted lock of his heart.

Marlene is gone, and in her place will be his child. He knows it's a terrible cliché, but he wills himself to believe it. To fake it and make it.

"I have to go," he whispers to Violet. "Right now."

"What? It's the middle —"

He rises and walks over her, knocking her sketchbook onto the floor. He knees Damien's left arm, forces the two kids to flatten themselves against the back of the pew. The parents wisely step out and away to let Joshua out. Every eye is on him now, but he doesn't care. Like a shark, he has to keep moving to stay alive. Since Abby told him of her pregnancy, he's been scared. That's the truth of it; he's been a coward. The notion that their baby will bring them together is preposterous, as realistic as a fairy tale. No, this baby's beginning is their end, of that he's certain, but an end is also a new beginning, isn't it?

The cold clarity he feels towards his future is so transparent that it almost doesn't exist. It is as if all the barriers he's been putting up around himself have fallen away. The door cannot open quickly enough. The light outside cannot shine in fast enough.

Ends and Beginnings

FROM THE BASEMENT, the egg timer blares its metallic ring, and again, the Word document on his laptop screen remains empty, the vertical slash of the cursor blinking like a beacon of his failure.

Josh grabs the timer and starts to turn it again to 60 minutes but stops. He wonders if today is one of those days, a wasted morning. It happens. He's never suffered from prolonged writer's block — frankly, that's always seemed like a luxury only really successful writers can afford — but two hours of zero productivity isn't unusual.

He pushes back on his chair and rolls away from his desk. He should just call it off, move on. He's got a list of little projects and errands scribbled on a Post-It, stupid stuff that'll take up the rest of this Saturday, like replacing the handle on the freezer drawer of the refrigerator, filling the backup sump pump battery in the basement with distilled water, braindead jobs that he frankly enjoys, even though he complains to Marlene every now and then.

Okay, he bargains with himself, *fifteen more minutes.*

And now that he's only got quarter of an hour, the pressure ekes out the words. Not many, just a paragraph, but it's a start:

> *Our story begins five years ago, on a cool and damp Saturday morning in the city of New York. The street is Fifth Avenue, downtown. Parked cars*

line both sides of the road, their windshields dotted with dew. We're a block away from Washington Square Park, the imposing arch squaring up its shoulders.

Josh reads that last sentence aloud, a little too proud of his final flair, the monument "squaring up its shoulders." But it is good, and now he can save and hibernate his laptop with a semi-clear conscience.

Since his return from Breitenbush, he's tried to start the novel several times. Who knows if these words will stick? Why he's gone with the first person plural, the "our" and "we" voice, he has no idea, but it feels right.

A month has passed since he sat on the plane with Abby by his side. She looked like she was about to burst then; surely by now she's a mother. He checks her Instagram page every morning, but the fact that there's a post of a tiny bird doesn't mean anything, as they can be scheduled ahead. He could email her, but now that their project has come to a close, it feels intrusive to contact her. It's odd, the emptiness he feels, but it shouldn't be so odd. For more than half a year, he's stared intently at Abby's works, into her works, through her works, and then Abby herself. It was a relationship, was it not? A platonic liaison of art and literature, but a relationship, nonetheless.

Now that he's done with writing for the day, he pays himself a treat, to get on the internet. Onward to the Instagram app on his phone, and today's feature is a stamp-sized pigeon. This has been Abby's obsession since Breitenbush, avian creatures of all kinds, curated by her followers as she sometimes paints photos people send her. This pigeon casts a shadow, which is different than the other birds she's done. Like how the first-person plural narrator of his initial paragraph felt correct, the shadow feels right, too. It gives this common pigeon heft, a hardiness, especially against the cardboard-box-colored board that serves as the canvas. The perfect frame for this New York City bird would be one made of corrugated cardboard.

LINES

Josh touches the airplane icon for a direct message and writes:

Hello, mother and artist!

But what if she hasn't delivered yet? Or even worse, something has gone wrong? He erases what he wrote.

Hope all is well with you

And deletes that, too. It sounds too distant, almost formal, and aren't they more than that now?

Hey Abby, if the pigeon is for sale, let me know how much and I'll

That just sounds crass, not even recognizing her motherhood and just going right for the money.

In the end, he sends her nothing at all as Marlene calls him from the top of the staircase, reminding him of their appointment with a lawyer.

The first thing Josh notices in the lawyer's big-ass office, which is located in a sunlight-drenched room of his big-ass house, is a photo of him in a TV studio. Fox & Friends, the signage in front of the large desk states, and surrounding him are the stars of the show, two guys in suits and a blonde woman. In a body-hugging pink dress, her smile is that of a hostage not wanting to anger her captors.

The lawyer's name, Biff Johnson, is etched into the clear prism in front of his desk, with the requisite "Esq." following it. If there was a more perfect name for a Republican, Josh can't think of one. He looks the part, too, with his buzz-cut hair and monogrammed vest.

"What a day out there, right?" Biff says, pointing to the green of his clean-cut lawn that fills three enormous windows. This office must've been added on, as nothing about it looks like the rest of the Victorian house; no fancy wooden baseboards or crown molding, the giant silver-metallic window frames like something out of *2001: A Space Odyssey*. Still, the view more than makes up for the room's clinical oddness, a calming effect that must be good for business.

"A great day to talk about our deaths," Marlene says, and Biff lets out a deep-throated laugh.

"You guys did an admirable job of answering the online prep questions, so let's now get our hands dirty."

Biff was just a guy Josh found in PayRight's corporate benefits. As it turns out, like physicians, lawyers, too, have their HMOs, and since they signed up for the plan, Marlene thought it made sense for them to create their wills. Sitting here next to his wife in this comfy armchair and listening to Biff drone on, Josh ruminates on the juxtaposition between himself and Abby; death over here, life over there. It's possible that as he and Marlene discuss the process of their respective demises, Abby is birthing a new person into the world. Is that irony? Could be. Josh has never really been all that straight about the definition of that literary motif.

"So I noticed that you, Marlene, wanted to include your burial plan in your will," Biff says.

"Is that all right?"

"It's not illegal or anything, but it's a bit 'cart before the horse.' Settling your estate and probate happens after your funeral, so it's possible no one sees your will and your instructions until it's too late. This is all contingency, of course — if either of you survive the other, you'll know what to do. At the same time, if this is years and years from

LINES

now, which let's hope will be the case, the remaining spouse may not be in a physical or mental state to execute your detailed desires."

As Biff and Marlene discuss a "final arrangements" document, Josh half listens and stares at the painting behind Biff's head, an autumnal forest scene with a leaf-strewn path that runs down the middle and fades into the horizon. It's something Abby could've painted, if Abby painted works larger than a few inches, but she doesn't. She's found her passion in her miniature art, and in her life, too, her life with Ted and soon with their child.

Has he found passion in art and life? Thinking of the end like they have been for the last week — filling out the questionnaire on Biff's website and perusing funeral homes and caskets online — has placed Josh in a mood of professional and personal evaluation. He's always considered passion in a negative light, something to be avoided. Doesn't it blind you, make you take unnecessary risks? No, he'll take contentment over passion, thank you very much. He'll never win the National Book Award, but he's written the book he wanted, on his own terms, and sometimes he even gets to write little stories about little paintings.

As he watches Marlene from where he sits, her index finger running over lines of text like the way kids learn to read, he feels a throat-tightening lump of tenderness towards her. It's always been the two of them, together. If they'd married younger, things could've turned out differently, but really, there were no regrets on the no kids front, even now as they craft their wills. He would survive if she were to go first, just as she would if he were to die; that's what humans do best, carry on. But they would both be lesser lives, of that he is certain.

"What about you?" Biff asks him, breaking him out of his reverie.

"Sorry?"

Marlene reaches out and places her hand on his thigh. "You okay?"

"Absolutely," Josh says, and keeps his tears at bay through his smile.

"I was just asking what you wanted for your funeral," Biff says.

"Oh, that," Josh says.

"Doesn't want one," Marlene says.

"Really?" Biff says.

Josh's phone buzzes, and he sees a New York area code he doesn't recognize. "You can literally throw me in a ditch for all I care," he says. "Would you guys give me a moment? I think I may need to take this."

"*Dead is dead* is one of his favorite sayings," he hears Marlene say as he steps out of Biff's office.

"A realist," Biff says. "I can relate."

Josh rescues the call before it flows over to voicemail. Out here in the hallway, photos of Biff and his wife and two children at various stages of life run the length: babies, toddlers, Little Leaguers, high school graduates.

"Hello?" Josh says.

"Hi, I'm trying to reach Josh Kozlov?" A woman's voice.

"You've got him."

"Great. I'm calling from *Hemispheres*?" She correctly assumes Josh's silence as confusion. "The magazine? United Airlines?"

Probably a millennial or even younger, as every sentence ends with a vocal fry. But her identity doesn't matter — if this is what Josh thinks it is, it's excellent news.

"Insomnia," he says.

"Yes! That's why I'm calling? It just happens that our next issue, which of course won't be out for another three months, features the intersection of art and literature, so what you sent couldn't have been more perfect?" She needs a signed release from both Josh and Abby for publication but only has his contact information.

"If you email it to me, I'll email it to Abby, would that work?"

LINES

"Totes! I'll send it off straight away, thank you!"

As soon as he hangs up, he feels the vibration of his phone, signaling the arrival of the email. Not only will they be published, but *Hemisphere* will pay $500, too. Half a grand for two hundred words — it's likely he'll never have a more lucrative ratio of letters to dollars. At the same time, he believes the magazine is getting the better end of the bargain, because is it not only the best of the stories, he believes it's the best thing he has ever written.

Josh forwards the message and attaches the original Word document to his email to Abby. He writes:

Hey there. If you're okay with it, we'll split the proceeds 50/50? I came across the magazine on our flight back. It was fate, destiny, and kismet all wrapped up in one. Hope you are living it up, Abby.

He clicks Send and clicks off the screen on his phone. That is likely the last Lilliput story he wrote. If so, so what? Should he have lingered over his missive, savored the moment more?

No, it's done and gone. Over. Dead is dead.

*

As Abby pushes yet again, as she balls her hands into fists and bears down to get this baby out of her, as the doctor tells the nurse that the station is now at zero, a thought pops into her head, a revelation, a gift: never has she felt more alive than now.

"Are you laughing?" Ted says through his mask.

"Yes, yes!" Abby says, and she tightens her belly with the last wave of her contraction.

"One," Dr. Jane says. "The station is now at one. Abby, you have two to go. You're officially past the halfway point."

Without the contraction, the urge to push subsides; time to rest. How long she's been at this, Abby does not know. It feels like hours, but it hasn't even been one. The doctor announces her contractions are now three minutes apart, the length of a boxing round, and the contractions themselves are lasting a minute, the time the boxers sit on their stools and listen to their cornermen. Dr. Jane is apparently a fan of boxing, something Abby never would've guessed in a thousand years. A good two inches shorter than herself, Dr. Jane is a few years shy of sixty and looks more like a baker of cakes than someone who watches grown men pummel each other to unconsciousness.

"I saw Mike Tyson fight twice in person, ringside seats," Dr. Jane says.

"I think you are pulling legs," Abby says.

"Not your baby's legs, though, because he or she's coming out head first like a good little soldier. I see a little tuft of hair, Abby!"

It's entirely possible her doctor has made up this boxing story to distract Abby from the business at hand. Before being rushed into the birth center, Dr. Jane promised she'd use every trick in her book to make sure this new life came into the world in the quickest and safest possible manner.

"How many rounds in a boxing game?" Abby asks.

"Match, not a game. Twelve now, though it used to be longer, fifteen. In fact, the last fifteen rounder was one of the Tyson matches I saw, when he knocked out Tyrell Biggs in the seventh. Now before you continue with your little quiz, how about another push...now!"

Abby thinks of Muhammad Ali as she draws in her breath — *fly like a butterfly* — and expels her lungful of hot air with yet another belly-straining shove that she hopes stings like a bee. Now here's something else she never imagined, that she'd be thinking of a heavyweight boxer

LINES

as she lies on her hands and knees, her head resting against the stack of pillows. *I'm so bad I make medicine sick!* That was one of his famous sayings. He was a fighter and he was a writer. Some people are blessed. Though Ali's blessedness ran out eventually, because he got sick with something and he couldn't speak anymore. He has probably passed by now, though Abby isn't sure.

"You're doing great," Ted says.

Behind his sky blue mask, she knows he's smiling because his eyes are. As he breathes with her, as he pumps his fist like Tiger Woods and cheers her on, he has never looked more helpless. *We are pregnant,* she's heard him say many times to many people, and it is sweet and right of him to say, but at this moment, she's the one pregnant, the one who feels as if she's been constipated for a month and has eaten the largest meal of her life. The creature living inside her wants to, needs to, get the hell out of her, and even though childbirth is nothing like what it used to be, safer and team-oriented and full of mechanical and technological sentries to safeguard the mother and child, in the end it is still those two beings, mother and child, together and alone in their opposite quests: for her an end, for the baby a beginning.

Spent from another session of simulated pooping — that is literally what the force of moving this baby down is like — Dr. Jane broadcasts to the room that the station is now two, and suddenly there's her mother, smack in the middle of her mind. Abby feels badly that she hasn't thought of her until now; it seems like she should've been there from the get-go, but the sad fact is, they are not close. How is that even possible, that a mother feels anything but permanently tethered to the child nurtured inside her? But once the baby grows up to be a petulant teen like Abby was, the bond of course can thin to a tenuous strand. They are cordial, phone calls for each other's birthdays, and Abby always sends flowers for Mother's Day, but after the family moved from Seoul to the States and her mother was confronted with a new world with its difficult language and mysterious people, she had to carve out her own life to survive. Her mother had to grow up, and Abby loves her for it.

"You're right at the cusp of crowning," Dr. Jane says, and the avalanche of pain — searing, burning, stretching — is nothing she's ever felt before. It's as if the lower part of her body is convulsing and exploding and twisting, and Abby just lets it out, screams as loud as she can, a wail that turns her hoarse. Her brain is a blank, white agony replacing all of her thoughts. She has become an animal, all instinct as her hips feel like they are being pulled apart.

"I can't!" she yells. "There is no way…I just can't."

"Yes you can!" Ted yells right with her. "Yes you can!"

"Just one more push, Abby, just one more big one," Dr. Jane says.

Sweat and tears and spit have pooled onto the white pillowcase in front of her, but that doesn't stop her from leaning her face into the mixture; who cares, it's *her* mixture. There are liquids leaking out of all of her orifices; this birthing bed is a gigantic petri dish of her DNA. Three years ago, she cycled all night in the Swedish countryside to avoid an oncoming hailstorm, an effort that turned her legs into jelly for two days, and she thought she'd never be so tired again. Wrong, wrong, wrong.

But in all that wrongness of her past cycling adventures is something quite right: a morning somewhere in northern France, three, four years ago? The peripheral information around this particular slice of memory, of this particular break of day, is fuzzy, except for what matters — the way it looked, smelled, sounded, felt. Of all the Lilliputs she has painted, there is one that is her favorite, and it is this one because no matter where she is or what she is doing, she can see it clearly, and as her baby's eyes and nose and mouth touch the air for the first time, Abby is no longer trapped in this brightly-lit square room of human creation. Instead, she's striding her bike, hovering over her seat as her feet step onto the pavement. She is still and so is this early morning air, and if not for her labored breathing, the world would be bathed in silence. As her heartbeat slows, she takes in the color of the sky, somewhere between gray and lavender, a delicate hue she desperately wishes to capture right here, right now, because literally, inside of a minute, it'll be gone forever. That's how it is with the blooming of dawn; there is nothing more ephemeral. The lightest wind begins to rustle the lightest leaves, and a few stray drops of dew kiss her forehead. It smells like a working garden here, as if fresh dirt has just been dug, plus a hint of mint, which must be growing near. It's all so alive, and she feels alive, her pulse slowing down after her bike ride but now accelerating because she's excited, and happy, and young. She closes her eyes, clenches her handlebar grips, and lifts her left foot onto the pedal and now her right foot and her eyes open and she's pumping down and up and down and up and the sun is out and the morning is upon her, and this is all that matters, that at this moment she's free to ride this French breeze, the trees a blur, the path ahead. Where it will lead she does not know, but no matter because the path is the reason. The ride is the reason. But now a voice calls her back…

"Abby! Oh Abby!" Ted says.

"Yes?" she says.

"It's a boy!" Dr. Jane says.

Beginnings and Ends

"IT'S A GIRL," Dr. Chang says.

It's a proclamation of neither excitement nor victory but rather relief and release, and Abby can't blame her — after all, the doctor has been here for the whole twenty-eight hours just like her. Every medical marvel for delivery that could be used has been used, from the intrauterine pressure catheter to detect the strength of her contractions to the electronic fetal monitor to make sure her fetus remained healthy despite the prolonged labor. What finally did the trick was Pitocin, an IV drip of oxytocin.

"It took a higher dose than we thought, but it made your contractions stronger," a nurse told Abby. "It's known as the 'love' hormone."

Ah, she thought. *Makes sense I'd be running low.*

But now it's over, and Dr. Chang brings her girl, covered in a few strings of blood and what looks and feels like fatty grease. "Vernix," the doctor says. "It protected her skin when she was inside your womb, but now she's got you." She places her child in the nook of Abby's arm. For a tiny thing, she's hot like a fresh loaf of bread.

"This is okay?" Abby asks, pointing to the umbilical cord still attached.

"We want immediate skin-to-skin contact with mother and child," Dr. Chang says. "Bonding."

"Franny!" Abby says, spotting her friend who's also been here for the entire duration of this marathon, peeking behind the doctor. "Franny, why are you hiding?"

"I'm not hiding, my little Korean dumpling, who just made an even littler dumpling," Franny says. "There was so much happening in the last five minutes that I froze like a deer in headlights."

While the doctor clamps the umbilical cord to have it cut, Abby turns her eyes into a panning camera and tries to see, really see, everything around her so she'll never forget any of it. It looks like the end of a raucous party, the two nurses and the doctor trudging about, discarded wrappers on the bed and the floor, hand-held equipment lying askew while the larger ones are pushed away at disorderly angles. She looks down at the miniscule person next to her, eyes shut and making little spit bubbles as she sleeps. There is indeed a fair amount of hair on this baby, brown curls more Joshua than Abby.

Joshua. First time I've thought of you in a while.

Before Abby knows it, the cord is cut, her baby is wiped down and swaddled in a soft towel, and when she returns, the nurse exposes Abby's right breast and places the baby's face near her nipple, and just like that, her girl begins to suck and Abby can feel the milk coming right out of her, a sensation not unlike peeing, a gentle liquid release. The automata of life in action: they're all organic machines with pre-existing instructions that fire off without any conscious decision-making. But oh, what a rush! As mechanical and predestined as this first-ever breastfeeding session may be, Abby has never felt such a purity of love for anything or anyone else. Not only love but protection and devotion, selfishness and possessiveness that even her paintings cannot rival.

This is motherhood. I am her mother.

LINES

Franny snaps a photo with her phone. "Your face," she says. "I've never seen you like that."

"What?" Abby asks.

"Like you could love and kill at the same time."

As always, nothing gets by her very smart best friend.

"I don't understand," Franny says. "I don't understand how he could not be here."

Abby shifts her left arm to cradle her baby closer to her. She doesn't even have a name yet.

"Could you check my phone?"

Franny takes off her blue cap, the highlights of her hair in harmony with the color of her smock. As her locks unfurl, they cascade down her back like falling water. Abby wants to tell her how beautiful she looks, but the gentle tugs of her girl on her nipple and the steady flow of her milk brings her to the edge of sleep, then falls right over into the darkness that awaits her.

When she awakes, everyone but her baby is gone, and she's in a different room, in a different bed. Was she so knocked out as to remain oblivious to being moved? She's always been a heavy sleeper, but this seems extreme.

In the small crib next to Abby, her girl emits the quietest snores as she snoozes. Bundled in a white blanket with just her perfect round face exposed, she almost doesn't look real.

Abby feels a buzz down near her waist and finds her phone. How that got there is another mystery, but all the mysteries will need to take a backseat to the one in her hand, an email from Joshua that's a forwarded message from a magazine, *Hemispheres*, that states publication plus payment of $500.

SUNG J. WOO

Hey there. If you're okay with it, we'll split the proceeds 50/50? I came across the magazine on our flight back. It was fate, destiny, and kismet all wrapped up in one. Hope you are living it up, Abby.

At the bottom is an attached Word document:

Insomnia (III)

Sleep has never come easy for her. Even as a child, she was an early riser.

"But you must sleep, you must rest," her mother said.

"If you do not sleep, you will not grow," her father said.

The fact was, she didn't want to grow. She liked being small, tiny, economical. She did not gauge any advantage in taking up more space. Her parents slept in a larger bed. Neither could sit in the gap between the two giant chests in the attic to read a book with a flashlight. She could hide, she could disappear, any time she wanted to. She'd just close her eyes, draw in her legs, wrap her arms around herself, and she was as miniscule as a period at the end of a sentence.

But of course, she did grow, slowly enough that she hardly noticed. As a child she fit neatly into the world; now she stretches the world so it fits around her. Most of the time, this doesn't bother her. But when sleep eludes her like it did last night, when she gazes at the lamppost across a deserted street before the break of day, she longs for the impossible.

    Abby reads the email again, but it still fails to make any sense.

    "That's for you," Josh says.

    The man who walks over and sits by her bedside is her husband, but he's also not her husband. Beardless, he looks ten years younger. It goes beyond his beard: the crow's feet etched at the corners of his eyes are simply not present, and neither are the deep corrugations of strain and worry carved into his forehead.

    "You wrote this story, for me?" she asks.

    "Yes. It's your favorite of the Lilliputs, is it not?"

    "How did you know that?"

    He shrugs and smiles, a combinatorial gesture so free and light that it turns him even further into a familiar stranger.

    "Because you're my favorite artist."

    He places a hand on her arm. If he is a figment of her imagination, she must also be imagining his touch, his warmth. She starts to cry.

    "Oh please, don't, Abby. You have your beautiful boy right next to you."

    "Boy? No, Joshua, it's a girl. Your girl. You missed it. You missed it all."

    "You also have a boy," he says. "In another life, a more pleasant existence for the both of us, you have yourself a son."

    Abby wants to stop her tears, but they come and they flow. She can no longer see Josh clearly, his kind face a wet blur.

"It's not so bad," she says. "We fight, yes, and we never have enough money, but I think we love each other. Or at least we used to."

"It sounds strange, you calling me by my full first name. Nobody calls me that anymore."

His words stab her like an ice pick, cold and numb. How could he not be Joshua? That's who he's always been, her friend, her lover, her husband, her enemy. Why wasn't he here? The bed shifts when he rises, and where his hand had been on her arm cools to the point of raising goosebumps. She reaches out for him but he's gone, but there's someone else in his place, a hand that grabs hers and squeezes it tight.

"Abby! Oh Abby!"

She's still in her birthing room, her baby girl firmly in the crook of her arm. Franny holds up Abby's phone to show the Caller ID of a phone call from hours ago from the New York Police Department and the voicemail that awaits her.

*

It is now 11:03AM. That's when Damien's text message arrives:

we planned to tell u after service but you ran the fuck away, so now embrace the news via text. our little story has been optioned by Paramount. notice the capital-fucking-P.

As Joshua walks on Madison Avenue, he plays the animated logo of the movie studio in his mind, the fancy newer one where the camera zooms slowly up the snowy peak and the circle of stars orbit the rocky zenith. Is there accompanying music? He doesn't think so. No fanfare like the 20th Century Fox one, the drums and the horns, just majestic

LINES

silence. He's seen various versions of that mountain for as long as he can remember.

That's amazing news, that the graphic novel the twins have been working on, the one based on his sad little existence, has found a cinematic champion. Or maybe it's a TV series — that's more likely since everything is TV in the era of streaming. Joshua feels like he should be more excited than what he actually feels: an odd kind of calm.

He passes by Le Pain Quotidien on 97th Street, a restaurant he never feels he can afford when he eats there. He glances at the plain, woody décor inside, the rectangular workmanlike communal table, simplicity leading to elegance. He and Abby can stop there when they leave, if she feels like it. She probably won't feel like eating after all she's gone through. Or maybe she'll want nothing to do with him and ask for a divorce on the spot, while holding their child in her arms.

The next street is the entrance of Mount Sinai Hospital, but when he traverses the crosswalk, there's Marlene under the walk-don't-walk sign. She's in a beige pantsuit with white shoes, shiny and bright under the late morning sun.

"Hey," she says.

"Hi," he says.

She's dead — he knows this. After all, not an hour ago he was at her funeral. This has to be a dream, but when you realize you're in a dream, can the dream continue to exist? Apparently so, because Marlene extends her hand to him and he takes it, and they walk up together to the blue and white triangle that overhangs the revolving doors.

As soon as he walks through, he's inside an elevator where Marlene pushes the button for the second floor: Steven and Alexandra Cohen Center for Labor and Birth.

"I don't believe in an afterlife," Joshua says.

The lights on the elevator's ceiling are dim, but he can still make out Marlene's bemused expression.

"That makes two of us," she says.

"Then I must be dreaming."

"Then you must. I don't know if it's important to know the how. Like you and I are married and have been for years, but I don't care to know just how or why I know that."

"So you never died."

"Not yet, thanks to you," she says. The elevator dings, and it opens up to what can best be described as an upscale dorm room: classy fake wood paneling on one wall behind the twin-sized bed, matching nightstand, a comfortable-looking plushy chair. The chair is pulled over next to the bed, where a man sits and cradles a bundled baby. Looking spent with messy, sweaty hair, Abby stares on with a smile overflowing with love.

"That's Ted, Abby's husband," Marlene says. "And that's their child, their son."

"Do I know him?"

"Her officemate, her husband — it's complicated when the lines cross. I don't believe you've met."

"Seems like a good guy."

"I can't say. The only reason why I even know this much is because you've told me."

"I've told you?"

"Yes, but the you I know has no beard and goes by Josh."

"Jesus Christ, there's another one? Isn't one of me enough?"

"No."

"I can't imagine going through life without this," he says, raking his fingers through a cheek full of hair. "It's my barrier against this awful world." His fingers feel sticky, a coagulation of blood, half dried, half wet. This should be a source of great consternation, but much like the Paramount news, it's all flattened out.

LINES

"I think it's time for you to go," Marlene says.

"Go where?"

"Back."

"If I don't want to?"

"It is a choice. In a minute, you can wake up," Marlene says. "Or not."

"If not, will you be with me? Here, wherever this is?"

"I don't know."

"What do you mean, you don't know?"

"I haven't decided."

"What else do you have to do? Aren't you dead?"

Marlene laughs. "You always could make me laugh, even under the worst circumstances. Like this one."

"Okay. Since I now have less than a minute with you, let's go somewhere else."

"Where to?"

"Hawaii," Joshua says. "I've always wanted to go."

"I know just the place," Marlene says, and when they turn to leave the room, they stand on the back porch of a small cottage, the deck painted white. Surrounding them are soft hills that look like they've been steeped in the greenest dye, the color of a summer lawn after a rain.

"Because we've been here," Joshua says.

"This past summer."

"In this other…line, did you say? There, we are happy."

"We're a good team."

"I'm not doing well here," Joshua says. "I don't mean right now. Obviously I'm not doing well at all at this exact moment, because my beard is caked with my blood. But, you know, overall."

"I don't know how to help you," Marlene says. "I wish I could, but you know what happened to me here."

"You and I could team up and murder the other you and me and take their place. Come on, it'll be fun."

Marlene takes his hands in her hands.

"Sadly, we're in no shape to murder anybody."

"I can't feel you," Joshua says, squeezing his hands as hard as he can. "Please don't leave."

Marlene says something, but Joshua can't quite hear her. Her words are like whispers because his ears fill with the piercing ringing of sirens.

He came out of nowhere, a woman says, her faraway voice frantic. *I swear, I didn't see him.*

Like at the church near the end of Marlene's funeral service, he feels his body being lifted, except it's happening for real this time, as two paramedics load him into the back of an ambulance. Pain shoots everywhere inside and outside him, and then he feels nothing at all.

It is now 11:04AM.

Acknowledgments

The first person to thank here is obvious — Dina Brodsky, who not only let me write about her paintings but further extended her generosity by having her artwork grace the covers and the pages of this novel. Much gratitude to three other New York Academy of Art graduates, too, Cara De Angelis, Nicolas V. Sanchez, and Alyssa Monks, whose works I reference in the book.

Thanks also to Katie Herzig, who granted me permission to excerpt the lyrics from her song "Lines," from her album *Walk Through Walls*.

Where would I be without my readers? Ava Sloane, Wendy Lee, and Stewart O'Nan – all my words would've been far clumsier without their support and guidance. I'm also hugely indebted to the fine folks of Unsolicited Press for making this book happen, especially Esme Howler and Summer Stewart. And a thank you to my agent Priya Doraswamy for always having my back.

Finally, a great deal of appreciation and love to my wife Dawn and our menagerie of pets: Mac, Koda, and Little Joe.

About the Author

Sung J. Woo's short stories and essays have appeared in *The New York Times*, *PEN/Guernica*, and *Vox*. His previous novels are *Deep Roots* (2023), *Skin Deep* (2020), *Love Love* (2015), and *Everything Asian* (2009). In 2022, his Modern Love essay in *The New York Times* was adapted by Amazon Studios for an episode of *Modern Love Mumbai*. He lives in Washington, New Jersey.

About the Press

Unsolicited Press is based out of Portland, Oregon and focuses on the works of the unsung and underrepresented. As a womxn-owned, all-volunteer small publisher that doesn't worry about profits as much as championing exceptional literature, we have the privilege of partnering with authors skirting the fringes of the lit world. We've worked with emerging and award-winning authors such as Shann Ray, Amy Shimshon-Santo, Brook Bhagat, Kris Amos, and John W. Bateman.

Learn more at unsolicitedpress.com. Find us on twitter and instagram.